JANIE

JANIE

KENDALL ROBERTS

atmosphere press

Published by Atmosphere Press

Cover design by Matthew Fielder

Atmospherepress.com

For Evelyn & Arianna.
You make me so proud everyday,
and I love you both so much.

⌒ PROLOGUE ⌒

Victory

Janie De Casas crouched in the street, sheltering behind the barrels from the Agents' gunfire. Three of them rained bullets on her position and on Will Covington's, who hid in a doorway down the walkway.

Less than a dozen minutes after riding into the town of Victory, the quartet of avengers, Janie, Will, Finn Hennessy, and David McPhail, had found themselves in another firefight. Granted, they had planned on robbing the local Revenue Office, and so this scenario had been on their docket, just not the part that included an ambush by twenty or so of Governor Hogg's Agents in the middle of the street. Back when, Janie could not remember how many months ago, in the town of Diffidence, Will had warned her that their little gang had a habit of making hasty exits from every town they visited. Janie only hoped they could succeed one more time, and then maybe she and her beau really could ride off together into the sunset.

Janie's world of more than eight months ago had eschewed desperate gun fights, attempted bribery, and burgeoning love. In fact, Janie's world of eight months ago had included little more than a hangman's noose.

After years of enduring her father's sober and drunken abuse, Janie had shot him dead. When the town sheriff and deputies had come calling to discuss the matter of patricide, Janie had sent them packing much worse off for the trouble. In the end, it had taken six of Governor Hogg's feared Agents, led by Agent Seward Garland, to bring her in. Four of the Agents died in the process, and Janie might have gotten all six of them had she not run out of ammunition.

And so, for the death of her father, a former member of Governor Hogg's personal posse, and the four other Agents who had come to arrest her, Janie had stood on the gallows one bright noon. First, the black canvas bag had come down over the head, then the rough hemp rope had encircled her neck, and Janie waited to join her mother who had died almost a decade before.

The trapdoor snapped open under her feet, but Janie had not died. In the penultimate moment, former Territory Ranger David McPhail shot out the rope before it could break her neck. In the dusty street beneath the gallows, Will Covington cut her bonds, and together with Finn Hennessy, the quartet escaped from Compassion and left Agent Garland fuming behind them.

The whirlwind of McPhail's quest to destroy Governor Hogg and rebuild the Territory Rangers of old swept up Janie as surely as it had Will and Finn. Over these past eight months, they had broken into the private residences of Hogg and his advisor, Horace Weatherwax, robbed another Revenue Office, waylaid a shipment of gold, robbed a bank, and blown up a railyard along with an entire town, all to arrive here in Victory.

Oh, and somewhere along the way, Janie, despite her best efforts and painful memories, had fallen in love with Will.

"Cover me." Will's voice broke through the cacophony of bullets.

Janie rose from behind the barrels and started firing.

Her first bullet caught one of the three Agents in the center of his chest, and down the man went. The other two ducked back under cover while her shots continued to riddle their concealing crates. Hitting them, though desirable, was not the point. Across to her right, the cover fire permitted Will to close the distance on the two remaining Agents. When Janie finished emptying both cylinders, Will was on top of the Agents' hiding spot.

The Agents must have been counting Janie's shots because even as she ducked down, both men came up around the crates to return fire. One of them even got a shot off that buzzed by her shoulder and dug into the dirt of the street before Will brought them down.

In the silence that followed, Janie reloaded both pistols. The heat of the chambers singed her fingers, but she completed the task and snapped the guns closed.

Twenty seconds passed. Across the street, Finn and McPhail surveyed the scene. Bodies littered the street, wooden sidewalks, and doorways. Once again, against all likelihood, the band of four stood tall at the end of the fight.

Janie poked her head up over the barrels and grinned when she caught Will's eye.

His grin might have swallowed hers.

Janie stood up and came around the barrels toward him, and Will stepped off the walkway into the street.

Up above and a building back, Agent Foster Callaghan uncovered his ears at the silence. He had been the lookout who spotted the gang riding toward Victory and alerted the rest of the posse. Agent Seward Garland had ordered Callaghan to take up position on this roof, but when the gang arrived, all hell had broken loose. Garland had gone down in the first volley, victim of that ex-Territory Ranger McPhail. Callaghan had been about to take a shot at McPhail, but shots from the woman drove him back and down from the building's edge. Twenty of Governor Hogg's Agents had lain in ambush here in Victory. Now, with the silence descending on the town, surely they had won.

Foster peeked over the ledge, and his jaw fell open. Two of the devils still stood in the shadows across the street, and the woman was below him and looking ahead to where the fourth must be out of Foster's line of sight. Sweat slicked his palms, but anger overcame his fear. He stood up with his rifle and aimed.

He had the woman in his sights, ready to put a bullet into the center of her back when one of the boys stepped into the street just beyond her. Foster Callaghan had been raised well by his mama and three elder sisters. He would not shoot a woman if he could avoid it. He raised his rifle barrel an inch and aimed for the center of the boy's chest.

Across the street, Finn caught Callaghan's movement on the rooftop. He raised his pistols.

McPhail spied the same movement from the corner of his eye and raised his guns. No one was faster than David McPhail, but he felt time slow, and his arm moved like it pushed through water. Thoughts and decisions rebounded in his mind. Will and Janie were both excellent gunslingers. They could be the foundation of a new group of Territory Rangers to fill the vacuum eliminating Governor Hogg and his Agents would create. But they were distracting each other from the true path. McPhail wanted both, but if he tried to keep both, in his soul, he knew he would lose them all.

McPhail beat Finn.

He beat the rifleman on the roof.

He waited to take his shot.

Janie did not see any of this. Will filled her vision. Somehow, despite the odds, they had survived. The wild adrenaline of the fight still pumped through her body. All her senses felt alive. In four steps, she would throw her arms around Will's neck and pull him to her and drown him in kisses. Her body ached to have his arms crush her to him, to feel the beating of his heart against her chest, to smell the sweat and fear and exhilaration on his body.

Will had promised Janie and Finn that after this assault on Victory, they were done. The three of them would bid adieu to McPhail and his quixotic quest to rebuild his fabled Territory Rangers. From here, they would ride off together, and just maybe she and Will really could build a life together. Maybe she could be okay for love. Maybe she was not as broken as she believed.

She gave a little leap and cried, "We did it!"

The red blossomed in Will's chest, deeper red than any rose, angrier than the raging explosion that had wiped the town of Forgiveness off the map. If a gunshot accompanied the blossoming, Janie never heard it, and she doubted Will ever did.

He wore a broad smile across his lips just before the blossom appeared, and his eyes had time to look puzzled before the shot drove his body back to the dirt.

Janie landed on him, screaming his name over and over. She tried to put her hands over the wound to stop the bleeding, but the bones in his chest just gave way, and so she lifted him to her and cried and cried and ran her bloodied hands through his hair.

The grin faltered as his lips slumped, and one of his hands tried to come up to touch her face. His lips moved without making a sound, and then the light blew out of his eyes, and his body slumped slack in her arms.

Somewhere in another world, McPhail and Finn were shooting again. Another body was falling to the ground. Janie heard none of that. Her world had just collapsed with the fading of those blue-grey eyes.

❧ PART ONE ❧

MORE WORLDS THAN THIS

Governor Alistair Hogg's boots made soothing susurrus as they slid over the heavy carpet lining the third-floor hallway of his mansion. The flame from the lantern in his hand cast a warm glow on the deep browns of the woodgrain at the edges of the rug and off the brass door handle to his study.

From two floors down, Hogg could hear the low murmur of the two Agents near the foot of the ground floor stairs. Another pair patrolled the second floor. Until three weeks ago, the Agents had only stood guard outside on the mansion grounds, but since that debacle in Victory, security and caution had become the new watchwords in San Alonso. The guards would continue like this for the next few days, at least through the Winter Gala, but by then, Hogg predicted the increased precautions would be moot.

He stepped into his office, the light filling the small space to illuminate the bookshelves, paintings, and his desk. The windows behind the desk reflected the light of the lantern and the dark of the San Alonso night.

Of its own accord, the door swung shut behind him.

Hogg stopped dead in his tracks and raised both of his hands to shoulder height. He did not need the reflection in the window to identify his late evening visitor emerging from the shadows behind the door. "Ahh, Miss De Casas, how pleasant to finally make your acquaintance."

"Quiet, Hogg," she rasped over the cocking of her pistol. "Don't move."

A cold circle pressed against the base of his skull, and a hand began patting down the sides of his coat and pants. "I can assure you, I am unarmed. I find it gauche to carry a weapon in my own home."

"Pardon me if I don't take your word for it."

Hogg chuckled, a warm sort of laugh. "I would be disappointed in you if you did, my dear."

When she finished her pat-down, Hogg heard the scrape of one of his chairs across the rug behind him. The cool metal left the back of his neck. "Set the lantern on the desk and sit down. Slowly."

Hogg nodded. Keeping his right hand up at shoulder height, he set the lantern down as if it were a delicate robin's egg. As he lowered himself into the chair, he raised the left hand back up with the right.

Only after he sat did his interlocutor circle around and perch herself on the edge of the desk. In her right hand, she held a large rosewood-handled revolver, which she rested on her thigh while keeping the barrel pointed toward his chest.

Alistair Hogg recognized Janie De Casas from the wanted posters that adorned most of the buildings of his capital, but he also knew her by her cheekbones and that cold expression on her face as the daughter of Arthur De Casas, a former member of Hogg's personal posse. Janie's long black hair, dark brown eyes, and lightly browned skin were all her mother's. Hogg had met Maria Montello on several occasions and had been sorry to hear of her death, though the fact she had died of natural causes and not by her husband's hand had come as a bit of a surprise. Her early death may well have been a blessing given the future Hogg would have predicted for her.

"May I?" Hogg looked from his hands to the armrests of the chair. When Janie did not object, he let them descend with the same delicacy he had used to set down the lantern.

He smiled at her. "Well, this just goes to show that I don't know women as well as I think. I predicted a seventy percent probability that you would have departed Jefferson after what happened in Victory."

Janie's eyes narrowed. "You didn't think I'd come here for revenge? You really don't know me at all." Her expression shifted, and she cocked her head. "Why all the guards, then?"

"You misunderstand." Hogg nodded and that warm smile never wavered on his face. "When the first reports from Victory came in, I assumed there was at least a fifty-fifty chance that my men had killed your lover." He watched the question marks dart across Janie's face. "Young people traveling and living together for almost a year, braving dangers together, united in a common cause: it would be natural that romance would spark under those conditions. Some biological drives are stronger than others." He shrugged. "My error lay in the fact that I thought Finn Hennessy the more likely wooer of your affections. He is taller and broader than Will was, and I thought he had the kind of face a young woman might prefer."

Janie wrinkled her eyes at him.

"Not that young Master Covington was not handsome," Hogg added. "I just assumed you might prefer the cousin. Hence, when I heard that William died in Victory, I thought it only a thirty percent likelihood that you would come here to San Alonso. I had hoped that you and Master Hennessy would head north or west and leave my state of your own accord."

Hogg shrugged and sighed. "Alas, that was not to be. As for the guards, they are here to guard against the unlikely event that Mr. McPhail was able to keep the three of you together and come here to mount an assault."

He met Janie's steady gaze and then gave her a lazy blink. "You're not here for revenge though, Miss De Casas. You're here for something else entirely."

Janie flinched back at that. "How do you know I'm not here for revenge?"

Hogg's smile blossomed again. "You haven't shot me yet."

"I still can." Janie raised the gun to eye level.

Hogg looked beyond the yawning barrel before him and into Janie's eyes. "You want William Covington back, and you think I can give him to you."

Tears appeared in the corners of her eyes, and her face scrunched up in pain, but her gun never wavered. "Will is dead. He died in my arms." Her left hand opened her vest to reveal rusty stains on the shirt underneath. "I still have his blood on my clothes."

Hogg gave a slight shake of the head. "Arthur, your father, told you a secret, my secret. There are more worlds than this."

Janie was ten years old when her mother died.

Maria had been delirious with fever for more than three days. Her body bathed in sweat, but her lips and mouth lay as parched as the ground outside did in August, her tongue a dark shriveled bluish prune in her mouth. Her breathing came in wet, rattling heaves that sounded like she was gargling syrup, though Janie had seen it was mostly pink froth and blood. Over the course of the night, the breaths came farther and farther apart until one forgot to follow the last. Her body gave one last tepid shake, and then she ceased to be Maria De Casas née Montello, wife of Arthur, mother of Janie and became a cooling, dry husk.

In the pale light of morning, Arthur dug the grave under the branches of the piñon tree on the little rise behind their house. While he labored, Janie washed her mother's cold body, dressed her stiff arms in her Sunday best, and combed out her tangled, shedding hair. By the time the November sun shone down from above and their shadows huddled about their ankles, Janie and her father carried Maria's body outside and laid her to rest in the cold late autumn earth.

Janie and her father clung to each other by her mother's grave. Red and brown dirt covered them with little dark rivulets where their tears ran down their faces and left speckled raindrops across their clothes.

Where his wife had been neighborly and friendly, a church-going woman, Arthur De Casas was a solitary man, and it never occurred to him to notify anyone that his wife had passed. Devotion to Maria and the rest of his flock led the local priest to come to their home not long after Arthur and Janie laid Maria to rest. He found them kneeling over the fresh grave. The priest offered a benediction after the fact and did his best to offer comfort to the dismayed young girl and her godless father.

Thanks to the priest, the women and men of the town of Compassion came and offered condolences, and brought warm meals and baked goods. The women, Maria's friends, arranged among themselves to deliver meals to the De Casas' house for the next four weeks which prevented the two from starving, and they also arranged to help take care of the household tasks.

That first night after Maria died, Janie caught her father reaching for the whiskey bottle in the top cabinet. When he turned, he saw Janie standing staring at him with her wide dark eyes shining with tears by the light of the lantern. Instead of pouring the whiskey into a glass or directly down his throat, he put the cap back on and the bottle back on the shelf. Then he knelt down and hugged his little girl to him. She was all he had left in this world, and he was all she had. If only Maria were still here.

That night, Arthur thought about that. If only Maria were still here. She lay outside in the cold earth, but maybe that was not the case *everywhere*. What he had seen in San Alonso as a member of Governor Hogg's posse had been too much to bear, likely one of the reasons he drank so much, but this was not the only world. Maybe she was not the only Maria.

A month later that thought had wormed its way so deep into his head that Arthur left Janie alone in their little house to ride over to the Hoover place. Charlie Hoover and his wife Natalie were the De Casas' closest neighbors and friendly enough. He came back in the late afternoon while Janie was preparing their dinner. She set the table and served out the food before her father finally spoke of his plans.

"You're going to be staying with the Hoovers for a space."

"Why do I have to go there? I want to stay here with you."

"I have to go on down to San Alonso, Pumpkin. Can't have you staying here by yourself."

"Why do you have to go to San Alonso, and why can't I come with you?"

"Journey's too far, and Governor Hogg'd never let me do what I need to do if I came there with a pixie like you in tow."

"But what do you need to do there? Why can't you just stay here with me?"

Arthur sighed. "You won't believe me if I tell you, and no one would believe you if you said anything anyway. I suppose you have a right to know, but I don't want you getting your hopes up."

Janie stared back at her father, solemn and silent. She had no more hopes, her face said, but her face lied.

"There's a place, 'neath the Governor's mansion, where you can see all the other worlds that are out there."

Janie made a face.

"Worlds just like ours, reflections. You ever hold two mirrors up to each other?"

Maria had owned a single hand mirror and then the larger, expensive mirror above the little dresser in her room. It had never dawned on Janie to hold the two of them up together, and she had no real idea what her father was talking about, but she nodded just the same.

"All those reflections jumping back and forth, one to the other, again and again out as far as the eye can see. All those copies in the mirror. Well, there's worlds like that, reflections of our world I reckon, but they're not very good reflections, like a mirror with dirt on it, or a crack or something. They're all a little bit different." He looked at Janie as if he expected her to understand, but her face remained blank.

"Well, if each world is a little different, maybe your momma didn't die in all of them. Maybe she only died in this one."

Janie's eyes widened at the thought of her mother, still alive and singing in the kitchen as she baked, leaning over Janie's shoulders to help her knead the dough for the bread, helping her stoke the fire in their stove, tucking her into bed at night.

Arthur cleared his throat. "I'm gonna see the Governor and ask if he'll let me into that room, and then I'm going to find a way to get your mother out of one of those worlds and bring her back to us."

"You're gonna bring Momma back?"

"Yes, I am, Janie. Yes, I am."

Of course, Arthur De Casas did not bring his dead wife or her reflection back to Compassion. All he brought back was alcohol and despair. Sometimes, over the next few years, when he was deep in his drink, he would talk about the room. "She's dead, Janie. Dead in all of them, and I killed her in most."

"He was right. There are myriad worlds like ours out there, and I know a place where you can at least see them all. I don't know why or how, and I don't know how to describe it properly." Hogg's voice was quiet and calm, reeling Janie in careful turn by careful turn.

"Some people think the worlds are like sheets of paper,

one lying atop the next, held together by some spike, some tower in the center, like that." He nodded toward his desk and the spindle of papers to Janie's left.

"Some people think they are like a necklace of beads stretching off either way as far as the eye can see. They say, if you knew how, you could step from one world to the next and the next and follow them on out until the end of the universe." He waved his hands toward the sides of the room but was careful to keep his movements small and slow.

"Others think the worlds are like soap bubbles foaming in the sink. Little bubbles of worlds jostling and bumping against one another. Maybe they pop. What happens if they do?" He shrugged. "I don't know.

"Much like your father did, other people think of them as reflections of our world. I don't know if any of those are true or not, but that they exist is true. Each is like our world, but a little different, one from the other. Imperfect copies or maybe just all the possibilities of the universe, all the turns we didn't take."

Janie swallowed hard. "My dad said Ma was dead in all of them. Why would Will be any different?"

Hogg repeated his languid shrug. *You're here aren't you?* that shrug said. *Whether he is or isn't is your concern, not mine.* "I haven't looked in many of the worlds since Victory, but in the ones I have..." His voice trailed off into the night. "Twenty of my Agents went to Victory. Twenty well-trained men, led by a veteran member of my own posse, went to Victory and lay in wait for four troublemakers. In how many worlds out there do you think any of the four walked away?" Hogg's eyes were hard. "What are the odds that any of you would walk away? Slim, and yet here you are, holding me at gunpoint."

The two sat there, letting the words sink in between them.

"The universe holds an infinity of possibilities. We know of one branch where Janie De Casas survived a childhood of poverty and abuse, escaped the hangman's noose, spent almost a year riding about the state of Jefferson robbing Revenue offices, stagecoaches, and banks, blowing up small towns, and surviving an ambush, all to arrive here in San Alonso and hold the Governor of the State at gunpoint to ask him absurd questions about fantasy worlds." Hogg snorted. "I imagine if you look hard enough, you can find one where William Covington managed the same. Whether you'll find a way to reach him after that, I have no idea."

Janie's dark eyes turned to flint. If she could have seen herself in a mirror at that moment, she would have been startled to see how much that look resembled Will's fierce look. "So there's no way to get to those other worlds? What good are they then, and what good are you?"

Hogg lifted both his hands in surrender. "There are always connections, doorways, between the worlds. I know where one of them is. Your father hoped to find his own and failed. Finding the connection you want may be even harder than finding the world you want. Kill me though, and finding your young man will be impossible."

The young woman and the middle-aged man sat and contemplated each other. Hogg still wore that faint smile. He did not need a host of worlds to know how this ended.

Janie nodded more to herself than her captive. "All right, so where is this connection?"

The corners of Hogg's mustache twitched. He understood people, even troubled, desperate young women. "In the sub-basement."

When she gestured with her gun for him to stand and head to the door, Hogg stood, but nodded to a bookshelf in the corner of the room. "I have every intention of letting you search for your young man's doppelgänger. Might I suggest another way so we can avoid my guards and any itchy trigger fingers on your part?"

"Fine. Lead the way."

Governor Hogg gave a little bow, plucked the lantern from

the desk, and walked over to the bookshelf. With a deft twist of the candleholder mounted on its side, the bookcase swung out into the room to reveal a tight spiral staircase leading down. "Please close the door behind you. Not everyone needs to know about my little thoroughfare."

The metal stairs spiraled down in a steep twist so that within a handful of steps Hogg's head descended in profile to Janie and only came to her waist. The air in the little chimney of a stairwell was close and humid despite the dryness of the desert air.

"So, may I ask what happened to Master Hennessy and the indomitable David McPhail?"

Janie was busy trying to keep the gun pointed in Hogg's direction and holding onto the center post to steady herself, all while fighting down the vague dizziness their swirling descent caused. "You can ask."

Hogg chuckled, still in good humor despite being held at gunpoint in his own mansion. "Fair enough." He nodded at a rectangle in the wall. "Second-floor conference room." They continued down. "You might be interested to know that a young man matching Master Hennessy's description arrived in Abstinence three days ago in the company of a native girl. He stayed away from drink and the infamous painted ladies. He and his new lady friend hopped on a stagecoach headed west toward North Cali as soon as the sun rose the next morning." He smiled back at Janie. "I wish the young man well."

Janie snorted. Hogg's story at least jibed with Finn's last plans when they parted company on Mount de Dios.

"As for your esteemed leader, my minions have seen neither hide nor hair of Mr. David McPhail. Any thoughts?" He raised his eyebrows at her. "I do hope *he* has come to harm." He winked at Janie.

Refusing to dignify the insinuation, Janie swallowed down a retort.

"First floor, parlor." They passed another rectangle in the wall.

They proceeded in silence to the basement level. "Here we could exit into the storage half of the basement. The other half contains some ... guest rooms." The pause between the words caught Janie's ear. Hogg gave her that same infuriating smile. "For special guests. In some worlds I have looked into, some of your little band joined me here for a stay."

The walls in the bottom quarter of the stairway gave way to red rock streaked with yellow and blue veins.

"Before Jefferson became a territory and a state, before the settlers came, even before the conquistadors, one of the great pueblos sat in this very location. The shamans of the tribe referred to this as the Seeing Chamber, the Scrying Cave, or the Smoke Room. The first Spaniards thought it was black magic, Satanic, or paganism. They tried to bring the cave down by razing most of the pueblo. I think in most of the worlds, that destroyed the delicate doorway. As near as I can tell, the Governor Hoggs in other worlds either don't know that this place exists or don't have access to it." At the bottom of the stairway, he led them down a narrow passage in the rock and then stood to the side and held up the lantern to allow Janie an unencumbered view.

About six feet ahead of them, an archway cut across the passageway. Strange symbols, runes, or petroglyphs adorned the edges of the arch. The lantern light would not penetrate beyond the archway. A faint shimmer danced across the opening like a heat haze or a thin waterfall that reflected the lantern's light.

"Through there are all the worlds in the universe, Miss De Casas." Hogg's smile was less jolly now, maybe it never had been. Janie suspected the smile had been more wily like a fox before, but now a wolf grin seeped in. "A word of warning, stepping through is rather unpleasant. You might consider holstering your gun. I would hate for it to go off on accident."

Janie returned a cold stare. "You first."

The Governor shrugged but held out the lantern to her.

"Once I step through, the corridor will be pitch black. You might want to hold onto this."

Janie did not move to take the lantern, only raised the pistol another inch.

"Have it your way, my dear." In three easy strides, Hogg stepped through the shimmer and all light vanished.

Janie retreated to the left in a trice until her shoulder brushed the passage wall. There she crouched and leveled her pistol at the spot she had last seen Hogg striding away. She strained her ears for any sound, prepared for the attack. He must have extinguished the lantern and was now either coming back at her or hurrying away through another exit.

Her ears adjusted in the silence. In front of her, a high-pitched whistle warbled like an echo reflected off mesa walls from miles away. It was hard to hear because the volume was so low and the pitch just at the very edge of her hearing, but the longer she sensed it, the more it made her eyes water.

At first, she thought her brain and eyes were playing tricks on her, but then she understood. A faint blue light marked the inner outline of the archway ahead of her. It seemed to make the dark behind it undulate in shallow waves. Whether the warbling caused the waves or vice versa, the light and sound marched in lockstep.

Hogg had walked through the archway and disappeared just as he had promised. Her father had only talked about his search for Maria when he was drunk, and Janie had never been sure what to believe, as the rantings were disjointed and shifted haphazardly from the past to present and from real to absurd. Always though, he had raved about "all the damn mirrors" and how he could not get the "whine of the giant cicada" out of his head. The blue shimmer was not a mirror, but the ululating whistle did remind her of the song of the cicadas.

Her father had gone through that archway, and in the end, Janie knew she had braved more than her father ever could, and at a much more tender age. If there was a chance of find-ing Will, she could handle a gossamer waterfall and some big annoying bug.

Janie stood up and walked into the shimmer with both guns drawn.

The feeling was like having the outside of her body crushed into a tight ball the size of her fist while at the same time having her insides inflated to stretch beyond even the walls of the mansion above them, like some giant rubber balloon filled to bursting. The whine increased, made her skull vibrate, and tried to burst her eardrums and rattle the teeth from her jaw. The pain lasted an eternity. It pawed through her memories and held every scrape and hurt and bruise and cut and sorrow she had ever endured and scoffed at how puny and insignif-icant they were in comparison to this pain, to this misery. It had time to roll out her entire life before her like an unfurling carpet, a topography of all her highs and lows, and review each section in minute detail. And at the same time, she barely had the opportunity to gasp, and she was through in no more time than it would take to step across a conventional threshold.

Janie collapsed onto her hands and knees. One of her guns thunked down into mossy earth, but she held onto the other and imbedded its side under her weight in the soft ground. She retched and emptied her stomach between the curtains of the black hair that fell around her face.

Somewhere, far away and distorted by the ringing still fad-ing in her ears, Hogg chided her. "I warned you." His footsteps approached, clicking like he strode across a wooden floor when all that lay about them was spongy, dark, moss-covered earth. As the ringing faded, his voice softened in sympathy for her plight. "Your father didn't have much of a stomach for it, ei-ther. You'll be better soon. The first time across is always the worst." His warm hand patted her shoulder.

Janie vomited again.

Her stomach was debating a third emptying, when Hogg's

fist grabbed a handful of hair and yanked her head back. Any sympathy vanished from his voice, and he pressed the cold barrel of her fallen gun to her temple. Hogg's voice became a low, harsh hiss. "Remember this. I could have killed you right now." He tossed her head forward and released her hair. The gun barrel fell from her temple, and the gun itself made a clattering sound on the pliant moss. "But killing you would serve no purpose, and I only do things for a reason."

He walked away from her, boots clip-clopping on wood. Next to the small pool of water, he sat down with his derrière incongruously supported by nothing more than air.

"Welcome to the map room, Miss De Casas."

Janie pushed herself up to her knees and wiped acidic saliva from her mouth with the back of her hand. The motion left a streak of green and brown across her chin and an earthy odor in her nose.

When she looked around, she found herself in a softly lighted wood either at early morning or just before dusk. A pool of water perhaps five feet across sat in front of her, and beyond it and off to the right and left as far as she could see, interspersed with some iconic-appearing but generic deciduous trees, lay identical pools of water. The light came from nowhere and everywhere, suffusing the world but leaving no shadows. The earth beneath her knees was moist and compliant, a rich dark brown to black covered in a thin layer of deep green moss. The only sounds were a burbling from the pools, her own breath, and a low whine from somewhere behind her.

She turned and there stood the archway with the same blue haze dancing over pitch darkness while flanking it on either side, marching to the distance, lay endless repeating pools and trees.

No birds fluttered in the trees or sang to their mates. No squirrels leapt from branch to branch as they hunted nuts. No insects buzzed past her ears.

It was like no woods Janie had ever seen and looked nothing at all like a map room. She turned back to Hogg.

The Governor crossed his legs and leaned back with his hands behind his head as if he were rocking back in some comfortable desk chair, even though no such chair existed in these woods. "Everyone sees it differently, my dear." The warm, indulgent smile had returned to his lips. "To me, this is a giant room filled with table upon table, each with its own map." Hogg's hand came down over the pool next to him and made a solid thunk in midair.

"I am told one of the old shamans saw plumes of smoke dancing over fires. Dick Warren sees glowing golden globes. Your father saw a veritable funhouse of mirrors. What do you see, Janie?" Hogg leaned forward, elbows on knees in eager anticipation of her answer, as if fascinated by the possibilities.

Janie looked around again. "A woods with tall trees and pools of water everywhere."

Hogg pursed his lips and nodded. "Interesting, I would have expected some version of mirrors. The pools must be from your mother's side."

Janie did not contradict him, but she knew that to be false. Now, as her senses came back to her, the pool reminded her of the little pool off their stream on Mount de Dios into which she and Will had tossed pebbles once upon a time and where they had bathed their feet together in the coolness of the mountain water.

Sitting back up, Hogg waved a hand at her. "Well, come on then. Take a look." He swung around in the air. His feet came close to the edge of the pool, and he leaned over a table only he could see.

Janie's nausea and disorientation had passed, but the dull ache where Hogg had yanked her hair still throbbed. She retrieved and holstered the fallen pistol and wiped the earth from the one still in her hand. She could feel the moisture on her fingers, and it left little dark stains on them, but the dirt fell away from the gun without a trace.

A part of her wanted to level the gun at Hogg and put a

bullet between his shoulder blades, but curiosity overwhelmed her desire for revenge. She took three short steps toward him.

Despite needing to maintain the secret of this map room, Janie realized that Hogg reveled in the idea of sharing his little observatory, this piece of magic. "Come on, step closer." He urged her forward with his hand before turning back.

Janie joined him on his right.

When he stood, a chair that did not exist scraped across a wooden floor that was made of moss and dirt as far as Janie could see. Hogg waved his arms and stared only a few feet from his face while Janie's gaze fell all the way to the pool in the ground.

"For me, it almost always starts around the San Alonso environs."

The pool at her feet reflected a bird's eye view of a sprawling city and the grand curve of a river. The view was similar to the view from the old hideout on Mount de Dios but more dizzying in height.

"By concentrating though, I can make it take me anywhere in this world." He turned to beam at her. "Would you like to see the Swiss Alps?"

Before she could reply, the pool below her spun in a blur of land streaming past, then ocean, more land, and finally an aerial view of snow-covered peaks, mountains that seemed impossibly tall, encased in thick white blankets. It made her shake her head and rock back on one foot.

"Or perhaps the Great Wall of China?"

The mountains spun away to the left across the pool followed by flashes of more mountains, plains, water, again mountains even taller than the last and settled on a thick grey-brown line stretching across a string of mountains, hills, and plains.

"I always prefer to check on my own reflections, though." Again the world in the pool spun in a blur back to the city by the river, but now the view expanded, the buildings grew large until the Governor's Mansion swept into view, expanded, and Janie seemed to fall through a window to a study and desk that she recognized. She had waited in that room for more than two hours, biding her time until her quarry arrived. The room looked the same except that the painting on the wall was now a bowl of fruit instead of a portrait of the Governor himself. An exact duplicate of Janie's companion sat at that desk reading a stack of papers. Exact that is, though, from the decor, this version of Hogg must be less vainglorious than the one she knew.

"See? There I sit, undisturbed by interlopers in the night, reading the latest reports from the Mexican lines in South Cali, if I am not mistaken." He sighed. "It is pleasing to know that somewhere I am accomplishing what I had planned for tonight."

He turned to look at Janie. His look was appraising, less excited to show off his toys, but slyer and harder again. "What about William Covington in this world?"

At her feet, the pool turned black.

"Finn Hennessy?"

Black.

"Janie De Casas?"

Black.

"David McPhail."

This time the pool lightened, and centered on the dying embers of a fire and a lanky figure wrapped in blankets.

Hogg's smile was crooked. "Seems our dear friend Mr. McPhail is the only one to have escaped the little showdown in Victory in this world. Fascinating."

Janie said nothing but could feel a knot churn in her stomach.

Hogg chuckled a chuckle that suggested he knew just how she was feeling. "Of course, I knew that already. This is one of the worlds I check regularly when trouble is afoot in ours." Hogg waved his arms about. "The maps closest to the archway seem to be most like ours. I walked once that way almost a mile." Here Hogg pointed over the pool and out into the distance. "The map I stopped at there was wrong. The time was off, night instead of day, and the terrain was wrong, geography changed. As near as I could tell, an ocean covered most of the area we call Jefferson."

He patted Janie on the shoulder. "Spread out some, but don't go too far from your doorway back. Good luck." With that, he picked up the lantern and strode back toward the archway.

"That's it?" Janie called after him. "You're just going to leave me here in your secret playground."

Hogg's laugh reverted to indulgent. "Well, what did you expect, my dear? I have business to attend to, and you have a great deal of work to do if you hope to find your lost love. Don't worry, my men will not disturb you here. It might be wise though when you leave to approach me in my study. They might not take kindly to you wandering about the mansion." At the archway, he turned back one more time. "If I don't hear from you in a day or two, I'll send Dick Warren in to check on you. Be a dear and try not to shoot him."

Alistair Hogg stepped through the archway and disappeared.

Janie turned in a circle, taking in the vastness of the space. As far as her eyes could see, pools of water shimmered beneath broad trees, all individual worlds for her to search. But was Will still alive in any of them? The follow-up question — Would he be the same Will? — she pushed down and ignored.

Her rotation brought her back to face the archway. It stood there in the middle of these woods, the only object to break the monotony of the scenery. She walked closer to it, and the whine increased, but as she passed by its side, the archway vanished, and so did the whine.

Janie stopped in her tracks and sucked in her breath. The archway was not supposed to disappear. Her exit was gone.

As she rocked back on her heels in surprise, her head passed the point where the archway had stood, and in a blink there it was again and so was the whine.

She rocked forward again and the archway vanished.

Rock back, and it reappeared.

She walked around and stood just behind where the opening ought to have been. She steeled herself, took a deep breath, closed her eyes, and stepped forward.

There was no squeezing or stretching, but once she completed the step, the whine returned. When she turned around, the archway stood there, wavering a pale blue haze over darkness. Now she had two important pieces of information. It really was a one-way door, and if she got too far away or looked from the wrong angle, she would not be able to find her way back out.

This room or woods or world or way station or whatever it was looked the same in all directions.

She walked back over to the pool Hogg had shown her. The water was clear blue now and seemed to be without bottom. In the earth next to it, Janie traced out an X and then an arrow pointing left.

She walked to her left, passed one tree, to the next nearest pool where she knelt down before it. The water stared back at her, placid and clear and bottomless. How did it work? "Compassion," she said aloud.

The waters swirled, and a bird's eye view of the town she had grown up near replaced the blue water. She could see the Johnson's Mercantile Shop, the sheriff's office, and the town square. The last time Janie had set eyes on the town, a gallows stood in that square, but now it stood empty under the light of the moon.

"William Covington."

The waters turned black.

"Finn Hennessy."

Black.

"David McPhail."

Black.

"Janie De Casas."

Black.

It was nighttime. Maybe they were all asleep somewhere really dark, like a cave, or maybe the water did not know their names.

"Avery Johnson." She had not wanted to say Hogg's name. Seeing her father's story come to life had brought her would-be suitor's name to the top of her mind.

The waters shifted to a bedroom with two dark forms asleep in bed facing each other. Avery had married Hannah Greeley, eldest daughter of a rancher on the opposite side of town a little over a year ago. In the dark of the room, Janie thought she could make out a smaller bundle nestled in the space between their pillows, Justin Johnson. Maybe his name was different in this world, or maybe Justin was Justine, but Janie did not stay to contemplate more.

She drew another X in the earth and an arrow pointing down before turning to head to the pond behind her.

Hogg had said that the closest worlds seemed most aligned with their own, but how much of a difference would a world need to be for Will not to die? Janie worked in a circle, visiting each pool around the archway until she returned to her starting spot. She added an upward pointing arrow to her previous marks and then marched forward to the next pool.

She marked time by the shifting light in the pools she visited on her widening spiral. She had confronted Hogg close to midnight in her own world, and now the grey light of dawn crept into the visions of each pool, though the light in the woods never changed. There was no sun to cross the sky and in truth no particular sky for it to cross. When Janie looked up above the tree branches, all she saw was a vague greyness, like an overcast sky, but no streaks or fluffy edges or any other sense of depth distorted the uniform grey.

Nothing seemed to change in this world, only monotonous identical pools and trees and sky. Every once in a while, she caught a whiff of something green and fetid, but she could never discern from which direction the odor emanated.

Janie had been awake for almost a day now and the fatigue gnawed away at her, that and the niggling of despair in her heart at the blackness that always greeted Will's name when she spoke it over a pool. She found a place behind the now invisible archway and lay down on the soft earth beneath a tree to shield her sleeping form and napped.

Waking in this unchanging world disoriented her. When her head cleared, and she sat up to reassess her situation, it dawned on her that she ought to be hungry or thirsty by now, but she felt neither. The slight fuzziness to her mouth on waking disappeared quickly, and by the time she sat up to get her bearings, her mouth and throat no longer felt dry, and her belly did not rumble for food. That was just as well because she had neglected to bring either food or water. Somehow the idea of walking back through the archway and up the long flight of stairs to ask the Governor for a glass of water and a bite to eat made her laugh. He really would think her a lovestruck idiot, but maybe she was just that.

It seemed to be midday in the worlds out there.

As she moved about the strange terrain, she began to notice fine little trickles of blue stretching from pool to pool like crisscrossing trails of ants. Most pools had at least five or six little trails branching off toward other pools, while some had more than a dozen. Once, she tried to trace out one of the lines, but it soon became so tangled amongst all the others that she gave up and returned to her more important task. What the little lines meant, she could only guess.

She worked that ever-widening spiral through the remainder of the day. Every time she spoke Will's name or her own, each pool turned black.

Alistair Hogg seemed to be a constant, and Janie felt like she traced his entire day from one pool to the next, each pool seeming to pick up where the other left off. In all the worlds out there, he seemed immutable.

Avery Johnson existed in all the worlds she tried, always working in the mercantile shop and always married with an infant from what she could ascertain. That made her happy. She no longer loved Avery, if that passing crush could ever have been considered love, but she wished him well. He had never meant any harm to come to her because of his attentions and had always been kind to her when others in her hometown had not.

Janie lost count of how many pools she visited the rest of that day, but it had to have been more than one hundred. Only once did she find Finn. He was in a locked room with barred windows set high in the wall. He looked pale and feverish with a bandage about his head. When she looked closer at the covers over his bed, he seemed to be missing his right leg below the knee. His color and the shivers that ran through his body suggested that if Janie returned to this pool in a few days' time and spoke Finn's name, she would find only darkness. She could do nothing for him and moved on.

David McPhail lived in one of every seven or eight worlds Janie guessed. Most of the time, she found him riding alone through the plains or mountains of Jefferson, though she could never tell where exactly he was. Several times she found him in a cell that resembled the one in which she had seen Finn. Once, she saw him with a bright red fresh scar that puckered his right cheek and set his mouth in a permanent sneer. That image sent shivers through her because Janie knew without a doubt that she had put that scar on his face. She was unsurprised to find no trace of Will, Finn, or herself in that world.

Janie remembered how after Victory, the now three companions carried Will's body back to Mount de Dios. They would not leave him to be desecrated by the townspeople or the Agents who would follow. McPhail would have buried him somewhere in the mountains to the west — he still wanted to push on toward San Alonso — but Janie brokered no argument. They needed to bury Will at their hideout. Finn nervously backed her, and so north and east they rode after Victory.

It took them three days to make the journey, but they never saw signs of pursuit.

They dug his grave near a little grove of trees overlooking the plains of Jefferson far below. The little stream burbled nearby and small purple and blue wildflowers grew in little patches about the clearing. It seemed peaceful. Janie hoped Will's soul would be happy there. She knew that she would have been happy to lie there and enjoy the view, listen to the birds and the stream, and smell the light sweet scent of the wildflowers.

No one objected when Janie kept Will's rosewood-handled revolvers. They were the only possession of any value Will owned, except for his share of buried gold high in Gorseman's Pass, and although he had left no will and testament, they all understood Will would have wanted Janie to have those guns.

Janie woke early the next morning and hiked away from their campsite. She missed Will, but now that he was buried, she could not sit by his grave, and so she found a new perch high up the mountainside to observe the world and think.

Finn found her maybe twenty minutes later.

"I'm leaving, Janie. You need to too."

She looked up at him in silence.

Finn knelt down next to her. He reached out to touch her but thought better of it and put his hand awkwardly on the log next to her. "Before Victory, we all agreed that was our last job with McPhail, that we'd leave. Nothing's changed. You can come with me if you want or go your own way, but you need to leave, and the sooner, the better."

"Everything's changed, Finn." Janie shook her head. "What does it matter? Will's dead. I don't have anything left, nowhere to go, nothing to do."

Although McPhail had been their leader from the outset,

Will had become the lynchpin holding the four together. He believed in McPhail, believed in the thirst for revenge. Finn followed because Will was his cousin, the last of his family. Janie followed because of her love for Will. Now, with Will gone, she had no one left to follow.

Finn bowed his head and groaned. "I didn't want to have to tell you this." The pain in his eyes was deep when he looked back up at her. "He let Will die. You couldn't see it, but I could."

Janie furrowed her brow and shook her head. "What?"

"We both saw the guy on the roof at the same time. I tried to get a shot off, but there was no time. You know how gawd awful fast McPhail is though. He had his gun up and leveled, and then he just waited. Waited for the guy to take his shot before he fired. He let Will die, I saw it."

"No, he couldn't have." Janie's head clicked back and forth like a metronome. "Why?"

"Because I thought he was going to shoot you." The voice was a whip from behind them. They both spun about and jumped to their feet.

David McPhail stood up the hill from them, an unlit cigar clamped in his teeth. He must have grabbed the damn things in Victory when he went into the store to fetch blankets for Will's body, while Janie sat in the street, holding Will, still coated in his warm blood.

Finn, galoot that he was, stepped protectively closer to Janie. Will would have understood that Janie did not need protection, and in any case, moving away from her, flanking their opponent, would have offered her the most protection. If McPhail had two targets to track, their odds increased.

The Ranger took the unlit cigar from his mouth and gestured with it in his left hand. His right hovered near his gun belt. "We are on a mission. We have a duty to the citizens of Jefferson to rid them of Governor Hogg and his minions and their oppression of the people. It is our obligation to destroy him and rebuild the Territory Rangers that came before." His eyes were wild, crazed with belief in his quest.

He was raving, and as long as the rave went on, time to act remained. Janie stiff-armed Finn and took a step to her right. At first, Finn made to follow her but stopped himself. Not all of their training had been wasted on him.

"Once upon a time, Will understood that duty, and so did both of you." McPhail leveled the cigar at Janie. "But you and he started distracting each other. You were losing your way." McPhail shook his head as if in sorrow. "I couldn't get you back, but I never would have acted on my own. In Victory, neither of you stayed ready. Instead of staying alert, all you could think of was running into each other's arms. There are natural consequences of losing focus. Sometimes nature is the best teacher. I just allowed nature to..."

That's when Janie drew. She felt the nearing of the rant's end, and just like Agent Wurst's rant in Kindness, Janie did not need to hear the end of it. In fact, the only thing she or Finn were likely to hear at the end of it was a gunshot.

Maybe McPhail was faster or maybe Will had been. Janie had been close behind those two, but she was always the most accurate of the foursome. Perhaps McPhail expected his words to mesmerize them or perhaps he had placed himself in a trance. By the time he saw Janie draw and pulled his gun free of leather, she shot him in the face, just as she had shot Agent Wurst.

She felt the tug on the edge of her calf where McPhail's bullet bit through her flesh, and she staggered. Her second shot missed McPhail's falling body, but her third struck his chest as he hit the ground. After that, she emptied the chamber into him just to be sure.

Her voice started as a hiss but rose to a yell by the end. "That's for Will. The natural consequence of letting him die."

When the sun went down in all of the pools, Janie found herself a dry patch of ground under a tree and curled up to sleep. She did not feel particularly tired just as she felt no thirst or hunger in the woods, but nonetheless, she fell asleep soon after her head touched the ground. When she awoke, the woods looked the same, but the nearest pool told her out in the world (worlds?) the sun had risen.

Long ago, sometime the previous day, Janie had lost her spiral and now her path wove in haphazard jigs and jags, one way and the next. She kept up her marks at each pool, hoping that when the time came, she could find her way back to the archway.

After midday, Janie dropped to her knees in front of yet another pool. The soft earth made a gentle squelch, and the moss released a minty aroma. "William Covington." Her voice croaked as much from the monotonous recitation of names as the gnawing despondency in her soul.

The pool before her turned black, and she almost stood, but then sunlight cut across the scene, and Janie realized that the pool was not black, only shaded. The seated figure was Will, or looked like him. The young man wore a dark suit with a black Stetson hat pulled down over his face. He sat crammed between two larger men in a small space, probably a stagecoach. Were they his guards? No, the one was portly, the other one old, and neither wore the Agent's black. They were just two more passengers jostling along inside a coach.

Could it be Will? The shape of the body looked like him, but Janie did not recognize the clothes, and he had no guns on his hips. If it was Will, how different a life must this Will Covington have led? What if he had never joined McPhail? What if he had never met Janie? Was it possible that in the world before her, they had never fallen in love?

The young man shifted in his seat and raised his hat. It was Will, but Will with a sorrow in his eyes that Janie had never seen. The flint remained, peering out the corners of his eyes, but despair filled the rest. Janie had seen that look in her own eyes when she gazed at her reflection in the mirror in Hogg's study. Will had lost something very dear to him.

"Janie De Casas," she whispered. Will vanished in a swirl of ebony. Janie swallowed hard and put a hand to her throat.

"Will Covington." He reappeared, looking out at her with those sad eyes.

Janie reached out to cup his cheek. Her fingers touched the cool surface and sent little ripples radiating out to the edges and rebounding back. The image in the pool danced and swayed but somehow stayed more coherent than her own reflection in a water basin would. Will noticed none of that dizzying dance. His coach unloaded the businessmen and a family with a teen-age girl, and Will stepped out with them into bright sunlight in the middle of a bustling city. He was standing in San Alonso, less than a mile from the Governor's mansion.

Janie stood up and turned, ready to run back along her torturous trail to the archway into the mansion and then out into the city and the coach stop and Will. Reason stopped her. Despite what the image suggested, Will was not disembarking in her San Alonso. He was only here, in this pool before her.

Janie knelt back down and watched him. She found that if she just touched the surface of the water with her fingertips, the scene would shift, changing her angle of observation. She could turn left or right or pull back to see more of Will's world. Mostly she watched, watched him wander the town, down one street and then another, turning suddenly at some sight or sound to which Janie was blind and deaf. Once he followed a woman in a maroon dress and long black hair. That puzzled Janie for a time, but then she remembered the town of Diffidence and the maroon dress she had chosen in the dress shop. Will was looking for Janie, even though he must know he would not find her in San Alonso.

Everywhere Will went, wanted posters hung on the walls with pictures of Will, Finn, and McPhail. Janie's face graced none of them. "Because I died in Victory," she whispered to the woods. "He shot me, not Will. Oh, Will." She had not cried since burying Will almost three weeks ago, but she cried now. Great tears streamed down her face, plummeted to the surface of the pool, and sent out reverberating rings over Will.

Was there never a world where they could be together? Of course, that was the point of this. Now that she had found him, Janie was going to make the world in which they could be together. She dried her eyes.

By that time, Will had found his way to a rough-looking saloon and a table with Finn. McPhail materialized right behind him. Their lips moved, but Janie heard no sounds. She watched them, fascinated by her three companions either dead or scattered to the wind in her reality, but still together in Will's.

She watched them through their meal and their journey out into the city as the sun set, as the gas lamps turned on and illuminated the Governor's mansion and all of the carriages and people. She watched them walk back across the town to a deserted building near the river. She also watched the dark figures who tailed them back to their hideaway, the one who took up position in a doorway not far away, and the one who hurried back toward the Governor's mansion.

"Get out, Will. Get out. Move. They've found you. Move now," she pleaded. She could not, would not, watch him die again.

Inside the building, Will paced back and forth in apparent frustration. Finally, Finn grabbed his arm and tugged his cousin toward the stairs.

"Not the front. Not the front. Find a back way out. They'll see you." Kneeling, Janie leaned out over the pool, hands on her thighs as she pleaded with the reflections in the strange mirror.

Will and Finn headed out the back door to the river edge.

Janie ran her hands over the pool, rotated the image, and found the lookout still ensconced in his doorway, oblivious to the departure of his quarry. Next, she combed back through the city to Governor Hogg. Instead of enjoying himself at his ball, he sat in a conference room with several Agents. The grin on his face told Janie that he knew where her companions hid.

"Please stay away, Will. Please stay away. Leave San Alonso."

Of course, he did not listen to her. By the time Hogg and his Agents rolled out of the mansion toward the wharves, Will and Finn turned and walked back toward McPhail.

In impotent horror, Janie watched the scene unfold. Finn and Will spotted trouble just a block before their destination. They took refuge in a nearby building as Hogg's noose tightened, and the Agents set siege to the safe house. Thank God, Finn was still with Will. When Will made to join the fray in McPhail's defense, Finn knocked him to the ground. As the firefight blazed outside, the two cousins made peace and snuck out a back door, grabbed a boat, and disappeared down the river.

Janie followed them downriver but backtracked every few minutes to look for signs of pursuit. No boats or horses chased after them. They sailed all night. By the time the sun rose, in that other world, the cousins beached their boat along the Great River.

Will and Finn slept under a cool blue sky. Much as she had in life, Janie lay down under a pale grey sky next to the pool and dangled her hand into the water to touch Will's stray hand on the sand. When she touched him, he seemed to stir in his sleep, and his fingers squeezed the empty air.

Janie's eyes opened before the cousins'. Somehow, her hand had stayed close to Will's in the night. Janie sat up and contemplated what to do next. Will had survived Victory. He had escaped San Alonso. Now all she had to do was find a way to get to him.

At first, she tried reaching deeper into the pool, but her fingers only scraped a sandy bottom that she could not see. She kicked off her boots and waded into the pool. In the center, the cold water came to her waist and a mixture of sand and coarse pebbles scratched her bare feet. On the surface, she stood less than a foot from Will and Finn asleep on the shore. Taking a deep breath, Janie ducked beneath the surface. When she opened her eyes, she could make out the blurry image of sandy earth devoid of any fish or plants or sleeping lost friends. When she emerged from the pool, water cascaded from her clothes and hair into the mossy earth, but when she licked the water from her lips and swallowed, no cool drops trickled down her throat. A minute later she realized that the wet clothes no longer clung to her body, and in fact felt perfectly dry.

Next, she knelt down to begin tracing the little blue lines, almost water but not quite, that snaked out from the pool. Were they connections between the worlds? A map of how the worlds joined or sat adjacent to each other in some higher topography? They soon lost themselves in tangles, and not knowing which to follow, Janie feared straying too far from what she now thought of as Will's pool and losing him again.

If she could not get through to him here, she would have to leave the pool and find another way. Janie went to the nearest tree and broke off branches. These she took to the pool and spiked them upright around its edge like a little half fence on what she thought of as the far side of the pool. Through all the trees, she hoped to be able to pick this pool out more easily with her markers.

Then, she began tracing her way back along her winding path toward the archway, always looking back from each pool to mark Will's as it receded from her. Her little fence helped, but as it began to disappear behind the foreground trees, she still could not see or sense the doorway back to her own world. The fear of losing him threatened to overcome her, but she pushed on.

At that last pool before Will's pool disappeared entirely, she built another screen of branches and then lay some on the ground pointing the most direct route back. She continued on.

About thirty minutes later, Janie had to build another screen of branches as a landmark. When she turned, she had not gone more than three more pools, before she spied one of her first two screens again in the distance, but this time she seemed to be looping around the pool's far side. Again, she marked her spot with branches and cut back across the intervening space.

It was Will's pool. The cousins were hiking up some mountains. Janie did not wait to see where they were going. They appeared safe, and now she had the first leg of the shortcut between him and the archway.

The remainder of her day — Could she call them days if the light never changed, and she never felt any hunger or thirst or other feelings of the passage of time? — Janie spent identifying the shortest distance between the pool and the archway. In the end, she had meandered far from the archway, but not nearly as far as she had assumed. Will's pool was located behind the magical exit, but far enough away that trees and distance would have obscured the archway from view even if the damn thing did not disappear if she looked at it from the wrong angle.

Janie wondered when Hogg came back to his map room if he would find gouges in the floor and broken pieces of chairs and tables to mark her progress through the space.

As night overtook their world, Will and Finn bedded down again further south along the banks of the Great River. Unbeknownst to them, Janie lay down at their side. When she did, Will rolled over and faced her in his sleep.

Now that she had her pathway marked, Janie spent the next day again attempting to trace out the thin blue lines that connected the pools. She also contemplated Will's reactions to her presence. Did he really sense her closeness, or were those movements a coincidence that Janie was conflating into something more?

In the end, the blue lines seemed a lost cause. One set did connect to one of the near pools, but the rest spun and trailed off into the distance as near as she could tell, and became such a tangle that they might well double back to Will's pool as connect with any other. Even if they did connect to other specific pools, she was not sure how that information would help her, since she did not know what the connections meant and could not access any of the pools any more than she could access Will's. Also, she had a growing suspicion that the lines changed over time. They were not fixed quantities but rather variables that she could not predict.

Janie had just sat back down to contemplate her next move and watch Will and Finn sail down the Great River when somewhere in the distance, someone called her name.

"De Casas." The voice came as a faint echo, lost among trees, but seemed to come from the direction of the archway.

The voice belonged to Hogg's Head Agent, Dick Warren.

Janie circled through the woods to approach the archway from a new direction and regarded him from behind one of the trees.

He was a heavyset middle-aged man who looked more powerful than overindulged, but he did have a paunch in his belly. He walked about the archway in little circles and shouted her name from time to time. On his third revolution, he remained silent until he came around to face her hiding spot. "You can come out now. I don't know what you think you're hiding behind in your version of this blasted place, but in mine, it ain't nearly as good."

Janie stepped out from behind the tree but did not approach.

"If I were here to hurt you, I wouldn't be bellowing your name and pacing in circles, girl. I may be getting on in years, but I ain't that daft." He gestured to a satchel on the ground next to the archway. "I come bearing gifts and tidings from the holy Hogg hisself."

Janie nodded and came to the edge of the nearest pool.

"The Governor did ask me not to shoot you if you came calling. I guess we can talk."

Warren snorted. "So what do you see? I see glowing balls on pedestals and columns everywhere. Always reminds me of some damn Greek temple I read about when I was a lad." He shook his head. "Hurts my head and hurts my eyes."

"I see a woods with pools of water everywhere."

He nodded at that. "That sounds nicer. Maybe that's why you can stay in here so damn long. Me, I go nuts if I'm in here more'n ten minutes." He retrieved the satchel and extended it. "Canteen and some food."

Janie just stared at him and refused to take it.

"Stubborn and suspicious, a woman after my own heart. You'll live a long time like that." He grunted a little when he sat down cross-legged and opened the satchel. "I bet you haven't eaten or drank since you came in. I try not to stay long enough to find out, but they tell me you don't get thirsty or hungry while you're in here." He pulled out a canteen and a wax paper package and placed them on the ground a few feet away from him. The satchel still bulged with the promise of more offerings.

Janie eased closer like some half-tame hare being enticed too close to the fire. She nodded and hunkered down by the canteen and food. Now that she saw the food and water, her stomach did grumble, not terrible, but enough to signal a bite to eat would not be unwelcome.

"It catches up with you when you step back out, though. Not all the way, but enough to notice. I'd recommend you eat and drink something at least once a day. Wouldn't be a bad idea to nap every now and again too. You'll do better when you come back out."

The wax paper contained a sandwich of soft bread, still slightly warm, with a thick slab of beef in a red sauce. The smell made her mouth water, and she could no longer resist taking a bite. The soft meat tasted even better than it smelled.

It seemed to melt in her mouth and redoubled her hunger.

Warren let her eat half the sandwich and swig some water. "You found him if I'm any judge."

Janie wiped her mouth with the back of her hand. "Why?"

"You don't look broken. If you'd been in here three days looking and hadn't found him, I'm not sure you'd even have come when I called. Someday, maybe somebody'd find your skeleton in here with one of them Ranger guns still in your mouth." Warren scratched his nose. "Your pappy might have done that I reckon if he hadn't had you to go home to. He could only stand it in here a day and a half. Seward and Justis found him on the other side, weak as an old woman and all cried out."

"Maybe I'm stronger than my father."

That made Warren laugh. "Ain't no argument there, little lady. Ain't no argument there." He poked at a worn spot on the side of his boot. "Trying to figure out what to do next, ain'tcha?"

Janie saw no point in denial and nodded.

"That's the rub. How do you get to them?" Warren waved his hands at the golden orbs that filled his vision. "Some people think the Injun priests could do it, but I always thought that they just made it up after smoking too much peyote." His laugh came out as a snort when he looked back at Janie. "You want me to getcha any?"

"No."

"Probably the only way they could stand to be in here. I gotta git." He shrugged and pushed himself back to his feet. Janie jumped to her feet in response, hand on the butt of one of her guns. He chuckled at that. "Suspicious. I could make an Agent out of you."

He left the satchel of food when he departed and promised to return in a couple of days with more supplies if she did not come out on her own.

Before Warren returned, Janie watched Finn die.

The night before, Finn and Will got drunk in a town Janie did not recognize. In the morning, as they prepared to leave, a priest whom they had met two nights previous accosted them. The trio exchanged words, but behind the priest, a posse closed on the town. The boys saddled up and fled toward the mountains with a dozen men in pursuit.

Janie missed what actually happened, but Finn and his horse went down hard a few hundred yards out of town. Will paused and started to go back to his cousin, but both Finn and Janie screamed at him to go, to run. In the pool, Will's head twitched as if he heard the buzzing of an insect when Janie yelled at him. He fled as Finn bid.

Finn held them off as long as he could. He lay trapped under his horse, with a broken leg or worse, Janie surmised, but he pushed himself upright and fired at the posse as they galloped up to him. In the end, he brought down three of their pursuers and injured four others, two enough that they retired to the town rather than continue their hunt for Will.

Janie forced herself to bear witness to Finn's sacrifice. Had he thrown away his guns, the posse might merely have taken him into custody and back to the town's jail and a doctor. Maybe his leg would have mended well enough for him to walk to the gallows under his own power. By fighting, he allowed Will a chance to attain the foothills and cover amongst the trees ahead of the posse. Even though the sight of the bullets tearing into his body broke her heart, Janie owed Finn that much. There was nothing else she could do.

Well, there was.

She had to make sure Will escaped.

From the bird's eye view the pool allowed her to take, Janie could watch the posse and Will as they wove through the hills. She would call out directions to him, tell him where to go, and although he did not always seem to hear, at distinct turns, he would pause undecided and perhaps at her guidance make the correct choice. By early afternoon, Will had ascended deep into the mountains, separated from his pursuers by two mountain spurs. Maybe Janie's prayers and directions had helped, maybe not, but he was as safe as the lone survivor of Jefferson's most wanted gang could be.

Now, she had to find out how to get to him.

Klah felt the presence of the spirit soaring above the village mesa. It seemed to spiral out of the clouds, like a feather fallen from an eagle, spun by the winds and updrafts, but always tugged and pulled to earth by gravity. As it came closer to the mesa, Klah sensed the desperation in it, as if that feather strained to rejoin its mates along the eagle's belly. No, that was wrong. The feather was searching, perhaps looking for the nest from which it had originated.

Klah narrowed his outer eyes and darted them about the room. He walked his fingers along his forearm to imitate the creeping of Coyote, the trickster. The little ones in front of him laughed at Coyote's guile, and that made Klah smile. He enjoyed his time telling the stories of Coyote and Raven and Jackrabbit and depositing the nuggets of knowledge the tales contained into the minds of the young ones. He would not let the spirit distract him from this vital task. It would wait.

This spirit seemed familiar with the pueblo. While he spoke the gruff voice of old Tortoise with his waking mind, his inner eye watched the spirit scamper about the village, flapping about Nascha and her brother Bidziil before moving on to old Doli and Atza. None of the four family members seemed to take note of the spirit, though Nascha swiped the air as if to shoo a fly. Having exhausted that approach, the spirit turned toward Klah and his classroom.

The story of Coyote concluded. The young ones stood and bowed their respects and thanks before running out to play.

The spirit hovered in the corner, watching Klah ruffle one girl's hair and hug one of the boys. The spirit was not a kin spirit of the village, nor did it seem to be of the People, but somehow it knew the pueblo. Intriguing.

The young ones gone, Klah fixed his outer eyes along with his inner ones on the corner where the spirit hovered. "Who are you?"

Waves of surprise and relief emanated from the corner. The spirit had not been sure it would be seen, but it did not answer him.

With a gesture for the spirit to follow, Klah left the classroom and climbed up the ladder to the small room he shared with Tsela. The old man's clouded eyes turned to Klah when he stepped inside. "You've got a spirit with you."

"It wants something."

"She."

Klah cocked his head. Tsela was right, the spirit was feminine. He had not noticed that at first amid all the anxiety, excitement, and hope the spirit wore like a cloak over a core of pain and distrust. "I'll be in the cave."

"Take the rosemary. It will calm her."

"She's in the Smoke Room, isn't she?"

"Very good." Tsela smiled and continued his weaving. "Not smoke to her though."

"The Smoke Room is gone."

"Not everywhere."

In the back of the room, Klah drew aside a curtain and stepped into the fissure in the rock. He carried a lantern and had to duck his head at the bend halfway back. That turn cut off the light of the outside rooms before the passage opened up into a small chamber.

He sat down on the soft sand near the center of the room with the open lantern in front of him. The dried rosemary prickled his palms as he ground it between his hands and let the pieces drop into the lantern's flame. He closed his eyes and inhaled the smoke carrying the aroma of the herbs.

Instead of fluttering about him, the spirit seemed to crouch opposite him, regarding him with caution, the hope and excitement bundled up tight and held close.

Klah took three more cleansing breaths.

He opened his eyes.

Then, he opened them again.

The young woman had long black hair and smudges of dried tears on her cheeks. The pupils in her dark brown eyes widened, and her body rocked back an inch or two in the sand. Her complexion was a mixture of the pale skins that had taken over these lands and the darker ones of the vanquished Spanish conquistadors of the south. Klah could see no trace of the People in her, but yet here she knelt in the lost Smoke Room of the People. Despite her foreignness, she seemed familiar.

He let his mind relax and float free. Wisps of smoke curled in the air between them, and behind her and in his peripheral vision, he could see more dancing smoke columns. When he refocused on her eyes, they reflected the shimmer of a pool of water and trees. Once again, blind Tsela saw farther than most.

Freed from concentrating on his initial conundrum, Klah's mind found the memory he sought. He smiled at her. "I am Klah. You are a friend of the Ranger. Your clan stayed in our village in the home of Doli."

The spirit woman nodded. "I'm Janie De Casas. I didn't know you spoke English."

The smile spread to his eyes. "I didn't know you spoke the language of the People, but in the Smoke Room, all languages are one, just as all the kin spirits come together as one."

Janie wrinkled her nose. "I don't understand."

Klah reached out to her. "May I take your hand?"

Something about his request repulsed her more than he

would have thought, even more so than the ones who hated the People. He could feel her revulsion bubbling out of the darkness she held underneath and watched her throat bob in a swallow over the memories hidden in that darkness. "No, but I can take yours." Her hand trembled when she wrapped her fingers around his, but they were dry and warm.

When she touched him, the Smoke Room shifted in Klah's eyes. He sat not in the wisps of smoke but on the cool surface of a pool of water in a quiet woods. The world in her eyes shifted to the smoke Klah knew and back to the pools of water. The shift made her gasp, but she held onto his fingers until the image they both saw settled onto woods and water. "There are many worlds out there. You sit between them, Janie De Casas."

She nodded an acknowledgment.

"The wisdom of the People knows that our own spirits have kin in those other wheres. In the right places, these kin spirits can reach out to other kin worlds. You found the sacred Smoke Room of the People and reached out to me. Why?"

Janie let her fingers slip from his, but the world remained woods and water. "I need help. I need to find Will, Will Covington. He was with us in your village."

Klah regarded her for a time with the tear-stained cheeks, the red rims to her eyes, and the tension and fatigue fighting each other in the muscles of her face and shoulders. "The kin Will Covington of your world is no more."

Her eyes squeezed shut, and a shudder ran through her.

He thought of telling her that if Will Covington died in her world, he had likely died in Klah's or that perhaps his kin spirit and hers were together in this world, but Janie had called Klah across the worlds, and she would know those to be falsehoods. "Kin spirits were not meant to cross over. You ask much and know not the price."

"I don't care." Janie gestured about at the woods between the worlds. "I've searched every other world out there. In all of them except this one, he's dead, and I am too. He's in danger in your world. I've helped him all I can, but I can't do enough here. You're the only one who can hear me. I need to make sure he's safe, even if I can't be with him. I need your help. Please."

Klah counted his breaths while he thought. "How have you helped him?"

Janie wrinkled her face. "I talk to him. He hears me, sometimes. Not always, but sometimes he listens to me, turns left instead of right. At night, if I touch his hand in the water, his fingers move."

Though not of the People, this young woman had managed to find the Smoke Room and communicate across the worlds. Her spirit was strong. Her kin-bond with this Will might be as strong. "You cannot stay in the Smoke Room. Spirits are not meant to live here." Klah held up his left wrist and jingled the obsidian bracelets. "Tsela gave these to me when I became Spirit Guide." He scanned the edge of the pond until he found one of the thin blue lines that looped out from the pool and back in again. His fingers dug into the soft black earth and plucked it forth with a delicate pop when the ends separated from the pool. They twisted in the air like the ends of a worm.

Without prompting, Janie held out her arm to him. The blue string felt cool and moist like the surface of the pools. When Klah touched the ends to each other around her wrist, they fused together and for a span of seconds became two streams of water flowing in opposite directions before slowing and hardening into a bracelet the color of turquoise.

"Now you have a connection to my world when you leave the Smoke Room." Klah held one of his bracelets apart from the others. "I can commune with the spirits of other kin worlds with these. Now you can commune with the kin of mine. Go find my kin spirit in your world. Show him the bracelet. Perhaps he will help you. For myself, I will do what I can to look after Will Covington in mine."

"Thank you." Janie's voice wavered when she spoke, and the tears touched the corners of her eyes.

Klah shifted his eyes off to Janie's right. "I must go now, Janie De Casas. Before I go, look deep into my eyes and see what I see."

She frowned but did as bid.

In his peripheral vision, Klah saw her pupils dilate when she recognized the reflection there. "Go now, Janie De Casas. Someone here wishes you harm." Klah closed his inner eye, and the woods vanished.

When he opened his outer eyes, Tsela sat across from him. The older man's gnarled hands danced in the smoke of rosemary above the lantern while his clouded eyes looked at nothing. "We'll make four bracelets, I think."

Klah nodded and began to collect more wisps of smoke. "How is she here?"

"Her mother's side, I think." Tsela smiled in a soft rebuke. "Just because you have only known the kin spirits of the People does not mean the people of other places do not know of their kin spirits. When you are old like me, you will see farther and know more."

Klah bowed his head in submission. Someday, he hoped to earn the wisdom of Tsela.

Janie had not known what to expect from the pueblo's Spirit Guide, let alone that he would appear before her, floating atop the pond like a bar of soap in the sink. When she had touched his hand, her vision shifted and for a few seconds, smoke burned her nostrils and stung her eyes. Even when the scene settled back into woods, the acrid taste of smoke dripped on the back of her tongue for most of their conversation.

Klah's explanations had not helped much, but he had promised to help Will, and that was what counted. If the bracelet could let her out of these woods without losing track of Will, maybe she could find a way to cross over to him. Klah's last reminder might be most important; she still dwelled among enemies, no matter how pleasant a veneer they might display.

Janie recognized the dark reflection in Klah's pupils as an Agent, too slim to be Warren but sent by Hogg or his Head Agent she was sure. As she rotated on her knees, the crunch of boots on gravel told her thoughts of Will and communion with the Spirt Guide had distracted her too long. Her right hand tried to draw her gun, and her left sought purchase in the soft earth to propel her to stand on legs numbed from kneeling too long.

"No, you don't, sweetheart," a rough voice said just before a bony shoulder ran into hers and wiry arms pinioned hers to her sides.

The impact jolted the gun from her hand. In his haste to reach her, the Agent lunged at her from an angle and they spun together as they fell. He hit the ground with a grunt but continued to fling her around and into the soft earth and ended up straddling her prone body. When they came to rest, their cheeks touched.

For Janie, the room darkened, and gravel bit into the side of her face and burrowed into her chest as hard little darts. Stalactites and stalagmites joined in narrow spindles where trees once stood and low rocky altars with coal braziers in the center replaced the pools of water.

The Agent grunted in surprise and loosened his grip. His world must have shifted too.

Janie flung her head back into the beak of his nose and the sharpness of his teeth. The blow sent a shockwave of pain through her, but his grip relaxed more. With a sharp elbow to his rib cage, Janie felt his weight lighten, and she rolled beneath him and tried to scramble away in the soft earth that had returned once their skin no longer touched.

The blow from her head had bloodied his nose, but his crooked teeth predated this fight. His eyes flashed in anger at her. "You're feisty," he said.

Janie pulled her right leg from under him just before he lunged at her. She caught him in the solar plexus with her knee but not hard enough to deflect his body.

When his hand clamped on her wrist, the dirt beneath her became gravel. Shielded by her knee in his gut, Janie grabbed a handful of the gravel in her right hand and slammed the sharp points into his cheek.

The Agent recoiled to the side which allowed Janie to break free. His hands scrabbled down her body and grabbed at her legs, but she kicked and regained her feet.

The woods returned, but hidden in the shape of the tree trunks lay the melted candle wick patterns of stalagmites, and over the pools, the ghosts of smoldering, coal-filled stone braziers stood guard.

Laughing without humor, the Agent stood up. He held a rosewood-handled revolver in one hand.

Janie touched her hips, but she already knew one gun lay in the moss (or gravel) behind the Agent and the other balanced in his hand.

"This wasn't gonna have to be hard." He spat red to the side. "I saw you talking to the Injun. Guess he wasn't sittin' inna fire like I thought, was he?" He glanced about the woods around them. "A dark cave and fires makes most sense to me, but woods 's okay too." The sharpness of his eyes slashed at her when he looked back. "What made it change?"

Janie's shoulders gave a little bob. *He sees the woods now too.* "We touched."

The gun barrel lolled off to her left. He grunted. "Guess I ain't ever touched anyone in here before." He dug a bloodied piece of gravel from his cheek. "You know how to talk to them other worlds. That's what the Guv'nor needs."

Janie contemplated running. If Governor Hogg wanted her alive, the Agent would hold his fire, the panicked side of her mind argued and tried to wrest control of her legs. The bitter side of her mind amended that he would just avoid shooting her in the important bits. In any case, with this crazy room, there was nowhere new to run to, nowhere to hide, and since it continued monotonous pool after pool, she might become lost forever, unable to get to Will or home or anywhere ever again.

With his free hand, the Agent undid his gun belt and dropped it near Janie's original dislodged pistol. "'Course now you an' I is gonna have some fun, and I'm gonna hurt you. Probably no worse 'n your daddy or them boys in your gang did, but it'll hurt. I'll make sure o' dat." He mused at the remaining revolver in his hand. "Don't think I'll be needin' this either."

When the gun hit the soft earth of Janie's world, she heard the ghostly echo of loose stone from another.

"Was you just for one'na them, or did they pass you 'round?" He took a step forward, and Janie retreated a pace. He sneered. "Bet you like being passed 'round."

The small animal part of her brain screamed for her to run, but Janie had never been the running type.

When he took another pace toward her, Janie dug the toe of her back boot into the earth. If this did not work, she knew the Agent would make good on his promise to hurt her. She focused on the ghostly altar over his shoulder and willed the world to change.

It did.

The Agent faltered on his next step as his world shifted too.

Janie's toe, now buried in gravel, kicked high to pelt him with a shower of sharp stones.

On instinct, he turned his head and blinked to protect his eyes. He expected her to run and whipped his head back around ready to pursue her.

Janie did run, but she ran straight at him. When his face spun back to track her, her fist met his already bruised nose and snapped his head backward on that long, skinny neck. The staggering blow allowed Janie to dodge past him toward the stone altar and the guns, but he was bigger and stronger. Despite the stars in his eyes and blood on his face, he snatched at her arm and kicked a leg into hers. Down they both sprawled again, not onto gravel, but soft dirt. When she had stopped concentrating, the world had shifted back to woods.

Janie clambered to her knees, but his hands grabbed her boots. She kicked to dislodge him, but the grip on her ankles tightened. He growled and yanked her legs back so she collapsed back onto her belly with the nearest gun more than two feet away.

Janie rolled to her left in an attempt to slip free. She kicked again but caught only air.

"Yeah, I'm gonna hurt you bad, before, during, 'n after." He crawled up her legs, pinning her to the ground. From his belt, a blade flashed under the dull grey of the featureless sky. "I'm gonna cut you first. Not yer tongue, 'cause the Gov'nor needs that, but maybe that purty little face of yours."

Janie's arms had been flailing above her, trying to find the guns, but to no avail.

The man straddled her waist with his boots locked between her legs and nailing hers to the ground. His left hand clamped onto her neck, tight enough to bruise and make this grey world dim more.

Janie tried to pry at those thick fingers, but they were too strong.

"Maybe yer eye." The cool metal of the blade froze her when it touched her cheek just below the left eye and ran a light trail down toward her mouth. "Prob'ly, but maybe somewhere a little mor' private first." The blade dug harder when he traced it down to the shirt over her collar bone and onto her chest and began to dig at the top button. Farther down, she could feel his excitement at having her at his mercy.

Her fingers brushed the cool of the pool, and when she turned her head that way, the memory of sharp rocks danced before her eyes. The sound of her shirt tearing under the blade competed with the pounding of her heart in her ears. Janie cupped her hand around a spirit rock the size of a large apple.

She pushed out the other sensations screaming in her body, she had learned to do that years ago when her father was alive, and concentrated on the rock.

The world shifted.

The cold, hard rock nestled in her hand.

Janie swung the rock to meet the Agent's temple.

The dull crack of rock against skull reverberated in her ears.

Stunned, he collapsed off of her.

Janie rolled atop him and brought the rock down on his face again. And again. And again.

For the first few blows, he groaned and flinched and twitched beneath her. When that stopped, he made little wheezing noises through what remained of his nose and teeth. Under the meaty thuds, like the sound of pounding a stone onto wet sand, the wheezing became gurgles which trailed away until all that remained was the sound of stone on sand.

When Janie sat back on her haunches, she knelt over a warm hunk of meat in a serene woods. She tossed the bloody rock to the side where it evaporated in the air before crunching on gravel in another world. She wiped off the blood from her hands on his shirt.

As much from fatigue as the after-effects of the adrenaline ebbing from her system, her legs wobbled beneath her when she stood. If there had been other Agents in the woods, they would have already intervened, but Janie surveyed her surroundings nevertheless. Satisfied she was alone, she took stock of her possessions. Her rosewood revolvers returned to her holsters. She emptied the bullets from the Agent's guns and stuffed them and the gun belt into the satchel of food from Warren. Her small knife lay nestled in her backpack, but the Agent's knife was bigger, and so she added its sheath to her gun belt.

Evening crept across Will's pool at her feet. Janie's fingers caressed his cheek, and he brushed at the side of his face as if a mosquito had buzzed by.

"Stay safe, Will. I'm coming." As she rose, she fingered the teal bracelet. Her dark eyes drank in that kin Will one last time before she made an about-face toward the archway and Governor Hogg's mansion.

While she marched around the pools and between the trees, she concentrated on the hidden shapes in the trunks of the trees and the ripples across the pools, and the shimmer of the grey light from above. The heels of her boots clicked on worn wood, and oaken tables with yellow maps took the place of pools. At a furrow of her brow, the tables contracted into pulsing crystal balls atop marble pedestals. Each new transformation made the next smoother. The crystal balls and pedestals flattened into mirrors reflecting images of a young woman Arthur De Casas might not have recognized. The mirrors dissolved into fumaroles belching puffs of grey smoke.

Janie brought the bracelet up to her lips and the woods came back into focus. At the touch of blue stone to pink lips, the stone became two streams coursing in opposite circles about her wrist. "Will Covington," she breathed onto the entwined threads of azure. He appeared in her mind, bedding down in a nest of pine needles between the roots of a slanting fir. When she let her hand drop away, the flowing rivulets on her wrist hardened into stone, and Will faded like the bloodied rock had evaporated from her woods.

Dick Warren trudged up the second flight of stairs toward Hogg's office with the satchel of sandwiches and a canteen of water bumping on his hip. A handful of years ago, he had bounded up these stairs, but a few years and more than a few extra pounds left him with a slight puff at the top. He paused on the landing for a couple of breaths to let his heart rate even out before proceeding down the hallway.

His headache, which had started before lunch with the kitchen staff complaining to him about his Agents snitching food from the larder at night, put on a head of steam when he stepped into that damnable crystal ball room. Forty minutes of wandering in circles and bellowing for that equally damnable De Casas woman solidified the thump between his ears into the continuous chug of steam engine wheels pounding on the track.

Now, he had to break the news to Governor Hogg that his pet parakeet had flown from her cage in the middle of the night. At least Warren knew who was raiding the larder. That thought reminded him of the satchel still slung over his shoulder, and he snorted in derision at himself. He should have left that downstairs. After delivering this news, he was going to be in no mood to eat.

Once upon a time... no, scratch that, never had this job been pleasant. Warren had served in the Territory Rangers, but even he had seen they lacked the organization and resources needed to manage the people and the land. The Rangers certainly had never been a force to govern the Jefferson Territory, only patrol and try and keep the worst of the bullies at bay. When statehood and Governor Hogg arrived, Warren had seen the way the wind blew with a strong, firm leader squaring off against a bunch of self-important hotheads. Warren had done his best to convince the cream of the Rangers to drift over to the other side before the hammer fell. Seward Garland, now dead in that debacle in Victory, had listened, and even George Hennessy bowed out under Warren's gentle prodding. Warren had even dragged off that pain the in derrière, David McPhail, one last time before the Governor made his move, but that tête-à-tête had been to no avail. McPhail had been as hardheaded and obstinate as his best buddy and rival in love, Joseph Covington.

After the Rangers fell, Warren suited up in black and joined Hogg's posse of Agents, and worked his way up to Head Agent. That had been a climb, and Warren had contemplated hanging up his spurs on more than one occasion, but as long as he was about, he could keep some of the less savory characters among the Agents in line and rein in some of Hogg's more capricious ways. Hogg was a good leader, but a bit like that Prince Machiavelli fellow, the ends justifying the means and all that. For all their faults, that at least had never been the Rangers' way.

Well, they were all gone now, even McPhail, if Governor Hogg's assurances were to be believed. Warren would not be assuaged on that matter until his own two eyes saw McPhail's body laid out in the cold earth. That man kept turning up like a pebble in your boot you kept trying to shake out, but as soon as the boot was back on your foot, up and stabbed you in the arch again. Warren was all that remained of the Rangers, and he often pondered if all the sacrifices had made a damn bit of good.

"Come in." Hogg's voice answered four seconds after Warren's initial knock.

Perceptive as always, Governor Hogg set down his pen, leaned back in his chair, and regarded his Head Agent over steepled fingers. "I'm not going to be happy, am I?"

Having long surrendered the need to be formal alone with the Governor, Warren dropped the satchel and canteen on the desk and flopped down into one of the red velvet chairs. "Someone raided the kitchen in the middle of the night, and she didn't show up after forty minutes of me calling for her. I think she scampered."

Hogg pursed his lips and nodded. Seconds ticked by on the clock. "We need her back. She's made contact."

Warren felt his face scrunch up. "Might have just scampered. Had enough of mooning and headed for the hills."

"You said she found him, didn't you?"

Shoulder shrug. "She admitted as much."

"And does she strike you as the kind of woman to just give up?"

Warren squirmed in the chair. "No, but maybe she saw something in there. Maybe he died in that other world or found himself another woman. Maybe just knowing he was okay was enough."

Hogg waved a hand. "If she saw him die, she wouldn't have come out to steal food. She'd look for another world or kill herself. Same if he found another woman. If knowing he was out there was enough, she would have left days ago." Hogg leaned forward across the desk. "Something changed. She made contact with one of the other worlds, maybe with him, maybe with someone else, or she thinks she found a way to cross over. That would be her only reason to leave."

Warren did not follow that logic all the way through, but years in this position had taught him not to question the Governor's reasoning, murky as it might seem to the Head Agent. He kept his mouth shut.

Hogg unfolded his lanky frame and turned to gaze out the window. "She might not even have made it out of the city yet. She'd have been exhausted and starving after that long in the map room, hence the need to raid our winter stores." Hogg turned on his heel. "Notify the rest of the Agents that De Casas is about in the city or its environs. We need her alive." He glared into Warren's eyes. "If she dies, I'll have the head of the man who did it. Make sure they know that."

Warren stood up. "Yes, sir."

Hogg's face relaxed again, his ferocity hidden once more by his implacable mask of a face. "Also, get some dogs and search the map room for Agent Palliser."

"Pardon me, sir?"

Hogg waved that dismissive hand again. "I sent Palliser in there to spy on her a few days ago." He smirked. "Don't give me that hurt look, Dick. You weren't getting anywhere with her. Palliser was to keep an eye on her, and if she made contact, to bring her to me." Hogg shrugged. "She's gone, and he's not back. You'll find his body near whatever world she found her beau in. That will be useful information too."

When the Head Agent did not move to the door, Governor

Hogg looked him up and down. "Chop, chop. You have a fugi-tive to find and an Agent to bury. Move along."

"Yes, sir." Warren clomped all the way down the hallway, fuming to himself. He liked to think himself the Governor's right-hand man, but once again, life made clear that Alistair Hogg spun wheels within wheels within wheels, and one cog in those wheels was as good as any other.

The hay prickled her skin. In the wee hours of the morning, the insect denizens of the hayloft had decided to make a breakfast of her arms and neck, and she thought in the middle of the night, a mouse had tried to bed down in her boot while her foot was still in it, but despite those indignities, Janie woke recharged and refreshed after just a few hours' sleep.

Down below, the sheep bleated and the smells of old and fresh manure drifted up after the sounds. Dawn stabbed through the gaps in the wood. The barn doors creaked on their hinges when the farmhand came inside to open the pens and shoo the animals out for the morning. Somewhere nearby came the sound of an ax splitting wood.

Janie tried to burrow deeper into the concealing hay without making excess noise, but the farmhand did not venture into the loft.

Across the loft, a calico cat regarded her from its perch atop a hay bale for a time before deciding Janie was neither a mouse nor about to produce a saucer of milk. It sat down and began grooming itself.

Janie ought to have left before dawn or never have crawled

into this barn, but last night, her thoughts had jumbled about confused inside her throbbing head.

Back in that woods between the worlds, Janie had waited outside the archway until by the nearest pool she had judged it close to midnight, and then she stepped back into the corridor hidden deep beneath Governor Hogg's mansion. This time, she had been prepared for the stretching and crushing and nausea, but the fatigue and hunger hammered her when her boots crunched into the dirt and sand of the dark passage. She swooned for a moment and caught herself against the rough rock wall, but did not drop the gun in her hand.

After a few seconds, she mastered herself and, by the thin blue glow thrown off by the archway, made her way to the stairway, past the basement, and out into the first-floor parlor. After a stop in the kitchens, Janie stole across the mansion grounds and out into the city. Her muddled brain directed her to the docks. Will and Finn left San Alonso by boat. She would do the same.

Sometime later, with the moon faded behind the mountains to the west, Janie awoke on a raft run aground on the shores of the Great River. She stumbled off the raft and down the road which she hoped led away from San Alonso. At the first farm she came to, a mile or so from her abandoned raft, she slipped into the barn and up into the hayloft. The whole way, she had been cramming food into her mouth to fill her empty stomach and replenish weak and shaky muscles. If Governor Hogg's Agents found her raft, all they would have to do was follow the string of crumbs scattered in her wake like a drunken Hansel and Gretel.

With the arrival of morning, Janie needed real plans and an exit from this farm without attracting attention. When she entered San Alonso, however long ago that had been, her face had adorned wanted posters throughout the city. Even if Governor Hogg had removed them, the locals might still recognize her and assume the reward stood. After that, she needed to find the Klah of her world and persuade him to help her. Klah would be in the big pueblo, and that lay to the north.

Her stomach growled loud enough to make the cat pause and eye her for a moment before resuming its morning ablutions. "Okay," Janie muttered to the cat as much to herself. "Food first."

Sitting cross-legged in the hay, Janie pulled out a last corner of bread, a hunk of cheese, a single strip of jerky, and a half shriveled apple. Get out of the barn, get some more food and water, and find a way to the pueblo while avoiding the Agents and human contact. Easy.

How long before Hogg realized she was gone? If he kept to his schedule, Warren was due to visit today or tomorrow, but might not be perturbed if she did not answer. He would likely just leave the satchel of food and check in later in the day or the next. What about the Agent she had killed? When did he report in and to whom? Probably to Warren or Hogg himself, but how often was the real question. She had to assume the man would report daily on her activities, which meant a posse might already be sweeping the area for her. Why hadn't she stayed on the raft or found a horse? At least then, she would be far off down the river just like Will and Finn had escaped.

Thinking of them so vividly, made her look down at the blue bracelet bouncing on her wrist. She held the bracelet up before her eyes and concentrated on the picture of Will in her mind. The hard blue dissolved into flowing intertwined streams. "Will Covington," she whispered as she closed her eyes.

And there he was before her, astride a horse, with the slopes of the Elephant Mountains and the sun on his right.

When she opened her eyes, Will's image dissolved and the bracelet hardened to stone once again. Still alive and on the move, and Janie could follow him as Klah had promised, even out of that strange viewing platform between the possible worlds.

She breathed a sigh before gathering her things. Time to go.

Downstairs, through the cracks between the boards, Janie

surveyed the farmyard. The open front doors of the barn faced the house and yard, but a small side door opened away from the house toward the river somewhere in the near distance. That same side door, though, exited toward a broad figure chopping wood.

At first glance, Janie took the figure for a man, but when the woodcutter paused to tip back her hat and mop her brow, Janie realized she was a woman. The woman had wide shoulders and strong legs built from hard labor on the farm. Her skin, fairer than Will or Finn's, was red as much from the sun as the exertion of chopping. On closer look, she wore a blouse, well mended, in a faded shade of blue, stretched over an ample chest, but she wore canvas pants rather than a skirt as she worked the wood.

The woman looked toward the crack of the barn door from which Janie peered deep in the shadows. "I hope you got a good rest. You can come out whenever you want."

Janie shrank back from the doorway and dropped a hand to the holster on her hip.

The woman continued to smile. She probably could not see where Janie's hand rested. "I was up across the field well before sunup checking on the cows. We've had some wolves coming down out of the mountains of late. I saw you come stumbling down the road and slip into our barn. When I got back, I warned Madison to keep an eye out for you but keep her distance. We don't mean you any harm." She stooped down to pick up a canteen of water and take a swig. "My name's Henrika, and this is my farm."

Janie did not see a point in continuing the pretense of hiding. Before swinging the door open, she glanced behind to be sure no one had crept up on her in the barn. Another quick check assured Janie that neither this Madison nor another of Henrika's friends lurked outside this side door, and she stepped into the sunlight. "I'm sorry for sneaking in. I'm just passing through and needed a place to sleep."

"Many a lost lamb finds their way to my ranch. You can stay as long as you need." The woman kept both her hands open in front of her and nodded to the hand Janie rested on the butt of her gun. "You know how to use those?"

"I've killed more than a dozen men, most of them Agents, my father included, and a crazy Ranger to boot with these or ones like them. Yeah, I know how to use them."

Henrika pursed her lips. "More wolf than lamb then." The two women regarded each other. "If you don't mind my saying though, a wolf without a pack if I'm any judge."

Janie shrugged. "If everything works out right, I'll have my pack back soon enough."

"Well, I wish you the best in finding them." Henrika cocked her head to the side. "In the meantime, you look like you could use a good meal and a bath and some clean clothes. If you'll refrain from shooting me and my girls, I'd be happy to accommodate you."

At the idea of food, Janie's stomach grumbled. Under the recent layer of old hay, she smelled of sweat and dirt, cordite, and the iron tinge of blood. In the sunlight, she could still see the dried blood of that Agent under her nails and rust-colored stains on her shirt sleeves. "How much would that cost?"

Henrika chuckled. "Nothing, my dear."

"Why would you help me? Why should I trust you?"

Now the older woman looked confused. "Isn't that what you came here for? Refuge? Help?"

"I was just looking for a place to sleep and to move on peacefully."

"You said that." Henrika looked Janie up and down again. "You don't know who I am or where you are?" She shook her head. "I assumed someone sent you, but you just stumbled in on your own." She tilted her head back and gave a chortle to the strange ways of fate. "Well, I'll be damned."

Janie shifted back a step. "I still don't know what you're talking about."

Henrika waved her arms in an encompassing gesture about them. "Well, Miss Wolf, you might consider this ranch a home for wayward girls and women, a refuge from the world at large." She inclined her head to the path around the side of the barn. "Walk with me." Without waiting, she headed toward the front of the barn and the house. "May I ask your name?"

Janie fell into step with the older woman. "Janie." She almost gave her last name but closed her mouth on the syllables.

Waving her hand in dismissal, Henrika smiled. "No surname is fine here. Janie Wolf works well for me. Many of my guests have pasts they want to forget. Some of them find new names here and stay, others move on."

Together they rounded the barn and strode across the front yard, Janie hurrying to keep up with Henrika's larger steps. To their left, a woman around Janie's age with short cropped brown hair leaned against the gate to a fenced pasture that accommodated the small flock of sheep that had bedded overnight in the barn. As the woman's head swiveled to watch them, the tan and white collie at her feet flicked her ears at Janie and Henrika before laying her head back on her paws. To the side of the house, two more women moved through a garden of small green shoots pulling up weeds. Off to the opposite side of the house, another woman worked the pump of a well while a fifth carried buckets of water across the yard toward a trough for the sheep. On the porch steps, a girl sat mending some clothes. When she spied Janie and Henrika's approach, she grabbed her things and ran inside.

"Some of my girls are wolves or at least coyotes," Henrika explained. She gestured with a cock of her head to the young woman at the fence. "Like Madison back there. Others, like Sally there, are more kittens."

Janie swung her head back and forth surveying the scene. "Just women. No men?"

Henrika shot Janie a sidelong glance. "A young woman who brags of killing her father probably can guess the rest on her own. When a girl or a woman or even an old crone has had enough, they can come to find a safe place on Henrika's ranch. No need to tell their story if they don't want. I've heard all of them before anyway. All I ask is that they pitch in where they're able."

The wood of the porch gave a dull clomp under their boots, and the front door creaked on its hinges when they pushed inside. Janie thought she saw a pair of bare feet scurry farther away into the homestead. In the kitchen, where they entered, a thin grey-haired woman, wearing a dress faded to the color of her hair, kneaded dough on a floured cutting board. "Thought I'd make us some pies for dinner," she said when the pair entered.

"I'm sure our newest guest would appreciate one of your pies, Lizzie," Henrika said.

The old woman looked up and gave a gap-toothed grin to Janie. "Welcome, young miss. I was thinking an apple and a rhubarb, but I might be able to find the fixings for mincemeat if that takes your fancy."

"I can't stay," Janie answered. "I'm looking for someone."

"That's what they all say. Maybe Winnie and Penny can go find themselves some berries to pick, and we'll have us a nice warm berry cobbler." Lizzie returned to her dough and allowed Henrika to lead Janie into a small sitting room with a little couch, a spinning wheel, and a loom where another young woman sat pushing the shuttle back and forth.

The weaver turned from her project when they entered. She looked a few years younger than Janie, but she wore a brand across her right cheek, under a milky white eye. Janie had seen plenty of terrible sights in her life, but at the sight of the disfigured girl, she had to suppress a shudder.

"Chrissy," Henrika said. "Ask the girls out front to prepare a bath for our guest and then see if you can find her some fresh clothes. The ones she has will need a washing and some mending."

The young woman jumped up, nodded, and ran out of the room.

Henrika gestured for Janie to sit on the small couch and lowered herself into a chair.

Janie's eyes followed Chrissy out the door. "Are all of them as... as her?"

"We all carry our own scars. Some of them are just easier to see than others."

Lizzie took that moment to come tottering into the room with an urn and two cups. Janie wanted to jump up and grab the tray, but a warning look from Henrika held her in her seat. The old woman wobbled to and fro but managed to negotiate the space between couch and chair to put the rattling tray down on a small table. She gave a little sigh and a groan before standing up and beaming at Janie. "Coffee," she declared and wobbled back to the kitchen.

Henrika leaned forward to fill the two cups. "She's still a proud woman and insists on doing things on her own. There's some other ones here more than happy to let you do all their chores for them." She leaned back and sipped her coffee.

Janie picked up her cup. The coffee was dark and bitter and only tepidly warm, but filled her with a kind of comfort. When was the last time she had sat enjoying coffee on the trail? Probably sometime before Will died in Victory. She fingered the cool stone of the bracelet but resisted the urge to call forth his image. Later, when she was alone, she would check on him again. Shaking herself from wistful thoughts, she glanced up to Henrika, who was regarding her over her own cup. "So when do the questions start?" Janie asked.

"No questions. Whenever you're ready to talk, we can talk. If you choose not to talk, I'll not pry. When your bath is ready, I'll finish chopping and join you and the rest of our little family for lunch."

True to her word, Henrika asked no questions. True to her nature, Janie remained silent. The two women sipped coffee and listened to the sounds of pots clanging in the kitchen and voices as someone else joined Lizzie to help prepare lunch.

As they sat there, Janie felt eyes on her. Trying to be inconspicuous about it, she let her head drift back and forth from one corner of the room to the other, but could find no one peering from around a doorway or from behind the furniture. Something niggled at the back of her mind and drew her eyes to the corner of the room behind Henrika. When her eyes alit in the corner, a cool tingle vibrated around her wrist. Janie gave a languid blink, and when her eyes closed, Klah appeared in her mind while three other figures blurred in the background. "Call us when you are ready," Klah's voice rang in her ears, and the four figures blew away like wisps of smoke.

When Janie opened her eyes, Henrika's hazel eyes stared back at her. She raised her eyebrows, but Janie gave a little shake of her head, and they returned to sipping coffee.

Eventually, Chrissy came back and led Janie to a small shed out back of the house with a small basin to stand in, and jugs of warm water to wash herself and rinse. A stack of clothes lay folded on a shelf, and Chrissy slipped off with Janie's soiled garments. Janie kept her holstered guns and backpack close by, though, and never removed the blue bracelet from her wrist.

After washing and dressing, Janie latched the door and sat down on a bench against the wall. She breathed onto the bracelet as she closed her eyes. "Klah."

The world swam for a moment, and then the tribesman appeared before her, sitting on a rug in the home he shared with the older shaman. "She's here," Klah said to someone else in the room, and then turned back to her. "Welcome, Janie De Casas."

"Thank you, Klah. Your bracelet works."

"Ours do too." Klah held up his wrist where another black bracelet, this one alive with streaks of green entwined in black, coiled about his wrist like a smoke ring blown from a pipe. Three more people stepped into Janie's view. The first was the older shaman with his blind eyes. Janie recognized him but could not remember his name from her visit to the village or when Klah had referred to him as his mentor. The other two looked like old friends.

"Nascha. Bidziil." Green and black smoke coils danced around each of the young people's wrists.

The young man nodded, solemn as ever, but the young woman smiled. "Welcome back, Janie." Her face took on a pained look. "Is it true you are no longer of our world?"

"Yes, I died in your world."

"I am sorry, Janie. I had hoped to see you again. But your young man, Will, still lives?"

"Yes, he does. I'm trying to reach him, or at least protect him."

"What of your other friends, the cousin Finn and the Ranger McPhail?"

"McPhail is dead. Finn went west with Sahkyo. I'm alone."

Nascha made a face. "But Sahkyo is still here. I saw her this morning."

"I'm sorry, this is all so confusing," Janie said with a shake of her spirit head. "My Finn escaped. The Finn in your world died, killed by Agents. He died bravely, protecting his friend. McPhail died in a fire in San Alonso. I saw it happen." Even as she spoke, Janie realized she had never looked for McPhail after the fire in San Alonso. Despite betraying Janie in her world, maybe he had remained loyal in Will's.

Nascha's face stretched long. "I feared as much. Sahkyo will be sad, but it is best she knows. I hope the Finn and Sahkyo of your world can find enough happiness for the ones in mine."

"Me too."

Klah waited to be sure the women had no more to say before speaking. "I told you, that I will do what I can to look after Will Covington. Bidziil and Nascha will each keep one of the bracelets. When they go to find Will Covington in our world, they will take Tsela's bracelet to him. Then you may speak with him, and see what the fates decree."

"Thank you," Janie said.

"Where is Will of our world?" Klah asked.

Janie thought back, picturing the terrain. "Somewhere south, near the end of the Elephants, I think. He's staying hidden from the Agents chasing him."

"That may be too far." Klah frowned in concentration. "You said he hears you?"

"Sometimes."

"Send him north if you can, toward our village. When he is close, Bidziil and Nascha will find him."

"I'll try. He seems to respond most when he's asleep. I'll try to speak to him tonight."

"You speak to him in his dreams," Tsela said. "It is the way of kin-spirits. If you are bonded as you say, he will hear you in his dreams and then in his waking if he becomes open."

"Find our kin-spirits in your world, Janie," said Klah. "Show them the bracelet. They will know what it is, and they will help you."

"Thank you Klah, Nascha, Bidziil, Tsela. Thank you."

"Tell us when Will Covington comes near, Janie De Casas." Tsela pursed his lips and blew. Waves of smoke stung her eyes and made her blink, and when they opened, she sat alone in the little shed on Henrika's ranch.

Lunch happened behind the house on two long tables pushed together. They ate biscuits with gravy, cold fried chicken, assorted vegetables, and a tangy lemonade that made Janie's tongue tingle.

Henrika sat at the head of the table while little Sally hid at the far end behind the other women and as far away and out of Janie's eyesight as possible. Fifteen women supped at the table, ranging from Lizzy who was by far the oldest down to

Sally who appeared the youngest, likely not much more than ten, but by Janie's estimation, most clustered in their later teens to thirties. All had tanned skin from farm work in the sun, but otherwise, their complexions marked them as the daughters of settlers, natives, conquistadors, and slaves.

This group served as the main workforce of the ranch, but a little farther back over a rise hid another bunkhouse where a handful of women cared for the babies and toddlers who had come with the women to Henrika's ranch, either in their arms or their bellies.

Chrissy bore the most visible scars of the cadre at the table, but Janie felt a kinship with each of these women pulling at invisible strings in her being.

Janie sat to Henrika's right and Madison on the matriarch's left, across from Janie. While many of the women wore dresses, Madison was in the significant minority who found pants and shirts more suitable to work on the farm. Like Madison, two of those women wore holstered revolvers and one leaned a rifle against the house when she sat down to eat.

Although they all greeted Janie in variations of friendliness or cordiality, no one pressed her for more than her name. She had expected questions about her hometown, her travels, and where she was headed, but instead, after the greeting, the women either ignored her or chatted about the day's work on the farm, the pleasant weather it was for late winter, or Lizzy's fine rolls.

Janie felt the weight of Madison's appraisal of her, but she spoke as little as Janie herself. Henrika filled in the conversation with platitudes about nothing in particular.

Once the meal was done, Janie stood to carry dishes back to the kitchen, but Henrika stopped her. "Leave them to the ladies. Come walk with Madison and me, will you please?"

They took a short walk together in the back of the ranch and up the little rise. At the top of the ridge, they could look back over the ranch house and barn toward the shimmer of the Great River. On the opposite side, the rise dropped away into a hollow where the other bunkhouse sat and small children played in the dirt under the watchful eye of their caretakers. Behind that rose more fields and rolling hills until they merged into the towering peaks of the Elephants.

"I told you I wouldn't pry into your business, Janie, but I do have a proposal for you." That was the first Henrika had spoken since asking her away from the table.

Janie had suspected as much and still feared what might follow a polite rejection. "I told you earlier, I'm looking for someone. I'm only passing by."

"I understand that, but I hope a bath, some clean clothes, and a fine supper buys us your ears for a few minutes." Henrika waited for Janie's fractional nod. "As I said and you've seen, we're a haven here for girls and women who have been abused. They hear about us through friends and word of mouth or stumble on us as you have. We give them a place to heal and to hide and to rebuild their lives."

"But some people don't like that." Madison picked up at Henrika's pause. "Fathers, brothers, husbands, fiancés — it doesn't matter. Sometimes they come to take back their 'property.'" She glowered at the world in general and kicked at a stone. "We don't let them."

The force of the other woman's stare almost broke Janie's reserves, but she refused to turn away from the sharp blue of Madison's eyes until she continued. "Four of the other women and I keep an eye out for anyone approaching and intercept them before they get close. Some of the other women help out, but mostly it's us five. At night, we set watches."

Henrika smiled at Janie. "Last night I was watching for metaphorical wolves."

"Most of them bluster a lot and cry and beg and plead and leave with their tail between their legs." Madison snorted with derision. "A fair number try to come back later, usually at night, sometimes with friends. Those that come back don't leave on their own two feet." She cocked her chin back in pride.

"What does that have to do with me?" Janie knew perfectly well what it had to do with her, but if they were going to ask, they needed to do it clean.

Janie expected Henrika to take back over, but Madison refused to relinquish the floor. Her look turned from prideful to earnest. "If you're who we think you are, and what you claim to be, I could use you. My team and I are good, but most of us haven't been in many real gunfights. You could teach us, help us get better, make sure no one hurts any of us again." She paused and swallowed the lump in her throat. "If you're really her, you could even lead us." Madison's voice trailed away at the end. The admission hurt her, but her mission to defend Hacienda Henrika mattered more to her than the blow to her pride.

That creep of vulnerability into Madison's tone dug claws into Janie's heart. She remembered when her own fears had broken her down, and how she had cried into Will's shoulder, admitting that she too needed help, needed someone. Moisture stung her eyes, and Janie turned away to stare down at the women and children outside the bunkhouse. Arms crossed over her chest, she spoke without turning. "You don't know me. You don't know who I am."

Behind her, Janie imagined Madison and Henrika exchanging a look. The older woman spoke. "We've both been into the city and seen the posters. You even made the papers off and on for the past nine months. If I remember, in the end, they called you and your wolf pack the Hennessy Gang, but it started off as the De Casas Gang."

"You sure do look like her anyway," Madison said.

"And you told me you've killed quite a few men, mostly Agents, as I recollect," Henrika said.

The silence stretched off on the breeze coming off distant mountains.

The shadow of a crow zipped across the ground.

Henrika cleared her throat. "You're a hero to the women

here, Janie. Most of them never saw the posters, but they listened to your stories in the paper and could read between the lines. You killed the person who wronged you, escaped the hangman's noose, and got revenge on all of them. You gave the women here hope. They wished they could have done what you did, and it broke their hearts when the papers said the Hennessy Gang was dead and gone."

"If your gang's gone, who're you looking for?" While Henrika had promised not to pry, Madison did not seem to feel bound by that oath.

The blue bracelet hung heavy on her wrist, and Janie fidgeted, rotating the stone around and around. So she was a hero to the downtrodden women of Jefferson, and Hogg had put out the word that they were all dead. Had Finn really caught a train out with Sahkyo, or had that just been a tale Hogg spun to reel her in? She wondered if she could use the bracelet to ask the Klah of that other world to look in on hers and find the big galoot, and if Klah could look, would he find only darkness? Janie spun back on her heel to face the women. Would anyone in this nunnery understand? "Will Covington." She said his name like throwing down a gauntlet.

This time, Janie saw the look Henrika and Madison shared, just as knowing and pitying as she expected. When Henrika returned her gaze to Janie, the woman's eyes reminded Janie of her mother's, but Madison stared at Janie's boots. "Papers said he died in Victory," the younger woman mumbled.

The memory of shattered bones scraped Janie's palms and the ghost of hot thick blood seeped into her shirt and burned her chest. "And I suppose they said I died too." Assuredly, in Will's world, they had.

Madison shrugged but did not look up. "Aye, that they did."

"Well, I didn't, and neither did he. We just got separated, but I'm going to find him." Strange how a lie could be true depending on which way you looked at it and how easy the half-truth rolled off her tongue.

"Is that what you want, child?" Henrika's voice caressed her, gentle as the wind.

"Yes." The huskiness in her voice surprised Janie with that rising lump in her throat and the burn in her eyes, but she would not cry in front of these women, and she would not break eye contact with the matriarch.

"Okay then." Disappointment, but not surprise, showed on Henrika's face. She had seen so many young women come through, most of them believing that special someone still waited for them or that the promise to change meant something this time. In the fullness of time, when the promises broke, some returned to Henrika while others never got the chance. "We'll give you what help we can. Where are you headed from here?"

"Better if you don't know."

Henrika bobbed her head with that pursed smile on her lips. "Hard to be much help if you don't tell me, but maybe if I were in your boots, I'd do the same."

Madison's head had been twisting back and forth like a weathervane caught in a crosswind. "Wait. You're not staying? We need you. You need us. We can keep each other safe. The Lord led you here, I know She did."

Janie shook her head. "No, Madison. It's better for you if I'm gone. I've got more trouble than you can imagine blowing on my tail. The sooner I'm away from your farm, the safer you'll all be."

"Who? More Agents?" Madison's voice was sharp, rising in fervor. "We know the stories. You're a legend. You stood up to them before, and you can do it again. Me and my girls will stand with you and send 'em packing back home or straight to hell."

Janie sighed. "Madison, I stood up to them with three of the fastest and best guns out there, and even then, the dice didn't roll our way." She let those treacherous tears that always seemed to hide just beneath the veneer of her strength well in her eyes now. "One of them's dead. One of them's lost. If there is a God, one of them's on his way out west with a woman to love, but more than likely he's as dead as the first. I'm all that's left, and when the Agents come for me, anybody standing with me is gonna find themselves six feet under or hanging by a noose six feet up."

The young guardian's face crumpled beneath Janie's stare, and Henrika laid a hand on Madison's arm. "She's right, Madison. It's for the best."

Janie had never felt a hero in her young life, never dreamed that someone would have heard her story and admired her, and now she felt like she'd just kicked a puppy. She exhaled. "I'll stay for a day."

Madison looked up with guarded hope.

"One day. To see how you and your girls shoot and take a lay of the land." Janie wagged her finger at Madison like Maria De Casas had scolded Janie in the kitchen. "I'm not an expert. I've never trained anyone in shooting or tactics, but I'll tell you what I can. After that, though, I need to go for your sake and for Will's. He and I stood by each other, protected each other, and he's still counting on me." *And I'm still counting on him,* she added to herself.

While Janie listened to Madison's pleas, Dick Warren knelt down, nose and mouth buried in his handkerchief, and looked at the body.

The bloodhounds had balked at approaching the gateway, but a bone from the kitchen was enough to entice the pair through. After crossing into that bizarre, tessellated world, the dogs lost their hesitation. A few sniffs from one of Agent Palliser's old shirts, and they set to their task, noses to the ground. At first, they spun in circles about the archway and then began to weave between the marble columns and plinths and orbs in Dick's version of alternate reality. Dick wondered what the dogs saw in their version of the world.

Whatever world they snuffled about in, their sense of smell led them on what must have been Palliser's preferred route, but when they caught the stronger scent of the man himself, they set off in a straight line. While Dick and Agents Neems and Macon and the dog handler Tracy dodged from side to side, the dogs bounded untouched through marble barriers that would have broken Dick's nose had he tried to follow on the dogs' heels.

Their ultimate path did not surprise Dick in the end. If the archway faced north, Janie De Casas had approached Dick from the northeast. He assumed she was playing at deceiving him. The dogs led them southwest, the same direction the Head Agent had wandered farthest this morning, calling De Casas' name when she had not appeared in the first few minutes.

"You sure that's him?" Moses Macon cocked his head to the side. "Not much of a face left."

"Dogs say it's him. It's him." Abe Tracy squatted and gave his two hounds deep scratches of appreciation along their rumps.

Big Ben Neems tapped his foot against the body's left hand. "That's that big old black mole on his wrist."

Macon whistled. "If you all say so. Whoever he was, he sure did upset someone. They done him in good."

Dick stood back up and shook his head. These were his men, all except Tracy anyway, and Tracy cared more about his dogs than he did about the doings of the Agents or even Governor Hogg himself. As long as Tracy got to roll around in the kennels with his four-legged friends, the rest of the world could go straight to heaven or hell, it made no matter to him. "It was De Casas that did this."

Macon jerked his head around to survey his surroundings. "De Casas? I thought the Gov'nor said we didn't have to worry about her or the Hennessy boy anymore."

"Well, the boy hopped a train toward North Cali, and the

Governor let De Casas into his little playground here. Problem was, he sent Palliser in to keep an eye on her." Dick kicked at the dead man's boot. "Could have told him this is how it would end."

"You think she's still around?" Macon rotated in a slow circle, hands on his guns.

"Nah, she flew the coop." Dick stood with his hands on his hips and heaved a sigh. The light in this damn place hurt his head. He tipped his head back, clamped his eyes shut, and thought.

So many men dead and gone in the past year or so, but when the Head Agent did the tallies, maybe it was not all bad. Murdock, who had died in the Serenity Valley at the beginning of this all, was no real loss, mean bastard that he was. Pryor and Reynolds' deaths out of Good Humor were a blow to Warren's plans. They were hard men, but good men who had not abused their power. Seward Garland lay somewhere in between, not a real impediment to progress, but a little too rigid. Losing his entire posse like that in Victory stung, but really, among the score of men, only one or two had really been the material Warren wanted to infuse into the rest of the Agents. Palliser had been even worse than Murdock, and if he had not been one of Governor Hogg's favorites, Warren might have bashed the man's face in himself come a time.

With all these open positions, maybe Warren could maneuver some of his own men into Hogg's personal posse. Both Neems and Macon were solid men, good men who did care about the people, the State, and right and wrong. Nelson showed real promise, though apt to be swayed by the wrong influence. The past year seemed a disaster to the Agents, but if Warren tried to think strategically like Governor Hogg, setbacks represented opportunity in disguise. If Warren could put his men in charge, he could push out the unreachable, rehabilitate the ones who had not gone bad in their core, and keep the good apples from spoiling. Then the Agents really would be the force for justice this state needed, while Warren would serve as Hogg's conscience.

"All right, well, we can't leave him here. If nothing else he'll stink up Hogg's playground. Neems, wrap him up, and let's haul him out. Macon, see if you can find any of his gear or any evidence of what happened. All I can see is damn solid marble. Tracy, hope your dogs can point us back toward the exit."

"Then what, Dick?" Neems asked.

"Put out the word to the Agents that Janie De Casas is still at large. No wanted posters for now. We keep it just in the family. We need her alive and unharmed, Governor's orders."

An involuntary chill ran up Macon's back. "That's gonna be a tall order." He nodded at Palliser's corpse. "She don't mess around."

When Dick glanced down, he noticed that the dead Agent's belt hung askew and the top button on his dungarees lay undone. "True, but I think Palliser here didn't understand the part about not hurting her. I met her, talked with her. If the right man finds her, he can reason with her, and then we can all go home happy." The Head Agent turned away and pulled out a cigarette. He detested the damn things, but those throbbing orbs in this world sizzled his brain worse.

Behind the Head Agents' back, Neems and Macon shared a doubtful look and a shrug.

In the end, despite her better judgment, good intentions won her over, and Janie stayed two more days with Henrika and her cadre of women.

By dinner the first evening, everyone knew Janie was "The Janie," the private hero of Henrika's ranch. The attention almost overwhelmed her resolve to stay. They fawned over her, even little Sally. Most wanted to touch her, run a hand across her shoulder, shake her hand, and they all wanted to hear her stories: how she had led the most wanted gang in all of Jefferson if not the Federation, gotten revenge on the men who had wronged her, and sought justice for all of the downtrodden and forgotten. If little of that story overlapped the truth, they did not want Janie to shatter the myth.

After her mother's death but before Janie killed her father, Janie's world had consisted of her little cabin and that father who had been loving, devoted, depressed, angry, remorseful, drunk, and abusive all rolled into one. She had learned to draw inside, remain quiet and motionless, unnoticed. In the past year or so, riding with an aloof, distant, and slightly crazed mentor, and the cousins, Will and Finn, as close as twins, Janie had managed to emerge from her cocoon, but even Will's attention had not prepared Janie for the flattery of a segment of the women and their naked need for Janie to be their champion. When farm chores did not occupy their hours, which thankfully seemed rare, the group hovered about her in a trailing cloud, Madison chief among them.

Not all of the women shared Madison's infatuation with Henrika's latest castaway. The sidelong glances and whispers that these women shared around Janie reminded her all too much of the looks the townspeople of Compassion had given her as the poor, bedraggled, and beaten daughter of the town drunk. If Madison captained the enamored, her fellow ranch guardian, Claire, led this skeptical faction.

Claire stood broad like Henrika with muscled arms, dirty blond hair, and a frown pasted across her lips even before she learned Janie's supposed identity. From their first encounter, when Madison brought Janie back down the hill to a dormitory that stretched off the back side of the ranch house to introduce her to the team of guardians, Claire doubted the veracity of Janie's story. Janie recognized the suspicion in the crossed arms, raised eyebrows, and the twitch of her nose when she looked Janie up and down. *Not my problem*, Janie thought to herself. *I've proved myself to better than the likes of you.*

All of the women on Madison's team were young, from late teens to early twenties, but carried themselves with a harder edge that belied their years, much like Janie herself. They included Abby, Beth, Claire, and Jessie, who based on her stance and deference shared a bond with Claire.

"We're twins," Abby said and offered her hand to Janie.

"Not identical," Beth said before Janie could even raise her eyebrows in surprise. Beth was as dark-skinned as anyone Janie had ever seen in her travels while Abby could be anywhere from a tanned white girl to a mixture of the various Spanish and native lines like Janie.

"I take after our mother," Abby continued.

"And I take after our father," Beth completed the quartet of lines, which sounded rehearsed.

Abby gave a shrug. "At least that's what our Abuela told us. We never met our parents."

"And she probably wasn't our Abuela," Beth finished. That last couplet sounded less rote like they only added it to certain people, and Janie felt honored by the admission.

The rest of the afternoon passed with a tour of the ranch and environs and pauses at each new knot of women to greet Janie.

With the sun setting and the temperature dropping, dinner took place around multiple tables in a dining room inside the ranch house. They left Janie in peace for dinner at a table with Henrika, Madison, Abby, Beth, and Lizzie, but afterward, they pushed back the tables, pulled their chairs into a double arc around Janie, and asked her to recount one of her exploits on the trail.

She chose Gorseman's Pass and the gold shipment, chasing the stagecoach, the fall into the river, and the harrowing ride down the rapids. "The current finally released us at the bottom of the mountain." She choked up at the memory of crying into Will's neck, the first person to whom she had admitted her father's abuse, of kissing him and falling asleep in his arms, feeling security for perhaps the first time since her mother died. "We managed to make a fire for the night, and Finn and McPhail found us in the morning," she finished instead.

"What about the gold?" Winnie asked.

"We buried it." Janie shrugged. "I suppose it's still there." The fortune in precious metal had never entered her mind since the last shovelful of dirt refilled the hole. Depending on Finn's fate, she might be the only living soul left who knew where it lay, and now she had planted the seeds of a legend of lost treasure in the hearts of a score of women.

That night she shared a small room and bunk bed with Madison. Henrika, Lizzie, Sally, and two older women shared the two bedrooms in the main house, and Chrissy preferred the couch in the sitting room. The rest of the women and girls slept in the dormitory in rooms of twos, threes, and fours in bunk beds or narrow pallets. Janie could not tell if Madison roomed alone or if Janie's arrival had displaced her roommate. Scrawled patrol schedules and sketches of men, some with X-marks across their faces, decorated the top of the table and small dresser, which made Janie suspect Madison slept alone, but the looks Claire shot raised shades of doubt about that assessment or how recent Madison's solo habitation might have been.

"Tomorrow, we'll all go out to the practice range. The girls and I want to show you what we can do, but we really want to see what you can do." Madison's voice drifted down from the top bunk.

"Don't get your hopes up too much." Janie laughed a little. "I'm only human. I'm sure you and your crew are good."

The pale oval of Madison's face peered over the edge. "You're great, Janie. Don't be modest. We all need to stand up for ourselves, no more getting pushed around." Her blue eyes sparkled in the moonlight through the window. "I'm so glad you're here. This changes everything." Before Janie could reply, the face disappeared. "Good night, Janie."

"Good night, Madison."

Janie lay awake in the dark and listened to the sounds of the night and Madison's breathing. Once the young woman above settled her rustling under the covers and her breathing assumed a steady rhythm, Janie ducked her head under her blankets and stared at the bracelet on her wrist. She contemplated reaching out for Klah, but the hour was late, and Will's well-being reigned preeminent in her mind. As she concentrated, a blue glow came off two intertwined rivers. She closed her eyes and whispered Will's name, barely louder than her own breath.

Janie was surprised to find Will sleeping on blankets on a wooden floor. By concentrating, she found she could pull back and turn and examine the scene. He slept safely in a farmhouse somewhere in the western plains of Jefferson. Janie turned back to Will's sleeping form. Had she been next to him in person, she would have been kneeling by his side, leaning over him. "You're okay, Will. I am too. I'll find a way to you, I promise. Stay safe. Go back to the pueblo. I'll meet you there." In his dreams, a smile played across Will's face. When she opened her eyes, the bracelet hardened, and Will vanished.

The next morning, Madison took Janie out to a shooting range north of the barn and away from the animal pastures. The nominal twins chatted as they trailed behind them while Claire and Jessie awaited the quartet at the targets.

The shooting gallery lay in the shade of a stand of pinion trees, heavy with branches and age. Weathered hay bales served as seats and tables. A stretch of fencing between two of the trees might serve as a balance beam for the younger children when they played here but now served as a stand for various types of targets from cans standing in small pyramids to pinecones. Three menacing scarecrows stood off to one side, armed with sticks to resemble guns. About fifty yards away, opposite the fencing and scarecrows, four boards painted like cowboys stood at attention. The holes and broken edges attested to their time of service to Madison and her crew.

Madison's excitement to show off her team of guardians suffused the air. She chattered about how often they came out to drill, the routines they followed, and how much they had improved over time. Initially, Henrika had tutored them, but as they all improved and then Claire arrived, Henrika spent less time with them, proclaiming how much confidence she had in their abilities, which had surpassed her own. Abby, Beth, and Jessie all beamed under the praise Madison sowed about them, and although Claire could not help but crack a small upturn to the corners of her mouth, she did her best to glower.

Janie contented herself with watching and adding small words of compliment and encouragement. She sat on one of the hay bales with her back to the sun. The breeze nipped with the mild chill of winter's incremental death, but the sun soaked into her long sable hair, tied to hang down to the center of her back. In time, the heat her hair absorbed would become uncomfortable even in the coolness of the day, and she would pull on her hat or move into the shade, but for now, she enjoyed the ability to just sit and experience the sensation without worrying about running and hiding or fighting. She rocked the bracelet on her wrist and when she let it dangle in the sun, it shone with the blue depths of hidden oceans.

From time to time, Janie felt a presence looking over her. Klah or Nascha or perhaps Bidziil looking in on her. She suspected Tsela had the patience to wait.

While none of the five women from Henrika's ranch would soon enlist with Governor Hogg's Agents, nor had any attained Ranger-level mastery, Madison and her four companions put on a commendable display of practiced potential. They stood, aimed, and hit their targets more often than not. Janie noted that none drew and fired, and only Madison and Claire attempted to hit multiple targets rapid fire, both with moderate success, more than likely good enough to drive off or kill spurned lovers, but not enough against a sustained assault by trained soldiers.

For a time, Janie watched Abby and Jessie, who took turns firing rifles at the distant decorated boards. Abby grunted in frustration when her second shot in a row missed her target's sneering lip.

"I've always been better with a pistol myself," Janie offered. "One thing to consider is a headshot might end the fight right away, but the body is an easier target. It might require an extra shot or two to bring 'em down, but you might have better luck there."

Abby nodded but still wore an abashed look on her face.

"You offer lots of advice," Claire's voice snapped from behind Janie. "Are you just gonna let those pretty guns of yours rust or what?"

And there it was. Since meeting Claire the day before, Janie knew this challenge would come. She had half expected it in the evening with all the women present. She thought Claire might wait until then, hoping to catch her out and humiliate her in front of the entire ranch. Perhaps Claire also understood that, if Janie really could live up to their expectations, then this more private setting would suffice for proof and allow Claire to save face if she were wrong.

Janie sighed before standing up. She had already lived a version of this moment with Will and Finn and McPhail. Back on Mount de Dios, Finn had wanted to know if Janie were any good with a gun when he goaded her into target practice on a dummy. Claire, and perhaps the other guardians, wanted to know if Janie was as good as the legend they read about in the papers. *That legend has nothing on you,* Janie told herself. *The only one who suspected what you're capable of died a year ago, but now it's time to show them what the De Casases can do.*

She wore a calm smile when she turned to face Claire. "What would you like to see?"

Claire nodded in approval. "You've seen all of us practice. How about you and me? Targets at twenty. May the best woman win."

"After you." Janie waved a hand toward the fence.

Beth and Jessie hurried over to set up the targets, battered tin cans standing in pyramids of three. Janie could feel Madison's gaze burn into her neck, but did not look to see if her new friend looked worried or confident in the match-up.

Claire took up position and raised her pistol.

"Do you draw from the hip?" Janie asked as the other woman settled in.

Claire's head snapped back, sending her dirty blond curls shaking. She scowled. "Yeah, I can draw and shoot." With a snort, she dropped the gun back into her holster.

"Me too," Janie said with a bland smile still on her lips.

Claire reset her stance in the dirt and stared down the cans. She took one deep breath and then drew. Raising her arm to shoulder height, she sighted down the barrel. Her first shot sent one of the bottom cans in the first pyramid flying and toppled the upper can to the ground. Her second shot hit the remaining can dead center. Shifting to the second stack, her third shot brushed close enough to send the top can wobbling, but without hesitating to let the can decide its own fate, her fourth and fifth shots removed the two supporting cans.

Claire's gun made a little click when it settled back into the leather of her holster. Around her, the other women, including Janie, applauded which deepened the smug look on Claire's face.

"Nice shooting," Janie said. She took Claire's place on the firing line, feet shoulder-width apart, and shifted to settle her boots snug into the dusty ground. Beth and Jessie busied themselves placing new targets. Janie cocked her head side to side, studying the placement of the new cans. "My dad was an Agent," Janie said to Claire who stood behind to her left, or maybe to Madison who stood behind to the right, or maybe just the world in general. "Despite being a drunk and a mean bastard, he got promoted all the way to Governor Hogg's personal posse because he was a damn good shot."

Beth and Jessie cleared away, and now all six of the women stood in an arc behind her, aching to see Janie shoot. "Abby?" Janie asked.

"Yes?"

"Can I borrow your bandana?"

Uncertain, Abby glanced about to her friends, but undid the dark blue bandana from her neck and offered it.

Janie turned her head but did not move those boots planted in the ground. "Come over here and tie it over my eyes."

Arthur De Casas' many areas of expertise included drinking, belligerence, and philandering. Over the course of his marriage and its aftermath, he managed to also cultivate wife beating and molestation among those dubious talents. Above and beyond all of that, Arthur De Casas was a crack shot, a marksman, a sharpshooter. In some worlds, they might have called him Gunslinger, had his moral character not gotten the best of him.

Maybe Arthur understood the darkness in his soul and tried to keep it at bay. Maybe he always wanted a boy to follow in his footsteps, and when no boy appeared, foisted his dreams on his daughter. Maybe, knowing both of the above, he became determined to give that daughter the tools she would need to defend herself even from her own father. Maybe, he just liked to shoot, and Janie's bravery and admiration won over his sorry excuse for a heart much like her mother, Maria, had done that handful of years before.

By the time Janie turned two, she had grown accustomed to the sound of her father's guns. By three, she followed him out of the house and across the fields to see him shoot and clapped and squealed with glee to see his tricks. By four, under her father's watchful eye, she wielded a small six-shooter of her own and a Winchester .22 rifle that knocked her on her rump as often as not. By five, the realization of the skill his daughter possessed pounded its way through the hardened bone of Arthur's skull. He did not know the word prodigy, but if he had been able to articulate to his wife what he observed in Janie's small frame, steady hands, and steely resolve, Maria De Casas would have known the word, but she probably would have kept it to herself lest Arthur assume she was getting up-pity and take it in his mind to bring her back down to earth. After he understood Janie's potential, his tutelage turned from pastime to obsession.

Around Janie's ninth birthday, more than a year before she would lose her mother, she watched her father, as she had on several occasions in the past, shoot the flowers off of a cactus, while wearing a blindfold. "How do you do that?" she asked with just the proper amount of awe and admiration she had learned to use with him.

That day was a good day. Arthur was sober for almost a week, their cow had given birth to a calf that in a year or so would fetch a nice price at auction, fine heads of yellow corn and full amber tufts of wheat swayed in their fields just itching for the harvest, and the small family strong box strained at its seams from the coins and script deposited two nights ago after Mr. Richards from the ranch four leagues north paid Arthur for a little side job, ostensibly work on the farm, although everyone knew that ranch work was not Arthur's forte.

"Well, Sugar Blossom, I just aim like always."

"But how? You can't see anything."

Arthur knelt down to meet her eye to eye. "I aim before I put the blindfold on."

Janie pulled a face. She raised her arm and sighted down the point of her finger at the cactus. "You have to see to aim."

Arthur's chuckle rolled over her, soft and warm when he lowered her arm. "Look at that flower there and remember where it is." Janie gave a solemn nod. "Now close your eyes." Janie obeyed. "Now without peeking, point where the flower is." Her thin arm jumped up, index finger straining ahead of her hand. "Open your eyes."

When Janie opened her eyes, her finger waggled close but up and away from the flower.

Arthur leaned in to sight down her arm. "Pretty good there, Sugar Blossom. You aimed first with your eyes, and your hand knew right where to go." He smiled when he ruffled her hair. "Once your eye knows where to aim, your mind knows where to put your hand and pull the trigger. A really good shot can aim with his ears too." He looked around as if checking to make sure no one had crept near to hear their secret. Then he leaned in close, his voice dropping into a fake whisper. "I once knew a man who could aim by smell. He shot a bear in the dark by the smell of its farts." At the same time, he let loose a wet raspberry of a sound from his other end.

That sent both of them into hoots of laughter. Janie held her nose with one hand and slapped him with the other. "Daddy, that's gross, and it did not happen."

"Might've happened. It just might've."

After they calmed down, he taught her to plant her feet firm and anchor her position. She started by repeating the pointing exercise again and again until her finger covered the flower in her vision every time. Arthur emptied the bullets from her pistol, and she practiced drawing. That threw her off. The motion of pulling the gun from the holster shifted her aim, and the weight dragged her arm too low on her first few attempts. Perseverance allowed her to master the empty draw within a few minutes.

When her father reloaded her pistol and offered it to her, he pulled it back when she reached for it. "Wait."

Janie scrunched her eyes and let her lips pout.

"You've gotten your aim down from here, but what about from over there?" He pointed five feet away from where she stood.

"Daddy."

"Sugar Blossom, you want to learn, then you need to listen. Move."

She did and readied for her first blinded shot.

"Where are your feet?"

Janie's eyes popped open and looked down at her feet standing askew one in front of the other. She replanted them at shoulder width and closed her eyes.

"Did you aim?"

Eyes opened again with a groan.

"Take a breath."

She did. Centered herself. Measured the angle and distance to the flower with her eyes. Closed them. Took another breath. Drew and fired.

When she opened her eyes, the flower grinned back at her.

"Missed low to the right. Try again."

Janie emptied her pistol twice and was halfway through the third when her father let out a whoop and the opening of her eyes revealed a rain of pink petals on the breeze.

The rest of that spring and summer and into the winter consisted of perfecting blindfolded marksmanship.

The coarse, sweat-damp fabric of Abby's bandana rubbed over Janie's eyelids and its point tickled her nose. Over the past weeks, she had cradled Will's guns, caressed them, weighed them, even shot with them. The rosewood-handled guns with their polished steel weighed more than her old guns and fired with more force but shot truer. Even the precious bracelet on her right wrist shifted her accustomed balance. Perhaps she ought to have considered longer before asking for the bandana. Hubris, another of her mother's words. Well, better to act now before doubt ate its way to her heart.

She remembered her father's lessons. Her boots remained planted. Her eyes knew her targets. The rest of the world dissolved.

Aiming has already happened.

She draws both guns.

She fires.

A double roar of thunder, louder than any of the other guns fired this morning, but beneath that, the sound of the top two cans flying away.

Shift.

Fire.

The two outermost cans fly away in her mind's ear.

Shift.

Fire.

The final two cans of the sextet leap from the fence, borne away by the passage of hot lead in one side and out the other.

The rosewood-handled guns, barrels just warm against her thighs, slide back into her holsters.

The trance broke.

Janie pulled the bandana from her face and opened her eyes.

The fence stood bare. Somewhere beyond it, four of the cans still rocked in the dirt, but the other two had gone still.

"It's a neat trick, but not very useful," Janie spoke to the silent crowd behind her without turning. "My father taught me everything he knew. David McPhail was a Territory Ranger, and he finished the job. I finished both of them: my father for what he did to my mother and me, and McPhail for what he did to Will and what he wanted to do to Finn and me."

She turned to face the six women whom all stood silent with mouths ranging from lips just parted to fully agape. "You're all good, really good." Here she looked Claire in the eye, talking to all of them, but addressing Claire. "You've got talent, and you work hard. Anyone can see that. You should be proud."

She swept her eyes from one end of the line to the other.

"I've never been a teacher before, but I'll do my best to share what I can in the next few days. I won't stay long. There's someone out there that still needs me."

She gestured around the shooting range. "Targets are great, but those men that come back aren't likely to stand still for you. You should hunt. At least once a week, some of you go up to the mountains and hunt deer, or shoot rabbits, or birds." She shrugged. "Anyway, we've been out here a while, and I'm hot. Maybe we should all get a drink, and come back after that." Janie walked past them and toward the main house.

The only privacy Janie found that day to check on Will came on her visits to the outhouse, but that left her little time to see where he was, and the impropriety of looking in on him at that those times cut her peeks short. He seemed to have stayed on at the farm, earning his keep with chores and lugging hay bales into a barn.

The sun's setting found Janie lying on the bottom bunk, wishing her roommate would go to sleep, and Madison sitting backward on the chair by the desk, chin resting on arms folded over the high back of the chair. Janie hoped the shadows hid her blush as Madison continued to gush.

"You're even more amazing than we read. I bet the Governor made the papers keep quiet. He doesn't want everyone knowing how good you and your gang are."

"Were," Janie said, but the negation failed to derail Madison.

"You even won over Claire. She means well, but she doesn't trust anyone. She thought you were a fraud, just pretending to be the Janie in the papers, and even when she decided you were who I said you were, she still didn't think you'd be very good. I've never seen anyone shoot as good as you."

"Lots of practice. I've been shooting since I was four or five years old. I ought to be good at it," Janie said. "'Bout the only thing I am good at," she mumbled, but Madison barreled on.

"After you shot out those cans like that, she listened to everything you said. She's done some hunting anyway, but she was talking to Jessie about going out once chores calm down around here. She also suggested to me, we start some of the other girls on target practice. I agree there. The more of us who know how to shoot, the better we can defend ourselves."

Janie rolled to her side and propped herself up on her elbow. "You've got a good team, Madison. You just need to work together, trust each other, and look out for each other."

The two women stared at each other. "You can stay you know. You could be part of our team. Everyone wants you now, even Claire."

Janie heaved a sigh. "I told you, Madison, I can't stay. I've got to find Will. He needs me."

Madison wrinkled her face in frustration. "Well, we need you too. What's so important about him anyway? If he's so good, he can look after himself. Men always look after themselves just fine."

"You don't understand." Janie flopped back down on the bed and opened her mouth to say, "I love him," but bit back the words. She had never told Will that she loved him. She had let down her walls with him, kissed him, held him, but never let the word "love" cross her lips. Saying she loved Will to Madison before saying it to him seemed a betrayal, and maybe even an admission that she never would have the chance to tell him. Why was Will so important to her? Why did she love him? "After my mother died, I didn't have anyone I could trust. I was all alone in the world. He rescued me, and then I saved him too, and he gave me the space to start to heal. I owe him." Images of Will danced in her mind: his wavy brown hair, his blue-grey eyes, warm and soft in one moment, as sharp as flint the next, the sound of his gentle chuckle, the feel of his arms wrapped around her in the night, the needy press of their lips against each other.

So absorbed was she in her memories, Janie failed to notice the chill of the room until the bitter edge in Madison's voice shattered it. "You don't think I understand what you've been through? We've all been through the same things as you, every woman here, same story, different characters, different scenes. You're not special."

This time Janie sat up in bed, her first instinct to fight tempered by the pain in Madison's voice and the tears in her eyes.

"We all found our salvation here with Henrika. We understand you. We know what you've been through. Maybe your Will says he understands, but he never will, never can. We're the family you're looking for."

Janie swallowed the lump rising in her throat and pushed down that primal urge to lash out. "I'm sorry, Madison. I've never known anyone who's been through what I have."

Madison rubbed the heels of her hands over her eyes. "It's okay." She turned and blew out the lantern. "It's always like this when a new girl arrives. I just feel like I've known you so long, but you don't know any of us."

In the dark, Janie sensed the shadow move across the room and climb up to the top bunk. Boards creaked above Janie's head, and the mattress sagged. "We understand you, Janie. Say what you want, but that Will of yours never can."

The cold bud of doubt bloomed in Janie's chest, sending shivers up and down her body. Because of Will, she had followed McPhail's giant circle of destruction around the state. Will had befriended her, earned her trust, and despite her resistance, had loved her, and persuaded her to love him.

Was Madison right? Could Will, who had grown up with parents who loved and cared for him even though he was adopted, who had only known real hardship in the last year of his life, understand a woman like Janie, who had known poverty, loss, and abuse all of her life?

And why had he been so drawn to her? Was she a project to fix like some broken down homestead in need of a new roof and plaster over the holes in the walls? Was he atoning for what had happened to his cousin Kali through Janie? Was it because underneath the gentle exterior he displayed to the world, he was just another lecherous man under a veneer of civility, and she was the only woman in his vicinity? What if their paths had crossed in a normal world where his parents had not died, and she had not murdered her father in cold blood? What if he had met her walking the streets of her hometown, Compassion, or seen her at a barn dance? Would he have asked her to dance or asked the blond or redhead next to her and never given Janie a second glance?

And if she loved Will as much as she thought, why had she not let him have what he wanted from her when she invited him into her bed, alone in their room in the pueblo? As much as Will wanted her, Janie had wanted to feel his body naked against hers, to feel him atop her, and inside of her. She had experienced the act so many times in the past, what difference would it have made to let Will have what he wanted? Had she been afraid their love was a mirage about to dissolve the closer she came to it? Had some part of her needed him to force her, to dominate her as her father had for so many years? And if that were true, what did that say about her?

So unsettled did those thoughts leave her that Janie did not check on Will. That almost cost him his life.

The echoes of carriages and carts rolling up and down the streets penetrated through the walls. In the corridors outside the room, legislators, lobbyists, and assistants bickered and argued and clomped past the heavy oaken doors. None of the noises could derail the Governor's train of thought.

"So we can all conclude that Ms. De Casas has departed San Alonso, most likely the night of her escape from the Map Room." Alistair Hogg paced the length of the conference room with his hands laced behind his back. "Where is she headed?"

He stopped where a map of the state hung pinned to the wall. Hand-scrawled circles, checks, and crosses marked various towns with solid and dotted lines connecting some of them. "Where would you hide?" he asked the paper.

Around the oblong table, Dick Warren, Rob Nelson, and Horace Weatherwax eyed each other, each voting for one of the others to speak.

Dick lost. "She might still be in the city," he said after clearing his throat. "It's hard to search everywhere in just a day. Maybe..."

"Shh." Hogg cut him off with a wave of his hand. Plucking a pen from the desk, he put a cross over a circle near the northeast end of the Elephant Mountains. "They robbed a bank and shot up Good Humor." His arm swung across the map and stabbed a check mark near the base of the Mescala Mountains. "Two weeks later, they blew up the town of Forgiveness." Dragging the pen back in an arc, he connected the two points in a swooping curve driving through the northern plains and the tablelands. "How long to ride that far, Dick?"

"Six or seven days, five if you pushed hard and changed horses."

Hogg nodded. "They stopped somewhere along the way." His eye roved back and forth across the path before jabbing his finger into the center of the tablelands. "The big pueblo."

Dick rubbed his chin. "McPhail used to be friends with some of the Indians back in the day. He spoke their jibber-jabber pretty well. That would fit."

Whirling about, Hogg beamed at his lieutenants. "The perfect fit. She's been there before, and I told her the Indians used the Map Rooms themselves when they squatted in San Alonso. She'll count on them to hide her, and she thinks they can help her cross over. She went north."

Weatherwax averted his eyes and continued to scribble entries from a stack of papers into a ledger. Years ago, Hogg had noted the man's habit to clam up whenever the topic of the Map Room surfaced and so chose to ignore his secretary's snub.

Nelson bounced his head up and down like a fishing lure bobbing in a stream.

Dick furrowed his brow, a sure sign his slow gears churned. "No word of any stolen horses in the city, and I don't think she had much money to buy one. Seems a long way to go on foot."

Hogg dismissed the objection with a wave of his hand. "Maybe she had one stabled, or she'll get one on the way. The big pueblo is the only place she can hope to find shelter, ergo, north is the logical way for her to go."

The Head Agent continued to contort his face in deep thought, which only exasperated the Governor all the more. Most days, Hogg tolerated the need to spell out his thinking to his underlings, but his patience was at an end. What he needed now was loyalty and quick action, not second guessing. He gripped the back of the chair and gritted his teeth. "They're the only friends she has left. Her gang is dead and scattered. Her hometown wanted to hang her. She'll go north over the Elephants or west over the coach road and then north to the Indians."

At that moment, the decision came to the Governor. Dick was a good man and Head Agent and loyal enough, but at heart, he was a better man than he was a loyal one. Agent Nelson was young, loyal, and followed orders without question. With the death of Seward, he was also hungry for advancement and power. "Nelson, pull together a posse from what's left of our Agent corps and get to that pueblo yesterday. I'll be sending a regiment on your tail in less than a day. Search the pueblo, by force if necessary, and bring me De Casas alive."

"Yes, Sir," Nelson barked and jumped to his feet with a salute out of place among the Agents and Hogg's leadership.

Warren cleared his throat. "Are you sure that's a good idea, sir?"

Hogg glared at the Head Agent and his near insubordination. "Yes. I. Am."

"Then let me take my posse," Dick said. "Some of them Indians will remember me if they remember McPhail. I can negotiate and get them to hand her over if she's there."

"She is there, Dick, but since you don't think we've finished searching San Alonso, you and yours can finish the job. Agent Nelson is perfectly capable of handling a few Indians with diplomacy if need be." *But with force more than likely*, Hogg thought to himself.

Janie woke the next morning to Madison alighting at the foot of the bed and pulling on pants and shirt. She averted her eyes from Janie, and although Janie watched Madison, she remained silent until the other woman slipped out the bedroom door.

Sleep had shorn the worst of her doubts, and the light through the window chased the rest into corners. "Where are you, Will?" Janie asked the empty room. The tingle of the bracelet on her wrist signaled that it knew the answer.

To her chagrin, much like herself, Will seemed to have settled in on a farm and still lazed about this early morning under blankets while the owner of the nearby bed seemed to have departed, perhaps to the outhouse, like Madison. "You're supposed to be headed to the pueblo," Janie told him. "Of course, so am I."

On the other hand, if Will had found a home, a family, and safety, then maybe he should stay. What right did Janie have to command him from afar? But much like her, forces pursued Will that meant him harm.

Who though?

"Dick Warren," Janie whispered. The man appeared, full as life, clomping along a street in San Alonso under the first rays of the morning.

Next, she checked on Governor Hogg who stood in front of

a mirror, adjusting the fit of his suit jacket.

Seward Garland revealed only black oblivion. Apparently, Victory had claimed him in Will's world too.

What other Agents did Janie know? Only the one who assaulted her in the in-between world. When she called his face to her mind, the scene of Will's world spun and turned, until Janie found herself looking into those cold eyes. Life in Will's world had not left him any more handsome or kinder, but it had given him a posse to ride with.

Familiar with these visions now, Janie pulled back until she found her bearings, the mountains, the sun, the plains. The posse rode north, straight like an arrow, and as Janie scanned the miles ahead, she found the township and farmhouse where Will lollygagged.

In a flash, Janie glided across those intervening miles. In life, she would have been kneeling next to him, hands shaking his shoulders, though the ghost hands she seemed to possess here failed to stir even motes of dust off his covers. "Will, wake up. Wake up, Will. It's time to go. You have to go now."

Despite her ineffectual shaking, Will rolled over and sat up in bed. Their noses might have bumped had they occupied the same world. His brow wrinkled in a frown. "They're coming, Will, a posse of Agents. You need to leave right now before they get here."

Will shook his head as if trying to clear a dream, but the set of his eyes and jaw changed. He tossed off his blankets.

"Janie?"

Janie gasped as if her name had passed his lips, but Will's voice had not pierced the worlds. With a blink of her eyes, Will vanished, and Madison stood in the doorway, face half in the room, back turned so she could flee. "I'm sorry about what I said last night, about your friend. You have to follow your own path. You know him. I don't." With that, she did bolt, vanishing in a scuffle of boots down the hallway, leaving the door to swing shut behind her.

Janie flopped her head back into the firmness of the cloth stuffed pillow. "Damn you, Madison." Her tone lacked the heat and conviction of her words, more rueful than angry. Three or four minutes of deep breathing calmed her heart before she could call forth the images from the bracelet. In those few minutes, Will had managed to be more productive than she had. She found him carrying a pack slung over his shoulder and headed for the barn and his horse. Janie watched him long enough to assure he had saddled his horse and waved away the objections of his hosts. "Go, north," Janie urged. "To the pueblo."

He trotted west, out into the plains, but at least he was moving. If the posse somehow knew Will had stayed on the farm, they would find him half a day or more gone when they arrived, a lean lead, but a lead nonetheless. She would have to check on him later, but much as it had been for Will, it was time for Janie to go.

"Fair enough. I knew you wouldn't stay long." Henrika sat at the breakfast table and dabbed her lips with her napkin. "We're all sorry to see you go." Janie had marched in and announced her plans to the matriarch with little preamble. As before, Madison sat at Henrika's left hand. Claire and Beth sat a table away while Jessie and Abby had either yet to appear from their night watch or had already gone to bed. Forks and spoons scraped on plates in the little dining room, but the voices of all the women had fallen silent as ears strained to hear what Janie and Henrika would say.

"I'm sorry too." Janie surprised herself that she meant those words. "I don't know if I'll be able to come back, but if I can, I'll try." She glanced about the room to the silent audience. "You've welcomed me in and given me shelter when not many people would."

"Our world is hard, but maybe not as hard as you'd think." Henrika gestured to a chair next to Madison. "Well, have a seat. No sense running off on an empty stomach. It'll take a while to get supplies ready for you."

Janie held up her bag. "I've got everything I came with."

"And that's not enough to go gallivanting across the state with Agents on your tail. Sit."

Janie sat.

Old Lizzie leaned across the table and began to scoop eggs and grits onto Janie's plate, leaving dollops in a line across the calico tablecloth. Chrissy appeared at her side to pour coffee from a battered urn into her cup.

Meanwhile, Henrika craned her head around the room until they alit on a brunette woman at Claire's table. "Winnie, if you're about done, get together some cooking supplies, a flint and steel, and a bedroll."

"Yes, ma'am," Winnie answered. She swallowed a last spoonful and hopped up to clear her place.

"Claire, you and Beth see what munitions we can spare when you're done eating." Henrika turned back to Janie. "After I'm done, I'll rustle up some saddle bags for you, and Chrissy and Lizzie will fill 'em with some vittles."

Janie felt dazed by the hubbub of activity her announcement created. "I don't have a horse. I came down river on a raft."

"Raft won't get you much of anywhere from here, I'm afraid. We can't spare a horse for you, but we've got a couple of mules, and we can part with one of them."

"But I can't even pay you for everything you've done for me already."

"You've paid us enough already. You've helped train my girls, and you've inspired all of us." Henrika gave her a wink. "Anyway, we take care of our own on my ranch, and you're one of us now, Miss Wolf."

"And if we give you a mule," Lizzie butted in while extending another scoop of grits to Janie's already full plate, "that'll give you a reason to come back to return it."

Parting gifts were not what Janie had expected. "I don't

know what to say."

As was her wont, Henrika gave a chuckle. "Thank you would be appropriate."

"Thank you," Janie said, still shaking her head in disbelief.

Murmurs of gentle conversation took over the room again.

Madison chased the last of her eggs around her plate. She made brief eye contact with Janie but then her eyes darted back down to her meal. "Where're you going?"

"I need to get to the big pueblo in the north. He'll meet me there ... I think."

"Which is more important, fast or quiet?" Madison asked.

Janie sighed. Her heart demanded fast, but her brain knew stealth would be more important. "Quiet, I imagine."

"Coach road and Gorseman's Pass are fastest but busy, and San Alonso's that way. Be hard to get through there unnoticed." This time Madison allowed her eyes to meet Janie's and hold her gaze.

Reviewing the map in her mind, Janie could see only one other option. "Going south around the Elephants will add a week or more. More time for them to catch me. I can't count on finding more friends along the way."

"There's another pass south of here. Can't take any wagons on it. Mostly used by trappers, but that'll get you over into the plains without the Agents or anyone seeing you. After that, if you stick to the foothills, you can avoid the towns and most of the eyes all the way to the mesas."

"Is it easy to find?"

"Not really, but it's only half a day's ride or so from here. I can go with you and make sure you find it."

"Thanks, Madison. I'd like that."

PART THREE

ON THE ROAD

Sometime after Janie's adieu to Hacienda Henrika, a trio of horses came trotting south down the main road by the river. Dick Warren rode in the center with Big Ben Neems to his left, Midnight Moses Macon to his right, and the sun beating down from above. On days like this, Dick wished Governor Hogg had chosen white for his Agents or at least a neutral tan. Black commanded respect and contrasted with Hogg's preferred crisp white suits, but damn if it did not soak up the heat like a mother.

Ben Neems was 'Big' because he was, well, big, a good six and a half feet tall and somewhere north of three hundred pounds. He sat astride the largest, thickest horse in the state, and the poor animal's back still swayed low beneath Ben's girth. If he had gotten a job in the circus, he might have been the jolly giant and made children laugh or wrestled bears to the oohs and aahs of the crowd. Instead, ten years ago, Dick had recruited the man and his generous literal and figurative heart into his own posse. Ben could be tough, and the best man to have in your corner in a tight spot, but he kept a clear head and looked for solutions that did not involve drawing iron or knocking heads together. When most people saw Big Ben coming, they saw the wisdom in finding common ground as well.

Most people assumed Midnight's nickname came from the dark shade of his skin reaching well beyond mere brown. In fact, Moses' mother nicknamed him Midnight the very day of his birth, when he crowned at the first stroke of midnight and dropped into the midwife's arms on the twelfth. True to his name, for the first year or more of his life, little Moses woke at midnight to gaze about the dark landscape of the world, gabble and play, rarely to eat except in that first handful of weeks, and then dropped back off to peaceful rest half an hour or so later. To this day, like as not, Moses' internal clock roused him at the exit of one day and the entrance of the next before allowing him to settle again.

In the shade of a cotton tree, not far from the banks of the Great River and a few miles south of the coach road over Gorseman's Pass, Dick called a halt and slipped off his horse. "All right, boys, y'all take a breather here and water the horses." Another hundred yards or so ahead of them, a stretch of dirt, thinner than the main road but still worn by wagon wheels, headed up toward distant fields and a ranch. "I'm gonna take a stroll up yonder and have a chat with an old friend."

Moses squinted toward the distant farmhouse. "You sure you don't want us comin' with you, boss?"

"Best if you don't. Don't wanna spook any of them."

"If you say so, Dick. Old Dusty here could use the rest." Big Ben swung one ponderous leg over the side of his horse and clomped down onto the ground. Dick could have sworn the horse sprung up two inches with Big Ben off his back.

"I say so. I'll be fine. Henrika and I go way back." In a show of adjusting his horse's saddle and bags, Dick turned the animal so her body blocked him from Moses and Ben. He slipped both pistols from his gun belt and tucked them into the saddle bags. "Make yourselves comfortable here. I may be gone more'n an hour. Don't come looking for me though unless I ain't back by sunrise."

"Whooee, Dick," Moses whistled. "Are you telling me we rode all this way for you to find some lovin'? Next time youse lonely, let Moses know, and he'll find you a nice fine woman closer ta home."

"Naw, Moses, you got it wrong," Ben laughed. "Old Dick's gots fillies stabled all over this state. He just got to go around and check on 'em every now and again. Why do you think he wanted the job of Head Agent anyhow? Gives him an excuse to leave Mrs. Warren and see his harem."

"Haw, haw," Dick snorted. "If Mrs. Warren hears stories like that from either of you, I will personally cut out your tongues and remove you of your manhoods, if Mrs. Warren doesn't do it first."

Moses elbowed Ben. "I think Mrs. Warren has had plenty of practice removing manhoods."

Dick just shook his head. "Rest. Sit tight. Do not move until I come back." He turned on his men's laughter and began the trek up the little road to the farmhouse.

The early afternoon stroll became a trudge. Halfway there, he regretted not bringing his horse. The wind blew off the river, and the dust his boots kicked up tickled his nose. Walking in the heat started little beads of sweat across his brow, and he imagined mopping with his dusty handkerchief must have left smudges.

The little colorful blobs around the homestead resolved themselves into women working the farm. All of them must have noticed his approach some time ago, but most refused to look his way, all that is save the formidable one who stood on the farmhouse steps with arms crossed over her bosom. At her feet, a girl not more than five combed the hair of a raggedy doll.

Her hair was shorter than he remembered and streaked with grey, much like his own. On level ground, they would have stood eye to eye, but from where she stood planted, Warren had to tip his head back and extend his neck to meet her eyes. Today she wore a long skirt and a calico blouse with sleeves rolled up to reveal the muscles in her forearms.

"Afternoon, Henrika," Dick said with a tip of his hat.

"Looks like the walk about did you in, Dick. Water pump's over there." She kept her arms crossed but nodded her head to the side. "Anna, be so kind as to fetch our visitor a cup." The little girl and her doll disappeared into the house.

Warren made his way to the pump and worked the handle. Crisp, cool water spilled into his cupped hand which he splashed across his face and the back of his neck. Before Anna made it back with the mug, he swirled some of the water into his hat, emptied it, and then replaced the damp felt on his head. By the time the cool of the water seeped into his hair, Anna handed over a chipped ceramic mug, and he downed two glassfuls.

Through all of this, Henrika remained rooted to her spot on the porch steps, surveying her domain and awaiting her visitor's return.

"Good to see you, Henrika," Dick said. The little girl scampered off the porch again to retrieve the mug and disappeared inside.

"Why are you here, Dick?"

"I'm looking for someone."

"You came to the wrong place then."

"She's a young lady that I thought might have found her way here."

"All the more reason to think you came to the wrong place, and you know that." Henrika shook her head with disdain.

"Her name's Janie De Casas. You may have heard of her." Dick watched Henrika's blank face. Either time had changed her little tells, or she had gotten better at hiding them because of all the women in Jefferson, certainly, Henrika Jamieson knew the name Janie De Casas. "I need to talk to her."

Henrika snorted. "Do you think you and your men showing up here in a show of force intimidates me, Dick?"

"Show of force?" Dick blinked and pushed back his hat. "My men are sittin' a mile or more away under a cottonwood tree. I hiked up here on my own two feet and left my guns in my saddle bag. How exactly is this a show of force?"

Caught on that point, Henrika scowled. "Head Agent showing up is always a show of force."

Dick sighed and shook his head. He stared at the ground before trying again with a softer tone. "You and I go way back, Henrika. I'm your friend."

"Me and my girls here don't recall too many friends coming out of San Alonso."

The ire rose into his eyes, but he pushed it back down. "Lots of people in this state have heard of you and your ranch, Henrika."

"And we welcome those that mean no harm and make sure the rest know the score and don't come back."

Dick sighed. "Of all the women and girls who find their way to your doorstep, how many of them have someone come after them? And of those that do, how many of them tell you they'll have the law come down on you?"

"Enough."

"And how often do they come back with the law?" Dick pressed.

Giving a shrug, Henrika averted her eyes. "Just a bunch of cowards able to beat on a single woman or girl. Once we stand up to them, they're all just bluster and scamper off with their tail between their legs."

"Aye, that's probably true for some. Truth is, there's plenty who come looking for their lost daughters, fiancées, wives, or whatnot." Dick took off his hat and ran a hand through his damp and thinning hair. "My posse and I are responsible for looking over San Alonso and its surroundings, including your ranch. When one of those men show up in my office, the smart ones say you kidnapped their loved ones, confused them. The dumb ones bluster about and yell that you've stolen their lawful property and me and my men need to ride on down here and string you all up."

Henrika harrumphed at that.

"My men and I listen, but we all know damn well why a woman would look for sanctuary here. Once they're done with their little fit, I inform them of that fact. We take down all their information, their name, where they're from, and who they're looking for. Then we take their guns and escort them to the edge of town and let them know that if they ever darken my territory again, my men and I will personally string them up and use them like a piñata." Agent and matriarch stared each other down. "That's why you don't see more turning up here."

"So you're doing your job, Dick, what the people expect of the Agents. Congratulations. Do you want a laurel wreath?"

"Believe it or not, we're both looking out for Janie's safety."

"I never said I knew the young lady," Henrika replied, but her tone had lost some of its sharp edges.

"Fine. Maybe you don't, but someday, she might show up here. If she does, I'd like you to pass on a message." When Henrika made no movement to object, he took that as passive assent. "I did not send Agent Palliser after her. That was Hogg. Hogg wants her back, unharmed, but I don't trust the other posses he's sent out not to harm her. I can guarantee, she'll be safe with my men, and we won't hurt her. I'd consider her a guest, someone under my protection. She should also know that Hogg thinks she'll head to the big pueblo up north. He's sending men to stop her, lots of them."

Henrika looked down at her boots. Her voice came softer now. "How do I know you're telling the truth?"

"I've never lied to you before, Henrika. Maybe you didn't like what I had to say, and maybe I wished I had found a different way to say it, but I never lied. I'm not lying now. If you have any contact with Janie De Casas, tell her to stay away from the pueblo and the tribes. If she doesn't, Hogg will have her for sure."

"And if she comes to you?"

This time Dick had the good grace to look uncertain. "She and I will talk. We talked before. I liked her. Maybe we can come to a resolution." He looked Henrika in the eye. "I serve the Governor, but more important, I serve the people of this state. I've done that since it was a territory. That's my calling. You and I may not always agree on the best way to do that, Henrika, but you know damn well that's what I've always done."

For the first time, Henrika uncrossed those arms. "All right, Dick. You've said your piece. If I run across this Janie De Casas, I'll tell her everything you've told me today. I'll also tell her everything I know about you. What she might decide will be her decision based on *all* the facts."

"I never asked for more."

"Good day, Dick."

"Goodbye, Henrika."

Once Dick Warren's silhouette had receded past the far fence, Madison came to stand at Henrika's side. "She's headed to the pueblo."

"That's what she said." Henrika nodded.

"We need to warn her."

"I don't like this, Madison. Dick's as good as you can expect from a man, but he's loyal to Governor Hogg." She stood watching the receding black oval of Dick Warren. "Do you think you can find her?"

"She doesn't know the pass like I do." That was as much truth as lie since Madison had only been over the pass once herself. "If not there, I'll catch her on one of the game trails."

If Henrika detected the white lie, she chose to ignore it. "Wait till they're well gone. Put Claire in charge of guard duty. I'll get one or two of the other girls to pitch in too. Then you can take Black Bessie and try to head her off."

Madison's heart skipped a beat. "You want me to go alone?"

"We're already down one mule and now a horse when you go. Can't spare any more." Henrika finally turned away from the mote that had once been someone dear to her. "She'll be hard to find, you know."

Madison nodded.

"In the end, Janie De Casas can take care of herself, I think. Can you, Madison?"

The young woman's throat bobbed in a dry swallow, but her eyes did not waver.

The Head Agent's walk back down the narrow trail from the farm to the road seemed twice as long as the walk in. If David McPhail had died at Janie De Casas' hand as Hogg believed, then Dick Warren stood as the last of the fabled Territory Rangers, and Henrika Jamieson was his last link to that past. When the line between friendship and justice had shifted, Dick found it strange how the two now stood, if not exactly opposite, at least askew of one another. Dick would do what he had to. He never had learned the skill of walking away.

The hike gave him time to mull the possibilities much as Hogg did, though the Governor seemed to shift through all the strategic options in the twitch of an eye, while it took Dick most of the walk.

Henrika might be telling the truth, and De Casas never showed up on her doorstep. In that case, his hunch had played out, and the search continued.

If in fact, Henrika sheltered De Casas, the only way to extract her would be to return in force with his whole posse, which would mean killing more than likely, and Dick loathed the thought of raising a hand against Henrika and her women. They had suffered enough. He would only come in force under a direct order from Governor Hogg, and if it came to it, that might be the time the Ranger in Dick would finally balk.

From what Dick had seen of Janie, he doubted she would let it come to a showdown on the ranch. Dick suspected she would surrender to spare the ranch if she could, but he would not want to test that intuition. On the other hand, the Head Agent showing up like this might be enough to spook her into the open.

The last option that Dick could see was that Janie had visited the ranch and already moved on prior to his arrival. In that case, if they knew where she had gone, someone might try and warn her.

When Dick sat down in the shade of the cottonwood, Moses handed him a canteen. Ben sat on the opposite side of a small fire warming some beans.

"What next, boss?" Moses asked.

"Lunch," Dick replied. "After that, Midnight, you head south, and Big and I'll head north a pace. Find a quiet spot and watch the road."

"How long?"

"'Til the morrow. If she hasn't come by then, come look for Ben and me near that big boulder at the bottom of Gorseman's Pass. If we're not there, we'll leave a sign which way we've gone."

"And if she comes my way, I'll do the same." Moses was not clear on which she he might encounter on the road south, but he knew enough to keep that to himself. Whomever he followed would be the correct she.

"Aye. If we don't see nobody, we'll come on back by noon and catch up with you." Dick leveled his finger at Moses. "Keep your distance. No one goes near her except me, and only when she's led us to De Casas if it's not her to begin with."

Moses smiled at that. Even his boss did not know who they might be following, and Moses had heard enough stories to want to stay well clear of Janie De Casas in any case.

Moses whistled a jaunty tune as he and his steed, Lightning, moseyed south along the banks of the Great River. On departing Warren and Neems, he had announced to his partners in an exaggerated voice that he would head south to check with the crazy ferryman in Endurance. He assumed that would be just the touch to throw any spies off the scent of their deception, though Dick had scowled. Moses spared scarcely a glance toward Henrika's ranch and followed the bend in the road behind some gentle hills a solid two miles away. He debated hiding over one of the rises, but instead elected to picket his horse in some trees near the river, and settled down to wait.

The afternoon found that perfect balance between the warmth of the winter sun and the gentle cool breeze off the river. He smoked a cigarette or three and waited.

The tedium began to wear Moses down, and he fought to keep his eyes from closing and sliding into Morpheus' oblivion when the sound of hoof beats jogged him back to alert.

A sable mare trotted down the road away from Henrika's farm. On the mare sat a young woman, either short-haired or with her hair tucked tight under her hat. The rider looked neither left nor right, only urged her mount forward. Moses imagined he could make out the furrows of worry across the woman's brow.

He waited until the horse and rider had hurried well ahead before he stirred in his cover and gathered his belongings. He walked Lightning back out to the dusty road. First, he cut an arrow into the dirt with the toe of his boot and then chalked one into the bark of a dying tree with a rock.

Before starting on the trail, Moses took the opportunity to examine the tracks on the road. The ground was hard, but here and there he could make out a set of small, sharp hooves and three sets of larger ones. The sharp hooves headed south, the same direction Short Hair rode. The freshest of the larger sets of hoof prints belonged to Short Hair, and overlay the sharp hooves and the other two larger sets. Of the remaining two sets, one headed south and the other north. The terrain lacked large swaths of soft earth, but Moses could guess that two riders had left around the same time within the last handful of days and only one returned, perhaps the same horse that was now headed south. Janie De Casas and Short Hair heading out, and Short Hair returning alone? Moses gave a low whistle of approval. Dick Warren had good reason to be Head Agent.

Moses remounted and let Lightning head off and at an easy rolling walk. Short Hair's tracks lay clear in the dirt. He needed to follow the trail, but Warren had said to stay back, and on that account, Moses felt happy to oblige.

Loneliness gripped Janie tighter than in the days following her mother's death. All those years growing up alone with her father ought to have inured her to the feeling, but a year traveling with Will and Finn and McPhail had awakened her desire for companionship. Hope and hunger for belonging with someone had carried her to San Alonso, through those strange woods, and on to Henrika's ranch. For two and a half brief days, Janie had become part of a community again, and now, she rode on her own, alone against the world, lacking even her father's confusing mix of love and abuse to keep her company.

Underneath the loneliness, perhaps its true cause, lurked vulnerability. Janie felt the harshness of the world. With no one to share watches and guard her back, she stuck to narrow game trails during the day and then forged far off the tracks as night crept on. She huddled cold without a fire, waking with every rustle of the leaves in the night. Her one comfort was that her life now paralleled Will's.

Of course, Will was a man on a horse with guns on his hips. While Janie might carry the same guns, she was a woman on a mule. She could defend herself against any opponent she encountered, but where Will's adversaries might be deterred by the hard flint in the way he carried himself, Janie's would not. A lone woman would seem easy prey no matter how much the killer she looked. Janie could not trust any face she met, no matter how friendly a countenance they wore.

Janie checked on Will throughout the day, as if they rode side by side again, not worlds apart. Once out of sight of the little homestead on the prairie, he turned northeast across a stretch of hardpan, almost doubling back on his course. His evasion proved wise. When Janie searched back to the posse pursuing him, she found the household that had sheltered Will eagerly pointing the direction he had fled.

Janie's warning had been prophetic. Even Will traveled in a friendless world. He must have heard her voice in the night and headed toward the pueblo. Janie could not bear to think his moves remained a coincidence of her wishful thinking.

Relegated to brush, forest, and rocky outcroppings, Janie's progress proved slow over the next handful of days. She could have covered ground faster by descending into the plains, or even the foothills, but fear of discovery held her to the high ground. The harrowing need to remain hyper-vigilant, to watch her back and sides as well as the path ahead at every moment, hindered her forward momentum and exhausted her.

The first night out of the pass, as Janie settled down to a cold dinner, she spied the telltale smoke of a fire wafting into the air from somewhere near the head of the pass. Janie had slept near the head of the pass the night before and managed to cross over without stumbling across any of the trappers Madison said frequented the area. Thankfully, Janie had left Henrika's farm when she did, or she might have been atop that fire right now, cornered by whoever traveled that road.

Janie closed her eyes and called Will's face to her. He had not made camp yet but seemed headed toward a stand of trees in the distance. He was making better progress than Janie, but the tablelands still lay several days' ride north and east. The posse, on the other hand, seemed to be biding their time in a town Janie did not recognize. "You're safe for now, Will. I just hope I am."

The next night, the campfire appeared again, perhaps some-where along her back trail, but the twists and turns along the mountain spurs made it hard for Janie to be certain. The night after that, the fire popped up near dusk again, closer than the first two nights. That a group of trappers followed the same game trail as Janie seemed too much of a happenstance. Someone was tailing her. The lack of subtlety suggested her pursuers feared neither her ability to elude them nor her ability to fight them off. They wanted Janie to know they were coming and to fear them.

Janie promised herself, she would not pick this fight if she could avoid it, but if they wanted her to fear them, she would make sure they feared her too before the end.

That's what she thought, anyway, until she heard the shouts.

Madison tossed little twigs and pinecones into the fire where they set off a satisfying series of pops and crackles. Her saddle-sore rump complained and almost drowned out the anxiety and frustration that vied within her for supremacy.

When Madison left the farm, Janie had only been a day and a half ahead on the little mule. Coming off of the pass after the first night, Madison had found little hoof prints preserved in the muddy banks of a small stream and followed them as they deviated from the main road and onto a game trail off the opposite bank. Here and there along the trail, she still found traces of the mule's prints, but no other sign of the actual mule or Janie for the past two days. A few times, when Madison came to the edge of one of the mountain spurs, she would cup her hands over her mouth and call Janie's name, but only echoes answered her. As evening set in, she saw no campfires but her own.

Maybe the little mule made better time than Madison thought. Being smaller, it could navigate the game trail and push its way through the brush better than her big horse. Of course, maybe Janie had turned up or down the mountain and eluded Madison, unaware she was being followed. Maybe the tracks way back at the main road had been from another mule, or maybe Madison was a terrible tracker and was following a big stag or a wild ass.

Last night, she had made a point of camping on the outer edge of one of the mountain cliffs and called Janie's name into the setting sun. Ranchers on the plains probably heard her, but if Janie did, she did not respond.

Now three days on the road and her voice was throaty, her tailbone ached, her stomach grumbled, and her spirits sagged. Why had she thought she could catch Janie? Looking back now, she knew offering to chase Janie down and warn her had been more infatuated fancy than a practical plan. How was a lone woman on a horse supposed to find a lone woman on a mule in the middle of the Elephant Mountains? Answer: she wasn't.

Madison's shoulders slumped with a deep sigh.

At that moment, thin fingers clamped around her mouth and an arm clasped her head close to a chest. "Shh," a low voice hissed in her ear.

Madison flailed, kicking her legs in the dirt and almost into the fire in her fright and effort to drive her assailant back. She grasped at the arm and hand over her mouth. Her attacker absorbed the momentum of the kicks and clamped the hand tighter over her mouth. An inch higher and she would be suffocating. She kicked again.

"Stop fighting, Madison." The voice rasped in her ear, but still not much more than a forceful whisper. "Keep quiet. It's me, Janie."

Madison struggled in the other woman's arms for a second more, before the words and the familiarity of the voice cut through her panic. "Janie?" She mumbled into the hand, but she could not even recognize the name in her own ears.

The fingers loosened over her mouth and the press of Janie's body against her back lessened. As the arm fell away, Madison turned to find her face inches from Janie's. The warm memory of Janie's encircling arm still lay across her shoulder. Firelight danced in her friend's eyes. "Janie!"

Janie's eyes flashed and her finger jumped into a salute against her lips. "Shh, keep quiet."

Madison dropped her voice to a whisper. "What's wrong?"

Janie ignored the question. "What are you doing here?"

"I'm looking for you," Madison said.

Janie's eyebrows arched in interrogation.

In the past few days, the overt purpose for this journey had subsided beneath Madison's real desire, her need to see Janie again. Whiling away the hours on horseback, fantasies of this conversation had percolated through her head, but those rehearsed words caught in her throat. The look in Janie's eye quashed those reveries. "I've come to warn you. The Agents are looking for you."

"For about a year." Janie rolled her eyes. "You're being followed by three of them right now. They're camped a mile or so back over the last ridge."

Madison's mouth dropped open. "What? How?" She had never spotted anyone on the trail. When had they started following her?

"Tell me the story."

After recounting the Head Agent's visit to the farm, and his warning about Hogg's men converging on the pueblo, Madison watched Janie sit back and close her eyes in contemplation. "Henrika trusts him," Madison added. Then she shrugged. "At least she thinks he was telling the truth about them looking for you in the tablelands and about wanting to talk to you."

"And once he's done talking, what then?" Janie's question was not directed at Madison, but the world. "So Warren delivered his message, waited for someone to leave, and then followed."

Madison hung her head. "I'm sorry, Janie. I shouldn't have come." The touch of Janie's hand rubbing her shoulder made her look back up in hope.

Janie gave her a weary half-smile. "You were trying to help. What's done is done. Question is, what next? Once they realize I'm here, they'll move in."

"Then let's run, now, before they wake up."

Janie's hair wagged when she shook her head at the suggestion. "It's dark, not even much moonlight. It'll be hard to get far. Plus, at least one of them's a tracker. If we go crashing about in the dark, we'll leave a clear trail for them to follow."

"Fight?"

"Not unless we have to. We need a distraction, something to make it hard or impossible for them to follow us. I'll need some time to figure things out, find out if Warren was telling the truth."

The two women sat by the light of the dying campfire. Madison broke the silence. "You hide somewhere around here. I'll keep going and lead them away."

"No." Janie's voice was sharp. "It's too dangerous for you. Hogg wants me alive, but he doesn't care about you. I won't let you be bait. We need to stick together."

The thought of sticking together buoyed Madison's guilty spirit. "But this is my fault. I'm willing to do it, for you." The last two words trailed off in a breathless mutter. If Janie noticed the emotion in them, she chose to ignore it, but given the way Janie's eyes drew inward, Madison surmised Janie likely had registered little of Madison's burgeoning feelings.

When Janie's eyes came back into focus, they shone with determination. "This is going to be dangerous if it works, worse if it doesn't."

Midnight Moses Macon rolled to his back and opened his eyes. His favorite constellation, Orion, the Hunter, hung above him on the canvas of the sky. Wisps of dark clouds drifted north to south across the view, causing the stars to alternate dimming and sparkling even more than usual. The smell of the campfire tickled his nostrils, and he scratched his nose with his right hand. This time remained his favorite part of the day.

A new realization snapped him from his meditative calm. They had not lit a campfire since departing that woman's ranch along the banks of the Great River.

Moses sat up in his bedroll.

A sliver of moon glowed to the west, but something else glowed to the north. More dark wisps wafted up over the ridge and across the constellations above.

"Uh, oh," Moses said. "Boss? Hey, Dick, wake up. Ben, we got trouble."

Dick groaned but sat up, while Big Ben required a firm prod before he stirred.

The three Agents followed the trail until they crested the ridge. Tongues of yellow and orange flames licked out in an oblate ring centered on Short Hair's camp. Already a wide swath of underbrush crackled merrily in the night, and the branches of several trees ignited into dancing fire demons, which sent embers scattering into the air. The winds, gentle but present, pushed the flames toward the three Agents and slightly upslope, creating the elongated circle.

"God damn," Moses swore. "Dumb girl gone and let her fire get away from her in the night."

Dick snorted. "Pack up, boys. It's movin' fast enough. We need to be gone before it gets here."

"What about the girl?" Ben ran his hands through his hair. "We should see if she's all right."

"We ain't getting through that," Moses said. "Too hot already."

"I expect she and De Casas are already far away out the other side," Dick said before he turned back to his camp and the horses. The smell of smoke had begun to send the three steeds pawing and snorting. "De Casas just better hope she knows what she's doing."

Confirming Dick Warren's worries, Janie realized that she did not know what she was doing. The idea seemed simple enough: start a fire across their trail, big enough to send the Agents packing and allow her and Madison the opportunity to escape. The first part, creating a large enough fire, proved simple enough in the dry brush, but the flames and winds conspired to make the second part, escape, dicey for the first two days. She had not intended to set the entire mountainside ablaze.

If she had started the fire closer to dawn, at least they would have had some light to follow the game trail by during their initial getaway. The two women had to tow their mounts along by the halters in the dark, stumbling and tripping on roots and ruts and blundering into thorn bushes in the night.

Dawn arrived with a sun, orange in the smoke. The winds stayed more or less southerly, but embers and flames kept drawing close when they stopped to rest. They spent all that day and another long night catching shut-eye when they could, and then hurrying away when the winds shifted. By late afternoon of the second day, the fire seemed to have spent all of its northward fury save for a few tendrils of smoke rising from the remaining hot spots. From the looks of the mountainside behind them where billows of smoke with orange and red bases signaled the fire still raged, Janie thought Warren and his men got the worse end of the bargain.

During their flight, Janie had angled uphill. If Warren and his men escaped the flames, she expected them to flee into the plains and try and catch her and Madison when they came down, and Janie did not want to oblige them.

The pair found a rough cave created after a cluster of rocks and boulders had collapsed downhill in a landslide some decades before. Snowmelt from the peaks above fed the bushes, grasses, and trees that had sprouted in the rubble, leaving only the outlines of the scar on the mountain.

Janie had been unable to check on Will, both because of the pressing danger of the fire, but also because she was loath to share the secret of the bracelet and the real heart of her quest with Madison. Although Madison had yet to ask, Janie had seen her companion's eyes drift down to the blue bracelet around Janie's wrist, drawn as much by the color as Janie's need to fidget with the cool blue of the stone. Will was close to the pueblo now, and she still struggled far behind. At least Klah would greet Will and shelter him, but would Janie be able to pierce the picket lines Warren implied lay ahead of her? The worry ate away at her spirit as much as the lack of sleep sapped her energy.

Janie unsaddled her mule and let the little animal free to graze while Madison did the same with her horse. Madison filled their canteens with stream water, and Janie hefted their gear over to the little cave.

In the coolness of the cave, Janie sat down cross-legged in the dirt. In a few minutes, Madison plopped down with her legs splayed across the opening, half in the sun, half in the shade.

Janie filled her chest with air and let it out in a weary sigh of resignation. "Madison, I have something I need to do. I'll try and explain later, but for now, please just sit quiet and make sure no one comes sneaking up on us."

Madison wrinkled her brow in suspicion. "Sure."

"And please, don't interrupt me until I'm done." Janie held up a finger, turning the plea into an order.

With her eyes closed, Janie whispered Will's name. The inert feel of the stone on her wrist became a cool trickle running about her forearm. In what seemed like another world, Madison gasped, but Janie pushed her friend out of her mind.

Will rode astride a chestnut horse deep among the mesas. His shoulders slumped. Fatigue and sorrow still reflected in red rims around his blue-grey irises, but over the blues and reds lay a sheer, gauzy layer of hope. Friends and succor awaited him just a few miles up the trail.

Much as Janie wished to hang there staring at Will, she knew more important tasks called her away. "Klah," she whispered.

In a blink of her mind's eye, the spirit guide sprang into her view. He sat on a ledge next to Tsela where both men worked mortar and pestle on piles of dried herbs. Despite the cataracts over his eyes, Tsela first noticed the change of his bracelet from onyx to smoke. "Welcome back, Janie of clan De Casas." The old man's lips no more than quivered, but his voice echoed deep and warm.

"Janie," Klah said when he looked up into the eyes of her spirit.

Janie reflected that she must seem to hover like a butterfly in the emptiness of space over the village terraces below. "Will is almost at your village."

Klah nodded and turned back to his task. "The braves spotted him. He should arrive this evening. He will be welcome. Are you safe from the flames?"

Janie knew she had felt eyes on her during the flight from the conflagration. "Yes, but I may not be able to reach your pueblo."

"Our kin spirit pueblo," Klah corrected without malice.

"I've been told the Agents seek me there, but I don't know if it is truth or a lie. Can you look into my world and see?"

Klah frowned. "We do not reach out to our kin spirits without great cause. Their worlds are not ours and can lead to fear and confusion."

"Please, Klah. I know I am asking you for so much, but I need to know if I can get there and ask your kin spirit for help. It's the only way to reach Will, or at least talk to him."

"When Will arrives, we will give him a bracelet, and then you will be able to talk to him."

"Please."

The younger spirit guide looked to his mentor, but Tsela appeared to be rocking his head back and forth to music only he could hear. "I will do as you ask. I will call to you soon."

When Klah blew, Janie felt swept by a great wind and crashed back into her body with a jolt. She must have jumped because Madison sat up straight. "Are you all right? What's happening?"

Janie held up the warning finger again. "Hold on. Not yet." She stared down at the bracelet, still circulating in its blue streams on her wrist. Rotation after rotation passed, and then, Klah's presence called to her, and the world shifted even as her eyes closed.

The two spirit guides had retired into their room. Tsela wore his same equanimous expression, but storm clouds circled Klah. "Our kin pueblo in your world has fallen. Soldiers and Agents in black patrol the streets, and my kin people cower in fear. It is not safe there for you or anyone, Janie De Casas."

Janie covered her mouth with her hand. "No, he wouldn't do that."

"He has done it. A person who can speak across worlds would be very valuable to the governor of your world, I think," Klah said. "I have done as you asked and offered you warning. Now, Janie De Casas, I need to know if the same fate threatens to befall my people in this world. Look beyond Will Covington, and tell me what we may face."

"Yes," Janie said in a timid whisper, but when she turned from Klah and Tsela she launched her spirit into the air of the mirror world like a great eagle leaping into the sky.

She rose in wide circles above the pueblo's tall mesa, trying to spy out the land below, but although she seemed to have the body of an eagle, she lacked the eyesight of a bird of prey. Even though she knew the direction he came from, she could not pick out Will against the background of scrub lands and red-orange rock. Scouring the lands closer to earth would take valuable time Klah and his tribe might need to prepare.

Janie thought.

If soldiers were to assault the pueblo, then surely Hogg or one of his close lieutenants would lead them.

"Governor Hogg," she whispered.

The mustachioed man sat at a table in his mansion with gentlemen in suits and ladies in fine dresses.

"Dick Warren," she said.

Entering the edge of the tablelands, the Head Agent appeared before her, riding in the center of his posse, two dozen strong, more than enough to capture Will, but not enough to endanger the entire pueblo. The duplicate of the Agent who had assaulted Janie in the woods between the worlds rode to Warren's right, but between them, on a grey horse, sat a tall lean cowboy, just as ugly and unpleasant looking as Janie remembered him. Perhaps directing them himself, David McPhail traveled with the posse hunting Will.

The Ranger had betrayed Will, Finn, and Janie in her world, and now his doppelgänger did the same in Will's.

The last rays of the sun bathed the slope around their cave in gentle orange flames. Janie and Madison sat shoulder to shoulder in the opening, both of them more entranced by the light reflecting off Janie's bracelet than the sun's rays off the leaves and rocks about them.

"So the medicine man from one of those tribes gave you that, and you can talk to him through it?" Madison believed in Janie's marksmanship with all her might, but this claim left her incredulous.

For her part, Janie had decided it best not to mention the "medicine man" lived in another world, a world in which Janie lay as cold and dead in the earth as Will lay in this one. "Something about a way for our spirits to focus and find each other. I don't understand." That was true. "When I call him or he calls me, the bracelet comes alive, and we can talk."

"And he knows where Will is?"

"Yes, he's in the tablelands near the pueblo, but there's a

posse after him, and the tribe might not be able to take him in." Janie had measured the distance. Will could beat the posse to the pueblo, but they would corner him there. With McPhail at the head of the posse and his connections to the village, the tribesmen might turn Will over to Hogg's men despite what Klah and Tsela might argue with the chief. And if it came to harboring a pale-faced fugitive versus preserving the sanctity of the pueblo, Janie would not fault the spirit guides if they offered up Will as a sacrifice. Both of them could see what defiance of Governor Hogg had wrought on the pueblo of Janie's world. So Janie had returned to Will, whispered in his ear to wait, to stop, to rest for the night, and he had listened to her voice in his mind and pitched camp beneath one of the mesas.

"So Warren was telling the truth. They're waiting for you up there."

"Yeah." Janie sighed. Maybe Tsela or Klah of Will's world could help her, but Klah had implied someone on her side would need to aid her if she wanted to reunite with Will. Hogg may have cut her off from the only source of that aid, and if Janie thought deep enough on that, the guilt for any harm that came to the tribe's people rested at her feet. She had run from the Governor knowing full well he would want her back, and the tribe was her only link to those other worlds and her only friends left in the state. Of course, Hogg would move against them. All the more reason Janie needed to distance herself from Henrika's ranch and the women there.

The sun dipped lower in the sky, flickering now between clouds and the peaks of distant mountains Janie would never visit.

"So what do we do now?" Madison asked.

"We?"

Madison gave Janie a defiant look. "We. Everyone needs help, even you."

Instead of barking back as perhaps Madison expected, Janie nodded. She did need help. This past year ought to have taught her that lesson, but what price would Madison pay for offering that aid? She stood up to take a few steps outside of the cave, breathed in more of the fresh air, and surveyed the surrounding landscape. Somewhere to the south, plumes of smoke marred the sky. "I don't know. I can't do anything for Will right now." She faced Madison. "We camp here, and I think."

Horace Weatherwax sat at his desk in the capitol building, sorting through the latest cattle figures, mining outputs, and tax revenues. He hoped to complete the report by the end of the week for the Governor's review, but as usual, collating all of the data into a uniform picture was proving troublesome given that no one ranch, cattle driver, or mine owner submitted the information in the same manner. Even the reports from the Revenue Offices required careful scrutiny. Most of the men making up the ranks of the State's revenue collectors specialized more in lead and intimidation than they did accounting. As Mildred often complained, what Horace needed was a secretary for himself, but Horace felt more married to his job and the Governor than Mildred these days, and if work kept him ensconced in the capital, then so much the better.

That being said, Governor Hogg seemed to be suffering from undue stress that was beginning to affect the efficient running of the government, leaving a larger volume of details and decisions to land squarely on Horace's narrow shoulders and hunched back. This whole De Casas affair was spiraling out of control. Governor Hogg might well have had brain fever given how obsessed he seemed to be over the young lady and that dank cave beneath the mansion.

Once, years ago, Governor Hogg had dragged Horace down the narrow rock corridor to that little rock archway. Apparently, Hogg had been impressed that some ancient people had carved this opening into another cave, but Horace's eye had seen the telltale signs of metamorphic rock rammed into an odd shape by the eons or the hand of God, not man. Still, he knew enough not to spoil his employer's little theater. He'd stooped his head just a bit to step into the narrow spot beyond. While Hogg pantomimed his little joke of some grand space full of maps, Horace had stood bemused in the darkness and uttered the appropriate polite oohs and aahs on cue.

Hogg had given him an irritated look. "Well, Horace, what do you see?"

"Well, really sir, it is quite a nice little cave, but I think of myself as more of a numbers and pen and paper man myself. Geology never really fancied me much back in school." He'd shrugged. "Rocks don't do much, just sit there. Numbers move things."

"Do you see nothing here, man?"

Horace looked around the narrow cavern and did his best to hide his irritation at being the butt of the joke. He pushed his pince-nez further up his nose. "It's quite a nice little cavern, but I have work to do so, sir. I will see you upstairs." He had turned and walked out with all the affronted dignity that he could muster.

After that, the topic of the little cave under the mansion dropped from Horace and the Governor's parlance, but from snippets of conversation around the capital, the Governor had gone on to bamboozle a fair number of his Agents into the delusion that some vast space full of maps lay spread out beneath the roots of the city. The bamboozled even included Dick Warren, whom Horace considered a very grounded, solid man.

Under normal circumstances, Horace felt he understood most of Governor Hogg's schemes and machinations and how they fit into the grander moving gears and cogs that kept the State running and free from the meddlesome hands of Federation-types back east and those heathens to the south. Of late, though, Horace had begun to question the Governor's sanity. Hogg managed to keep his ravings about the little cave beneath the mansion and those purported other worlds behind closed doors, but they dominated the lion's share of his time and the government's resources of late.

Take sending Agent Nelson along with a whole regiment of conscripted soldiers to march against the big pueblo to the north. Someday, the Indians might rise up and unite with those heathens and half-breeds below the border to steal land that rightfully belonged to the settlers from the Federation, but there had been no signs to suggest they were preparing to do that. Maybe making an example of the biggest tribe would keep the smaller ones in line, but Horace could not fathom how doing so at this juncture forwarded the best interests of the State.

Beyond that, Hogg claimed the move was all in the name of capturing that young De Casas woman. Horace had heard the exaggerated tales of her pistol prowess and that she was a comely enough lass, but how the value of one woman outweighed peace with the tribes and the expense in men subduing the Indians and searching her out lay beyond Horace's ability to comprehend. How she related to Hogg's strange cave obsession must plumb even deeper depths of the Governor's madness.

Horace wished he possessed a true ally, someone else to help judge Governor Hogg's continued fitness for office. Lacking a kindred compatriot, Horace toiled on doing his best to keep the ship of state upright and, if not under full sail, at least with prow on course.

A sharp rap sounded at Horace's door. "Come in," he called to the interloper.

Bobby Rawlings stuck his head through the door, brandishing a small yellow paper. "Telegram for the Governor, Mr. Weatherwax, from Agent Warren."

Horace rose and took the paper from the seventeen-year-old young man. Bobby yearned to be an Agent someday and had pleaded with Dick Warren to let him ride out as part of a posse, but the Head Agent had declined the offer. Horace thought the young man really ought to be grateful. Death swirled about the Agents these last months with unprecedented zeal.

"Thank you, Bobby." Horace reviewed the missive. "I'll give it to him straight away. Wait a moment. He may have a reply."

Striding across the common to the door to Hogg's office, Horace gave a light knock but opened the door before being asked to enter. "Telegram from Head Agent Warren out of the telegraph office in Deference."

The Governor leaned back in his chair and made a spinning gesture with his finger. The shadows of circles nestled beneath Hogg's greying eyes. His suit, though spotless, had a rumpled look, and even the ends of his mustache drooped in fatigue, though the noon hour was yet nigh.

Horace held the telegram up to his nose. "De Casas in Elephants STOP Send reinforcements STOP," he read.

"I told him to stay close to San Alonso. She's heading into my trap, and he's scaring her away." Hogg's resonant voice growled more than it sang. "I suppose he thinks my orders are optional now." He glared up at Horace. "Send a message back: Return to San Alonso forthwith."

"Yes, sir." Horace bowed at the waist and backed out of the room. He would not want to be the Head Agent when he returned to Governor Hogg's side. On the other hand, though touched by the addled belief in caves and maps and imaginary worlds, Dick Warren might be the most leveled headed authority left in the State. Horace would have to speak with the man and gauge his reaction to Hogg's condition.

The chill of the night in the thin mountain air prickled at Madison's cheeks, but in the dark, she thought they must be flushed more from the emotions roiling inside of her than the cold.

After the sun set, Janie decided to forgo a campfire against the remote possibility the Agents had managed to track them through the wildfire. The horse and mule ended up standing close together in the looming dark, while Janie and Madison bedded down together in the cave.

They huddled back to back under shared blankets, using each other's warmth to stave off the cold. An old hand at sleeping on the trail, Janie's breathing leveled into a steady rhythm in minutes. Madison lay awake, body atingle, and heart skipping beats for a long time afterward, fighting the urge to twist and turn and wriggle lest she disturb her companion's rest.

The next day passed. Janie spent chunks of the day sitting cross-legged on a boulder, looking out over the western plains and meditating over the bracelet on her wrist. When Madison came close, she could hear Janie muttering unintelligible words to herself. The strange swirling and bright blue of the bracelet at once entranced Madison, making her want to reach out and caress the twisting bands, and at the same moment, repulsed her, making her want to reach out and smash them to pieces. The worry lines on Janie's tanned face and the welling in her eyes represented her sole concessions to the anxiety within, and that upset Madison more than the dark feelings the bracelet imbued within her.

Madison foraged, finding a berry bush with tart but edible fruit and a few tubers they could boil. Between scrying sessions for her missing love, Janie joined Madison to hunt, and they bagged a quail and a rabbit to supplement their depleting rations.

By the afternoon, with no sight of another human for days, they risked a campfire. Janie dressed their catch, and Madison gathered firewood and kindled their fire. With the rabbit, tubers, and dried spices courtesy of Lizzie's larder, they soon had a merry stew simmering over the fire and a bird roasting on a spit.

They had whiled away the day. Janie stood up from the meditation boulder and came back to join Madison next to the fire that burned away the cool evening air.

"Stew's ready, I think," Madison said.

"I know. Sitting downwind's making me hungry." Janie took a seat at Madison's side by the mouth of their little cave. The breeze blew down the mountain over their heads, pushing the wisps of smoke and the smell of roasting fats out across the clearing and into the heavens above and the plains below.

Stirring the pot, Madison watched Janie out of the corner of her eye. "How is he?" All day she had avoided asking about Will or the Indians or Janie's strange communication, a telegraph without wire.

"Running." Janie exhaled and then took a sip from her canteen. "I thought the posse would get slowed down at the pueblo, but they didn't. He's staying ahead of them for now." For the umpteenth time that day, silver pools of moisture began to well in the corners of her eyes, and Janie blinked them away. "I can't help him, and neither can Klah. He's on his own."

Judging the quail to be done, Madison pulled the spit from the fire and set it aside to cool. They would save that for tomorrow. Instead, she began to ladle out scoops of steaming thick soup. "Well, if what you've told me is true, he can take care of himself." She handed over a bowl and began filling her own. "You've managed."

Janie sniffed. "As you pointed out, I've had friends."

"He'll make friends."

Madison caught a bristle in Janie's eyes at the suggestion, but it vanished with a twitch to her head. Janie blew on her spoon. "Mmm, it's good."

Madison took a bite and made a face. "No, it's not."

Janie laughed. "It's edible, and better'n some of the food McPhail cooks ... cooked."

"Well, I tell you, it makes me miss Lizzie and Chrissy and the women back home."

Janie regarded Madison over her bowl. "So the ranch is home for you now?"

"Only real home I ever had." She set her bowl down and

looked at Janie. "Was it your dad who hurt you?"

That froze Janie for a moment. A flurry of emotions darted across her dark eyes, but Madison's question was more about asking permission to speak than probing Janie's past. Madison hoped Janie understood the need to share vicious thoughts and memories as if that might somehow ease their weight and blunt their fangs. Janie acquiesced with a fractional nod of her head. "My mom died when I was ten. Dad started in on me a few years later."

Madison took the admission as permission to share. "I never knew who my dad was, but that was probably for the best. My momma didn't either. She was a prostitute, and Dad was just some cowboy. Maybe he was a regular or maybe he disappeared on the next cattle drive. She moved around so much, she didn't even know where she got pregnant with me."

She looked away from Janie and gazed over her bowl and into the fire. "Eventually, she settled down in Purity and worked most of the whorehouses there. I had a brother three years older and a sister two years younger. We lived in a little dirt floor shack on the edge of town next to the shacks of all the other little bastard whore kids and their whore moms."

"My brother was a troublemaker from the start. Stole things, not to survive, just to do it. Ran a gang. When Momma wasn't around, he'd hit me and my sister to keep us in line or just for the fun of it. When he learned to smoke, he'd burn us with the butts if he thought we'd crossed him, but only places that didn't show." Madison turned her head and pulled down her shirt collar to reveal two puckered pink circles where her neck blended into her shoulder.

She heard Janie's swallow.

"Momma always told me I was pretty and would make some good money when I was old enough. She used to tell me all about the men and how you had to read them, which were easy pickings, which ones you could wheedle extra from, who'd be quick so you could move on to the next one and make more money, which ones would hurt you. I think she planned on retiring when my sister and I were old enough to take over the 'family business.'" She snorted at that thought.

"When I was thirteen, I bled for the first time. I tried to keep it secret, but my brother found out I'd become a woman. A week later, three of his friends paid to take turns with me. Needed to start pulling my own weight, he said."

Madison felt the vacant, haunted look in her own eyes, and when she gave Janie a sidelong glance, she saw the kinship of someone who knew that feeling.

"I told Momma as soon as she came home. I'd never seen her so mad." Madison shook her head. "She gave me four good lashes and beat my brother senseless because she said a girl's first time can always fetch the most. She'd already picked out a local mine owner who liked to high-grade all the new girls. He'd have paid five times what my brother's friends paid for me all together, and now *we'd* gone and soured the deal."

"Momma brought me to work two days later. Tried to pass me off as 'fresh' to the miner, but he took one look at me and knew I'd already been 'broken in.' Still had his fun with me, just didn't give Momma all she wanted."

Appetite gone, Madison set her bowl down and pulled her knees to her chest. "Took me three months of working like that before I was able to scrape together enough supplies and courage to run away. Chopped all my hair. Joined a cattle drive disguised as a boy and helped out on the chuck wagon. Of course, the cook figured out I wasn't a boy, probably knew from the moment he set eyes on me when I came to ask for a job. About four days out, in the middle of nowhere, he tells me he knows what I am, and I need to start servicing him. If I didn't, he'd let all the cowboys on the drive know they had a playmate along for the ride, and I'd spend the next six weeks being passed from cowpoke to cowpoke for some poking."

A shudder ran through Janie's spine as if she were weighing all the years that had passed with her father against all the months and men Madison had endured. Which was worse? Who could tell? The story only reinforced that Madison had been right, she understood Janie in a way few others could.

Janie's shudder did not derail Madison's tale. Once started, the story had to flow out all at once, regardless the consequences. "Well, guess we weren't too good about keeping the secret, 'cause a week or so later, one of the drovers announces to Cook that he seen what we've been up to and wants in on the action too. Cook was mad as hell but had no choice, and neither did I. That arrangement lasted another week until they got in a fight over me, arguing about whose night it was. The trail boss got wind of it all and broke them up. Next day, he put me on the back of his horse. He said he'd take me somewhere safe and dropped me off with a preacher man at a little church in some no-name town. The preacher weren't much better than the cook or the drover, but he was older and didn't bother me nearly as often, and I had nowhere else to go."

"A few weeks later, a traveling nun came through the area. She knew what was going on all right, but didn't say nothing to no one. When we were alone, though, she told me about a woman named Henrika who had it in her heart for wayward girls. Made me memorize the name. After she left, I ran away from the preacher and found my way there. That was six or seven years ago. I've had a home ever since."

They sat there listening to the sounds of the fire crackling, the coo of a dove, and the rustle of a small animal somewhere in the brush. Madison picked back up her bowl and took a few more bites.

"I'm sorry, Madison," Janie said.

"Nothing for you to be sorry about. You didn't sell me off to the highest bidder."

"But I doubted you. I didn't think you'd understand what I went through."

Madison met Janie's eyes for the first time since starting her recital. "That's one of the first things I learned at Henrika's, you're never alone as you think. Plenty of other women have been there before you, and plenty more will come after you."

"That's grim," Janie said.

Madison shrugged. "Not all of us tote around six-shooters and know how to use them. Sometimes, nothing else you can do but pick up and move on. Knowing you're not alone helps though, a lot."

Janie looked back at the fire. "It does."

The fire burned down while they ate the last of their stew. The company improved the taste.

When Madison's spoon scraped the bottom of her bowl, she sighed. "So what's the plan now?"

Janie tipped the last of her stew back into her mouth before answering. "I can't go to the pueblo. Will's not there anymore even if I could. I think I know where he's going, but I'm not sure." Shaking her head, she set her bowl to the side and stared at the fire. "Warren'll be looking for me heading north. I guess we go south. That's the long way 'round, but maybe I can still catch Will before they do."

Reflections of flames danced in Janie's eyes, and Madison watched the fire kaleidoscope as tears filled her friend's eyes. Janie bowed her head and ran her fingers through the thick of her hair before looking up to the stars. "I don't even know if he's my Will anymore. This could be all for nothing." She looked back to Madison, forlorn and spent. "What if I do all of this, and he doesn't want me anymore?"

Every word Janie said, all the doubt and worry and pain, stabbed into Madison's heart. "How could he not want you? You're brave and strong. You've outsmarted Hogg and all of his Agents." Here she reached out to tangle locks of Janie's black tresses in her fingers. "You're beautiful." She stared into Janie's black pupils as they swam in the dark pools of her irises and sparkled with the light of their campfire. "Anyone'd want you."

With that, Madison leaned forward and kissed Janie's pale

pink lips. Madison had wanted to kiss Janie since reading her story in the papers and seeing her face on the wanted posters, and so the fact that her body chose that moment did not surprise her. What surprised her was that after an initial hesitation, Janie kissed her back.

Janie lacked words to describe her relationship with Madison.

Growing up, Janie's friends dwindled away after her mother died. Her hometown, Compassion, was small with a bare handful of children her age, and her father's short temper, rages, and alcoholic binges tended to keep other families away, while Janie's pride and shame prevented her from reaching out herself. During the past year, her friendship roster had burgeoned with Finn, if perhaps only a friend of necessity, and Will who had leapt well beyond friendship in her heart.

Janie's last female friendship had been almost ten years in the past, and she did not know what to make of Madison. The women on Henrika's ranch all appeared to get along with little rivalry. Some groups seemed closer than others, cliques within the larger family, and pairs like Claire and Jessie even closer than that. Best friends maybe? What did friendship with another woman even look like? Janie had dim memories of her mother's friendships, but few of them mapped precisely to the invisible ties she felt on Henrika's ranch or the bond forging between her and Madison.

By day, Janie and Madison rode together, talked, laughed, and shared little bits of their lives. Under the eyes of the sun, they did not speak of what passed when the moon shone and the starlight sparkled across the wide canvas of the sky.

The second night by the cave, the night before they started their return journey southward, Madison kissed her by the fire and again when they lay next to each other in the cave, bodies close against the cold of the night.

Janie remembered her mother's kiss, a soft peck on the cheek or the top of her head, full of affection and love.

Now and again, her father had given her those types of kisses too, though those moments became more strained, awkward, and forced as she aged and their relationship shifted. Even on the nights when he had abused her, he had never kissed her on the lips.

Will's kisses had been restrained. The passion and heat behind them radiated into Janie when their lips joined, but she could feel the reins inside of him, fighting to hold back. His restraint charmed her and assuaged her fears as much as his lopsided grin and blue-grey eyes did, and the flex of his toned muscles under her hands had made her heart flutter. Since they had parted ways in this world, Janie spent every night longing to hold Will against her and let him loose those reins inside.

Madison's first kiss had come quick but timid, even a little afraid. Janie had felt the pressure of it coming just before Madison leaned in, and had been chagrined as much from its unexpectedness as by her curious desire for it. Had she ever seen her mother kiss another woman? *Yes, but on the cheek,* she thought.

When Janie had returned the kiss, rather than pulling back as part of her urged, more kisses followed. Those subsequent kisses lacked the initial timidity but also the mad delirium that underlay Will's kisses. Madison's kisses warmed Janie with their sincerity and persistence. Janie returned those kisses in a measured manner, as she tried to determine what she and Madison meant, and where their journey led them.

A journey. In the quiet of her mind, Janie thought that the best analogy. Beneath the sun, Janie led their journey, meandering as it may be, groping about for a way to reconnect to Will and the life she dreamed of. Under the stars, Madison led their journey, touching her and opening her in ways Janie did not quite understand, evoking tingling and sparks of areas she had only dim awareness of before. She enjoyed that time, and felt the pull of its fascination, but the significance eluded her. Sometimes in the night, when she closed her eyes and luxuriated in the touch of Madison's lips and hands and body, she pictured Will in her mind and vowed to tutor him when they reunited. When she returned Madison's affections, the illusion faltered at the edges, but that level of intimate connection with another person filled the void that had lingered in Janie's soul for so long.

Were they friends? Lovers? Could women be lovers to one another? If they could be, what did that mean if she ever found Will? Those questions flitted through her consciousness like butterflies in the mountain breeze, beautiful and effervescent, dancing across the vista before flickering away only to materialize again from another direction.

While questions about Madison and the nature of friendship and love fluttered about the landscape of her mind, several large boulders dominated the scenery.

Of course, the largest boulder represented Will, the anchor to her thoughts day in and day out. During her peeks into his world, she found him bound where she would expect, the only safe place left that he knew, their hideout on Mount de Dios, but Janie knew it to be a safe haven compromised. Lacking that one crucial piece of information, Will fled, heedless of his peril.

The second boulder protruded like some cancerous growth from the first, or maybe it had eroded into the first. Janie's imagination could not decide which. David McPhail rode with Dick Warren and his posse, and from what Janie could tell, he surmised Will's destination. Judas that he was, the Ranger made no effort to thwart the posse's efforts. He led them straight to the mountain and Will.

And Janie had no way to warn Will. She still tried to whisper in his ear, shout in his ear even, but though the cock of his head or the spark in his eye demonstrated he heard her more, he seemed to listen less. A singular, dark fixation had taken hold of him, to get to Mount de Dios, and he employed all his remaining energy in doing so. Maybe he could sense his end approaching.

Orbiting around those two thoughts, impotent as Janie, came Nascha and Bidziil. They had been unable to contact Will in the mesas, but they followed the posse at a distance. The siblings rode double on a single pony with one of the mongrels from the pueblo romping about the pony's heels. They could not overtake Will, and in the end, they would arrive too late to offer any aid against the two dozen Agents scouring the plains that separated them from Will.

Between Janie and Mount de Dios lay the crest of the Elephant Mountains, the Great River, the peaks of the Santo Domingo Mountains, and the long northward stretch of the plains up to the Mescala Mountains with Mount de Dios at their crown. She could never make it to their old hideout in time to make any difference, never mind that her there and Will's there lay worlds apart. She could stand on the slopes, in the very spot where his boots dug into the dirt, but would never touch him. Her bullets would never find his enemies, and once again, she would be unable to throw herself in front of the slugs determined to take her love from her one more time.

Was it any wonder that as the sun sank, Janie allowed Madison to distract her from the nightmares preying on her in the dark?

Later, when she had time to clear her head, Janie would curse herself for not paying more attention. After days of traveling in the high mountains without sight or sound of another human save Madison, contemplating her fate and Will's, and luxuriating in the attention and admiration Madison showered on her, Janie relaxed her guard.

They broke camp soon after dawn. A world away, Will had begun his ascent of Mount de Dios, a good day's ride ahead of McPhail, Warren, and their cohort of cowboys and desperados.

Somewhere in that late morning when the sun had chased away the frost of the night, but before it beat down enough to raise a sweat across her mule's back, Janie found herself smiling at Madison's laughter. It jingled and jangled off the rocks and tinkled back to them in faint echoes out of the canyons. The sun revealed red highlights in her friend's brown bob and a flush of joy in her cheeks.

Distracted at the next tight turn around a crag of rock, Janie missed the acrid smell of burnt tobacco on the breeze. She was looking toward Madison whose neck craned back with laughter, and so Janie's first hint of danger came when Madison leaned her head forward and choked off her laugh with eyes widening to reveal whites all around.

Out of the corner of her eye, Janie saw a black shadow among the rocks, but when she whipped her head around, the shadow resolved itself into a man who sat planted on a waist-high boulder in their path.

His frame was all sinews with bulges of lean muscle under the black of his Agent's garb. His callused hands wore a grey patina of dried skin, but underneath their weathered appearance, his hands and face shown a deep ebony to rival his uniform. Curls of white smoke snaked from the tip of his cigarette and caught under the brim of his hat before the breeze sent the sharp aroma toward the two young women. His irises were a deep rich brown, reminiscent of the ones Janie saw peering back from her own reflection in the last watering hole they passed, but the scleras resembled tans more than whites. He looked as if some creator had taken the color of a hundred men and crammed it into a single body, creating a beautiful walking shadow in the middle of the day. Despite the visceral loathing the black Agent uniform summoned in her gut, his darkness struck Janie as startlingly handsome.

That did not stop her from pulling her mule to a halt and drawing one of her pistols over the animal's head.

When the women spied him and reined their mounts to a halt, even though he stared down the gaping maw of Janie's rosewood-handled revolver, the Agent grinned wide to reveal ivory teeth that veritably glowed between his dark lips. He held up his palms with fingers spread wide and let the cigarette dangle from the corner of his mouth held in place by the barest of saliva. "Het, tet, tet, tet, tet, tet," he clucked. "No need for that, ladies. I'm just here to talk."

"Not interested in talking." Janie's eyes darted around, looking for the man's comrades who must be lurking near.

Madison had pulled up her horse at the sight of the Agent but had been slow on the draw. Her gun pointed more at the dirt than the Agent. "How did he find us?"

"Doesn't matter." Janie pulled back the hammer of her pistol.

A bead of sweat ran down the man's temple, from the morning heat or nerves, Janie could not tell. "Let's not be hasty, ma'am. Head Agent Warren just sent us to talk with you."

"Us?" Janie risked a flick of her head behind them, but no one had snuck up their back trail.

When she returned her gaze to the Agent, she saw that four of his fingers had folded into his hand, leaving the index finger wagging up to her left.

"Me and Agent Neems." The click-clack of a cocking rifle accompanied the Agent's reply.

Madison swore and swung her gun up high. Silhouetted against the climbing sun, a second black-clad figure loomed above them with his rifle pointed down at Janie.

"Head Agent Warren promised us you'd be reasonable, that we could talk with you." The dark Agent shook his head. "I sure do hope Dick was right about that." His Adam's apple bobbed when he swallowed.

"Talk then." Janie kept her gun leveled at the center of his chest.

"Hard to talk looking down the barrel of a gun."

Janie nodded her head toward Agent Neems above them. "I am."

"Then you're a better soul than me." The Agent held her gaze for a few heartbeats and then sighed. "My name's Agent Macon, Moses Macon. Been riding with Dick Warren for going on eight years, Big Ben up there for six of them. He trusts us, and I trust him." Agent Macon looked up to his partner. "Big, lower the rifle. If shooting starts, I'm the one who's goin' down first. I'd prefer we avoid that eventuality."

Agent Neems snorted but lowered his rifle.

Out of the corner of her eye, Janie could see Madison's gun hand trembling. "It's okay, Madison. Put it down."

Madison's nod was almost as shaky as her hand, but she let her pistol drop to her side.

For a split second, Janie contemplated pulling the trigger. She could kill Agent Macon easily, and probably be fast enough to take down the big one before he could aim his rifle, but the man had the high ground and the sun at his back. If she was a little too slow or he was a little faster than he looked, either she or Madison might catch a bullet, and Janie would not take the chance. With a twist of her wrist, she flipped the barrel to the sky and lowered the hammer gentle as could be. Then she dropped the pistol into her holster, leaving her hand on the grip. "Talk."

Agent Macon did not lower his hands but pointed to the red handkerchief protruding from his shirt pocket. "May I?" When neither Janie nor Madison objected, he pulled out the red cloth, lifted his hat, and patted his brow dry.

He flashed those brilliant whites at Madison. "First of all, we got lucky, I'd say. I guessed after you figured out there were too many Agents north, you'd turn back 'round. I figured you'd stayed out of the plains so far, and so you'd keep that up, but I didn't know if you'd stay on this side or cross over at Gorseman's Pass." He shrugged. "Lucky us. Picked up your trail late yesterday, but figured creeping up in the middle of the night was likely to get us shot. Waiting almost did anyway, though."

Janie flushed a bit, wondering if the Agents had spied on them last night. She did not detect any leering on Macon's part, and Neems was too far away to make out his expression in any case. "So what does your boss have to say?"

"To the point. He likes that about you." Macon stamped out his cigarette on the bottom of his boot and tossed the butt to the side. "He wants you to know Hogg was the one who sent Palliser into the Map Room after you. He was a mean bastard, and Warren's glad you killed him."

Macon watched Janie's eyes and received only a languid blink in reply. "For what's it worth, I'm glad you offed him too. Anyway, Warren wants to meet you, one on one."

"If he wants to talk to me, why did he send you?"

"Because Hogg called him back to San Alonso but didn't mention me or Big."

"I'm not going back to San Alonso."

Macon shook his head. "And he doesn't want you there. He wants to meet you in a little town called Endurance, near the south end of the Santo Domingos."

Janie recalled a mop of tangled shaggy hair and a crooked grin. "I know the town. When?"

"Morning after the new moon."

Janie calculated in her mind, about three weeks away. "How do I know there won't be a whole posse of Agents waiting for me if I show up?"

"How does he know you won't show up with a whole gang of your own?"

"He knows I'm on my own now, and I'm not the one asking for a meeting."

Macon let his head swing toward Madison and back again. "Dick Warren is a man of his word. Me and Big'll be in the area I imagine, but he promises he just wants to talk to you, hear your side of the story, and have you hear him out, and then you ride away, any way you want to."

Janie raised her eyebrows. "And no one follows me?"

"Not then." Macon spread his hands. "Depending on how things end up, maybe later, but not then."

Janie sat staring at Agent Macon. During her little lunch with Warren in the woods between the worlds, he seemed honest enough. At any point, he could have tried to mine her for information or trick her into giving away some secret, but instead, he remained affable and sympathetic. He could never be her ally, but nor did he want to be an enemy. "Okay, I'll meet him after the new moon. Just him. There's a hill half a mile or so from the town, you two can camp out up there if you want, but no closer. I might bring a friend." Again the image of Marvin the ferryman came to her. "Or two."

"Fair enough, fair enough." Macon unfolded his wiry frame, each movement slow and easy. "Big and I will be headed back to Gorseman's Pass." He pointed a thumb back over the rise behind him. "Horses are back there." He turned to leave but looked back over his shoulder to tip his hat. "Best of luck to you, Miss De Casas. Have a right pleasant day."

Above them, Agent Neems was already trekking back along the ridge toward the purported horses.

Madison nudged her horse closer to Janie, and they watched until the two Agents disappeared over the ridge. Their heads made another brief appearance when they mounted their horses and headed off. Agent Macon even gave a cursory wave before the pair disappeared again.

Once she felt assured the Agents had truly departed, Madison spoke. "Why'd you agree to meet him?"

Janie curled the corner of her lip. "If I'd said no, do you think they would have just ridden off like that?"

"So you're not meeting him?"

"I don't know." Janie looked down at the bracelet protruding from her shirt sleeve. In her gut, Janie could feel Will making plans she could not change, and in her heart, she feared the outcome. While she plodded along, Will's fate raced like a bronco across the plains. "It all depends on what happens in the next few days. We're moving slow, but Will's moving fast."

Not for the last time, Madison gave the bracelet a sour look.

Neither Janie nor Madison was happy about the need to check on Will so often that day, but their reasons differed. Madison doubted the Agents would head off back to San Alonso. Janie doubted they had come alone. The congruence of their worries pushed them on with nary a stop, but Janie could feel Will's flight nearing its climax.

Trusting her mule to keep trudging along in the wake of Madison's mare, Janie would nip her avatar over into Will's world for brief flashes while they tried to put miles between themselves and the Agents. Janie also hoped that by communing with Will's world while they rode, Madison would keep her disapproving looks to herself.

When she first checked on Will, Janie found him digging a hole on a small plateau partway up Mount de Dios just outside a winding narrow pass. Nearby, a small wagon baked in the sun. A few hours later, she became more puzzled to find Will bedding down on the opposite side of a zigzag pass that led to their old hideout. He had a small campfire smoldering next to his bedroll where he lay as if to nap while the sun still hung high in the sky and the posse continued to close the distance behind him.

After his siesta, once he had started moving again, Janie had assumed Will would make his way to their old hideout, but again he frustrated her expectations. That night, she found him rolling up an old coat for a pillow and lying down in the bed of the earth far from the cave, the stream, and the little glen of blue and purple wildflowers. Whatever plan he had in mind remained opaque to her, but that the plan neared fruition sounded clear as the call of the jays off the mountain slopes.

Janie's mixed emotions and divided loyalties saddled her with burgeoning guilt as the day wore on. When they stopped to set camp, rather than let herself fall into Madison's arms, Janie suggested they set watches overnight to guard against Hogg's Agents.

If because she feared the Agents still tailed them or because she trusted Janie's judgment, Madison accepted the change in their nighttime routine. "Don't forget to wake me," Madison said before giving Janie a kiss, a kiss that Janie returned with half a heart.

During the first half of that night, Janie spent as much time examining Will, the posse, and his sleeping world as she spent guarding her own encampment. Fatigue overtook her sometime passed midnight, and she woke Madison before burrowing under her blankets and falling into a sleep frustrated by questions she could not answer. In her confused dreams, she kept finding herself flickering about the dark landscape, from Will to Warren and McPhail to Nascha and Bidziil. Under the blankets, a blue light flickered and winked off and on, like the last flames of a dying fire, sometimes bright and other times extinguished under the breath of the night.

By morning, Janie deduced Will's plan.

Daylight found him making a treacherous crawl back down the mountain, not through the narrow pass where his passage might leave a trace, but over sheer rocks and slopes of scree and shale. He arrived at the small plateau with the wagon and the hole she had watched him dig the day before. All of yesterday's work had produced a false trail for his pursuers to follow. A small part of Janie hoped that he planned to conceal himself and then steal back down the mountain after they passed, but if that were his intention, he had no need to lie in wait on the trail. Will planned an ambush.

During their months together, Will and Finn had joked about dying with their guns hot, staring down a bullet to make a final stand, to die shot down in a blaze of glory while taking as many of Hogg's Agents with them as they could. Although in her heart Janie had always suspected that was how they would all end (indeed it had already ended that way for Will in her world and most of the worlds out there), more and more of her ached for a long ride into the sunset, side by side, headed into a lifetime together.

Instead, she would have to watch him die a second time, just as impotent as before to prevent it.

But maybe not.

With her ability to view the entire landscape, she might be able to warn him, direct him in some way.

"Madison, we need to find a quiet spot off the trail." Janie's constant checking on Will had only allowed them to move in fits and starts since breaking camp that morning. Guessing they had traveled more than two miles would have been a generous estimate.

Madison rode in the lead and grimaced at Janie's words. The reasons Madison might want to find a quiet spot off the trail and Janie's surely lay incongruent with one another. "What's going on?"

"He's setting an ambush, but there's more than two dozen of them." Janie stood in her stirrups, craning her neck to look about them. "Up there by those boulders." She tugged on the reins and directed her mule through the brush and up the slope.

Madison and her mare paused and then turned behind. "How can you know all this?"

"It's the bracelet. I don't know how, but I can see him."

"You said you can talk to the Indians. How come you can't talk to him?"

"Klah, Nascha, and Bidziil all have bracelets. Will doesn't."

"But I've heard you talking to him."

"Without a bracelet, he can't hear me." Janie shook her head. "Well, sort of, but not really. I don't know if he knows it's me. It's complicated."

On the far side of the boulder, Janie reined in her mule and jumped off. She had to look up into Madison's face, her friend's expression hidden by the shadow of her hat. "Madison, I need to do this. Please help me. Just stand guard for me, and don't interrupt no matter what you hear me say." She swallowed hard with a dry throat. "I think I can help him."

Madison lowered her head and rubbed at the back of her neck. "Okay," she mumbled. "I'll take care of the animals and watch your back. Do what you need to do."

Janie felt her lips split into a wide smile. She reached out to stroke Madison's calf. "Thank you."

Janie located a comfortable niche where the boulder cast a shadow and sat down with her back against the grainy sandstone. On closing her eyes, she whispered into the bracelet, "Will Covington."

Events had moved apace in Will's world. He hunkered down in that hole covered by the backboard from the wagon while all about him milled a mix of Agents and deputies. She recognized Agent Macon among the crew, but could not see McPhail, Warren, or Palliser, but really, the three could only have gone in one direction. In a trice, she sent her spirit down the trail, passing Agent Neems and another Agent riding back toward the plateau and confirmed her suspicions that McPhail, Warren, Palliser, and another man waited by the faux encampment Will had created the day before.

So far, Will's plan appeared to be working, but did he really comprehend the odds against him? Maybe. Did he know how close Janie was, how they could be together again? No, or rather he likely only knew one way to rejoin her, in another life.

She whispered his name again and found herself kneeling next to him, almost a part of him, in the dusty oven of a hole. Tension radiated off of him, but boiling underneath came anger. Through the thin rays of sun sneaking between the boards above, Janie saw him raise his guns and prepare to stand. Too soon.

"Wait," she said into his ear. Her ghost arms encircled him to hold him down with their ephemeral touch. "Not yet. It's not time."

And just like that, Will responded. His guns lowered to the floor of the little pit, his head bowed, his shoulders slouched, his breathing slowed, and the echoes of his pounding heart spaced themselves apart.

Janie stood, her phantasmal body slipping through the wood. She felt as though she sat on the lip of Will's hiding spot while she watched the posse about her.

Wisps of cloud glided over the sun, their passage marked by little dips in the heat from above, but Janie could not tell if that transpired in her world or Will's.

Agent Neems and another man emerged from the pass. On their appearance, the men on the plateau perked up. The second Agent barked orders, and soon everyone mounted up to ride into the narrow defile in twos and threes.

"Stay down, Will. Stay down," Janie kept whispering. He could still retreat down the mountain with his pursuers none the wiser. McPhail would lead them to their old hideout, but by the time they searched the area, Will could meet up with Nascha and Bidziil and disappear. Of course, Janie's logic ignored the fact that Will did not know the two young tribespeople followed him nor that if they reunited the trio would have only a single pony on which to escape.

The number of Agents in the open space dwindled. Janie could sense the tension rising again in Will. She could not stop him, but maybe she could still help him. "Hold back. There's still seven of them, too many."

Two riders guided their horses between the rocks walls.

Three minutes passed. The next two urged their horses forward.

"Only five left, Will."

If Janie had been flesh and blood, the wooden covering would have struck her in the face and knocked her backward.

As it was, she flinched in both worlds, and when she opened her eyes again, Will stood in front of her, his guns blazing under the glare of the sun. Two Agents fell from their horses, and she traced his aim with her eyes as his arms shifted to the second pair. Each of those men took two bullets to bring down. The fifth and final man died with a shot from each of Will's pistols.

His opponents down, Will leapt from the hole. One man on the ground still struggled to bring a pistol to bear, but Will dispatched him. He pressed himself against the rock wall and reloaded. Unbeknownst to him, when he ducked into the defile, Janie sprinted ahead, scouting the terrain.

At the first corner, Will encountered a trio of men and felled them as quickly as the first five. Only one of the three managed to get off a shot in Will's direction, and he missed, perhaps because Janie's ghost hands pushed on his arm.

No sooner did Will finish with those three, than he had to duck behind a boulder while two more riders charged him. Again, Janie knelt unseen at his side. She estimated the distance to the lead rider. "Feint right, and go left. Closest is on your left," Janie whispered in his ear. "Go, now!"

She never knew if he truly heard her, but he did indeed feint right and rise to his left firing into the closest rider's horse.

And so the battle continued. Rider after rider fell before Will's guns while none of their bullets found a resting place in his flesh. Janie felt a pang of guilt when Agents Macon and Neems fell to a ruse from Will two bends later, but in Will's world, they had chosen the wrong side.

Sometimes Janie shouted orders at Will, other times she tried to dazzle his opponents or obstruct their aim. She could not tell how effective her efforts proved, but Will still lived. He kept drawing breath after breath. His heart pumped blood through his arteries, and Janie felt as though she stood at his side again, facing their enemies and vanquishing them together. In the red haze of battle that descended over her vision, the showdown ahead faded from her mind.

Together Will and Janie's ghost neared the end of the long ravine that had become an abattoir. The pathway narrowed one more time before widening out to a broad path that could lead up to the peaks of Mount de Dios or down the back slopes of the mountain.

Janie concentrated on the two men laying in ambush on the other side of the opening. "Duck," she called to Will just before the first man whirled around the corner. Will dove down as both barrels of a double-barreled shotgun roared a spray of buckshot into the space Will had vacated the moment before. The shotgun-toting Agent proved less fortunate when two bullets from Will returned his way.

"There's one more to the right," Janie warned Will, though the man's shadow in the opening had already betrayed his presence.

Will dove through the opening to come up in a roll beyond the man's aim and shot him dead.

Both he and Janie turned to survey their surroundings. Warren, Palliser, and a third man lay sprawled in fresh pools of mud red blood. Standing over them with a cigarette bobbing in his mouth stood Ranger David McPhail with a set of his rosewood handled revolvers strapped to his hips, the guns of the Territory Rangers of yore, McPhail's earned by deeds, Will's by birthright.

"Don't trust him, Will. He led them right to you," Janie whispered in his ear. She watched Will's pupils dilate in surprise or even happiness for an instant, but then confusion flashed across his countenance before his pupils constricted again and his eyelids narrowed in determination. Whatever bond he and the Ranger shared snapped. They now stood on opposite sides of some imaginary line, and perhaps they both thought their side glowed with righteousness, or maybe they both just hoped to die with their boots on like all good cowboys. That hardening in Will ensured this showdown would end in blood.

For the first time, Janie saw the scarlet blotches running down Will's left arm, the arm that held a rosewood-handled revolver leveled at his former mentor, and a revolver that contained six empty cylinders. Winded and wounded, Will faced one of the fastest men on the draw with one empty pistol in his hand and a loaded one in his holster. Janie prayed that McPhail would not be able to make out the empty chambers from his vantage less than ten yards away.

McPhail's lips moved as he spoke words Janie could not hear.

Will's answer was terse.

McPhail shrugged.

Instinctively, Janie backed out of the line of fire between the two men, but neither of them could physically harm her, only emotionally. She turned on McPhail.

The Ranger nodded to something Will said over Janie's shoulder. McPhail reached up with his left hand and flicked the cigarette off to the side, away from his gun hand.

Both Janie and Will recognized the ruse McPhail had used on Agent Seward in the town of Victory (*Triumph*, something in her brain whispered). "No," Janie yelled and flung her body at the Ranger's right arm as he went to draw. Even as she leapt, behind her, the hammer of Will's left gun fell on an empty cylinder, but surely he would be drawing with his right while he tried to shoot with the left.

The roar of one big revolver followed half a beat behind the second.

Once Janie dropped down by the boulder and lost herself in the hypnotic rings of blue around her wrist, Madison turned her back and tried to ignore her friend.

Friend?

Crush?

Love?

Star-crossed, ill-fated, doomed, and one-sided more than likely, but yes, she loved Janie.

In her early years, Madison always preferred the company of other girls, and the starkness of that contrast with her friends only accelerated with time. As they grew older, while she remained the same, her friends changed. They giggled and talked about various boys, and how handsome or kind or strong this one or that one was. They might sigh over them from afar, wave to them, the boldest going right up to talk to them. Over the years, their conversations drifted more and more to what it would be like to get married, have a family, who would make a good husband, who was cute but would not, and who tried to steal a kiss at the town dance.

Madison participated in those debates, but could never quite see the point. To a girl, they were the daughters of prostitutes and other reprobates. Not one of their mothers was married, or rather had been married for any length of time, or perhaps were serially and polygamously married to any number of drunk cowboys who promised to take them away from it all in the dark of the night, but then rode off with the cattle in the morning, never to return. What made any of those girls think they could escape their destiny to follow in their mothers' petticoats and bed linens?

Even if that was not the bald truth of life in the slums of Purity, the men and boys never sparked Madison's fancy. She preferred her girlfriends, their hair and braids, their mannerisms, the soft curve of their bodies, the sweet perfumed smell of their sweat, and all the more so as she matured. The coquettish ones who played shy had a certain appeal; Madison could appreciate what the boys liked in them, but overall, she preferred the bolder girls. Oh, they might wear ribbons in their hair and pretty dresses with a splash of color on their lips and cheeks, and a spritz of perfume now and again, but they would be just as happy to leap out of bed, roll up their sleeves, get dirt under their nails, and give as good as they got to anyone out there, boy or girl, man or woman. Red-headed, freckle-faced Sheila fit that bill.

Madison imagined finding a little farm out in the nearby mountains with Sheila, her best friend and first crush. They would live their lives far from the noise and drunks and cat-calls, just she and Sheila farming the land, raising some chickens, pigs, and sheep during the day, and curling up in a big bed next to each other in the night. Understanding the heresy of those thoughts, she kept the dreams to herself.

On a deeper level, all the girls in Madison's neighborhood understood where life directed them. Carmen and Felisha, two and three years older than the others, had already started working the brothels and returned with tales to titillate and chill their young friends. On one memorable evening, seven of the friends congregated, for the two worldly young women to tutor their friends in the arts of love. Madison's mother lectured her enough about the men she serviced that Madison did not need to hear more from Felisha and Carmen, but she attended because Sheila wanted to go. Under the pretense of acting, the girls drank and hooted and laughed while one would pretend to be the man and another the woman. Madison had melted when Sheila's moist lips pressed to hers and felt a tingling she knew no man could ever conjure in her. When she had opened her eyes, instead of finding the passion she felt reflected back at her, she found only mirth on Sheila's face.

"You take it all so seriously, Maddy." Sheila laughed and gave Madison a little shove to roars of laughter from the rest of the girls.

"Make them love you, Sheila, just like that," Felisha praised.

"That's how you get the big bucks," Carmen said.

Madison had hunched into a small hot crimson ball while the rest moved on to another lesson. All of them except Sheila, who turned back to Madison. "Come on, Maddy. It's all just fun." Then she leaned in to whisper in her ear. "You're good at kissing. Who you been practicing on?"

A week later, Madison bled for the first time.

Perhaps Madison might have been able to tolerate working the whorehouses with her mother and her friends. It was the life she had been raised for, but the memory of kissing Sheila echoed in her dreams. A week before she planned to flee Purity, in an awkward and mortifying display, she begged Sheila to run away with her so they could live together, yet Sheila had no interest in running because she just knew in her heart that Bobby Gilchrist was going to ask her to step out with him. He was the son of one of the saloon owners, and Sheila would be able to get a job there, cleaning up and serving the drinks rather than servicing the men. And what were she and Madison supposed to do if they ran off together anyway? They weren't likely to find husbands way off in the mountains all alone unless they stumbled on some dirty trappers or something, and was that the life Madison wanted?

Broken-hearted and fearful Sheila might let slip her plans to run, Madison joined the cattle drive two mornings later and left Purity as Mikey, assistant to the cook.

Since Sheila, Madison had two other brief loves while on Henrika's farm, but neither had lasted. Although most of the women on the farm no longer had much use of men per se, the majority professed to want to live their lives in peace on the ranch, Madison knew a good portion would leave if they found that elusive good man to love. A smattering, because of what they had endured, still looked for love but had turned to other women for that need, and a handful like Madison had never felt an attraction to men to begin with.

In her heart, Madison knew Janie belonged to the first group of women, her obsession with this Will testified to that fact, but Madison loved her nonetheless, and a part of Janie returned that love. It peered out from the corners of her eyes when she laughed at Madison's jokes. It echoed in her voice when they sang songs together on the trail. It smoldered in her fingertips and the swell of her body when they made love in the night. Yes, the attraction was more of convenience than anything else, but maybe, if Madison could nurture that love, she could bring it to full blossom in time.

After unsaddling their mounts and setting them loose to graze on the shrubs, Madison climbed atop the boulder to scout the territory. She stared back along the trail, both up slope and down slope, but spotted no pursuers. Somewhere below her, she could hear Janie's mumbled words. Once or twice, she let out a little cry that startled Madison, but the cries must have been from the imaginary enemies in her hypnotic trances.

Madison scrambled back down the boulder and hunkered down in front of Janie and just stared, contemplating what to believe. Where did the truth end and fantasy begin? And who's truth and who's fantasy did she mean?

Maybe Claire was right and you are crazy, Madison thought at Janie. The bracelet did turn from stone to water, glowing like it had a sun hidden inside, but whatever Janie saw, Madison could only see a growing obsession. What if the bracelet was like that opium Jesse talked about or one of those plants the Indians smoked? Maybe the bracelet was eating away at Janie's soul, deluding her with fantasies of a savior so many of the women on the ranch dreamed of. Maybe Janie still needed to discover she was her own savior, or that Madison could fill that role far better than some man on the other side of the state could, a man whom all the papers claimed had died more than a month ago anyway.

With a tremble in her hand, Madison reached out toward Janie's boot. If she touched Janie, would she see what Janie saw? The worn leather felt warm and soft under her fingers, but Janie did not stir under the light touch and no visions flashed before Madison's eyes. She allowed her fingers to walk up the sides of the boot to a denim-covered calf. Janie twitched, but that seemed to be more about whatever world danced behind her closed eyes.

The blue light pulled Madison's eyes away from Janie's face

and to her wrist. She let the hand on Janie's calf fall away and stretched out with her other toward the swirling blue lines. Her fingertips hovered inches away. The blue spoke of ice and snow and cold rivers and deep pools, but the twin threads gave off a faint warmth even against the heat of the day.

Before Madison's fingers could make contact, Janie's eyes flew open, her lashes splashing tears into the air. Anguish engulfed her face and voice. "He shot Will."

While Janie De Casas sat in a trance leagues away and Will Covington fought for his life in a world away, Dick Warren walked down a hallway in the Capitol building side by side with Horace Weatherwax. A cold shudder ran up and down his spine, causing him to take a stutter step. Next to him, Horace raised an eyebrow. Warren shook it off. "Someone just walked over my grave is all."

"I'd not joke if I were you. He's in a foul mood." Horace glanced about the men and women in the hallway and decided it best to hold his tongue here in public. "He's in his office meeting with Nazario."

Dick knew Ovidio Nazario, head of the Revenue Office, well. The man may have had an accountant's job, but he reveled in the bullying aspects available in his position, and that type of leadership bled down to the Revenue Men quicker than Warren's attempts at fairness trickled down to the Agents. More often of late, Warren wished Governor Hogg listened more frequently to the better angels of his nature than to the capricious ones. Nazario qualified as the latter.

The two men stepped into Horace's office. While Warren secured the door to the corridor, Horace placed his ear to the inner door, which lead into the Governor's office. Satisfied, he turned back to the Head Agent. "They're still jawing. We have a few minutes."

"I'm trail weary, Horace. Spit it."

Horace pursed his lips and then went to his desk to fuss over piles of papers. "I'm worried about him, Dick. I think all the losses in the past year have eaten him up. He's become obsessed with the De Casas woman."

Guessing the silent accompanying concern, Warren gave a resigned sigh and pitched his voice low. "And the Map Room?"

Horace scowled at Dick and went back to aligning already straight stacks of papers parallel to the edges of his desk. "Yes, and the Map Room. These delusions are dangerous."

Dick's nose made a phlegmy snort, and he plopped down into a chair that groaned under the pressure. "I won't debate you about the Map Room, Horace. You see what you see, and I see what I see." The Head Agent rubbed at his eyes and brow. "Ignoring all that, I may have to agree with you. What use Miss De Casas is to him or any of us, I have no idea." Well, he did, but the impropriety of it had been weighing on him these past weeks. She was a young woman dealt a terrible hand in life ricocheting from the control of first her father, then McPhail, and soon Governor Hogg because all the forces of the State lay arrayed against her. Dick could not see how she could escape.

"Then we agree at least this needs to be over."

Dick's cheeks puffed out as he exhaled. "Yes, this has to end." *And then I need to rebuild the Agent corps*, he thought to himself.

"So convince him, Dick. Talk some sense into him."

"You and I both know he didn't call me back here to get my advice."

Horace shook his head in dismissal. "He's mad, but that will blow over." He shot a glance toward the door where the murmur of Nazario's voice interspersed with Hogg's. "Believe it or not, he trusts you, Dick. You're his conscience, and he knows that."

Dick just raised his eyebrows at Horace.

"Fine, think what you want," Horace grumbled. "If you

can't or won't convince him to forget about her, then eliminate her."

"You want me to kill her? She's barely more than a kid."

"Well, that is what you do, isn't it?"

Before Dick could respond, the inner door swung open and Nazario strode out with an even deeper smirk across his face than normal. "Dick. Horace." He nodded to each man in turn.

Dick rose and adjusted his belt. "Ovidio."

Behind the Revenue Man, the lean shadow of Governor Hogg stretched to the top of the doorway. "Remember, you have two weeks to finalize the arrangements, but I'll expect a list in three days."

Nazario turned and gave a half-bow to Hogg. "Yes, Governor. I won't disappoint you." When he swung back around to leave, he gave Dick a contemptuous up and down with his eyes as he headed for the hallway.

Dick ignored Nazario's look and regarded the Governor with a little nod of his own.

Hogg did not return the nod. "And speaking of disappointments, the wayward Head Agent has returned."

"Back as ordered, sir." Intuition or perhaps foreboding tugged at him. "May I ask what list Revenue Man Nazario will be bringing you?"

Hogg twitched his nose. "We're running dangerously low on Agents of late. Nazario will be choosing which of his team will join him when he moves over to the Agent corp. I believe he will be an improvement over the late Agent Garland." The grimace on Dick's face warmed the Governor's heart. "Well, let's get this over with, Agent Warren. Come in."

Inside, Dick took a seat across from the Governor, who drummed his fingers on his desk with little rat-a-tat sounds for almost a full minute. "I believe I told you to stay in the San Alonso environs."

"Yes, sir. I patrolled my territory and played out a hunch."

"A hunch?"

"A hunch that De Casas may have gone south instead of north." Dick knew he tread on a thin branch. The two had never discussed Henrika or her ranch, but Hogg knew everything about his state. Likewise, Dick had never mentioned his former association with the woman, but Hogg always kept extra cards hidden up his sleeves and vest pocket and waistband and boots, and that was one of those shiny trinkets of information the Governor tended to keep filed away. If possible, Dick hoped to avoid directing the Governor's attention in the direction of the ranch.

"And why exactly did you think she would go south?"

"Agent Nelson and the soldiers were covering the north. The river runs south, though. It seemed prudent since my men and I were not required to help with the Indians, we might make ourselves useful and scout the area." Warren shifted in his seat.

"And you did not mention that because?"

"No sense in disturbing you if we were barking up the wrong tree."

"But it turns out you were on the right tree."

"We got lucky, sir. We picked up her trail a couple of leagues from the ferry crossing down south. She crossed the Elephants there at a little pass hardly anyone uses anymore."

Hogg reclined in his chair and steepled his fingers. "And you did not send a message. What happened?"

"No towns or telegraph in the area. We followed her through the pass and then north. She realized we were tracking her and set a fire, burned most of the southern half of the mountains, and we lost her."

"So my prediction was correct. She was headed toward the pueblo."

Dick nodded. "She was headed north, sir."

"And instead of capturing her, you may have scared her off."

This time Dick's nod was more bow than a bob of concession. "She has proved elusive this whole past year. If she's determined to get to the Indian village, I doubt she'll turn away now."

"And that is your only saving grace right now, Agent Warren." Hogg leaned forward to level a bony finger at the Head Agent. "I've trusted you a long time. You've done good work for me, and until now, you've done a fine job of making the Agents the force of order in this state. This past year, though, has demonstrated some shortcomings in my Agents. A measly gang of four miscreants ran roughshod over them and my state. As Head Agent, that does not look good on your resume, and you are flirting with insubordination. I am the Governor of this state. My word is law. I encourage healthy debate among my closest advisors, but when I give an order, I expect it carried out. Is that clear?"

"Yes, Governor."

Hogg pushed back his chair and unfolded his lanky frame to tower above Warren, who remained seated. "I'm shaking things up, Dick. Mind you don't find yourself shaken out with the rest of the detritus."

Warren pushed himself to stand, but still had to cock his head back to meet Hogg's eye. "I understand, Governor." All in all, he took it as a good sign Hogg had reverted to his first name.

"Good. You're dismissed, but I expect to be informed before you start chasing down any more hunches."

Warren's hand had just curled around the doorknob when Hogg's voice brought him to a halt. "Dick, if Miss De Casas does not surface soon, I'd hate to have to send our new Agent Nazario and his posse downriver to ascertain you did not miss any important information at one of those ranches while you were playing out your little hunch."

∽ PART FOUR ∽

THE OTHER SIDE

The sun shifted past its zenith to beat against the right side of Will's face as his appropriated horse carried him up the slopes of Mount de Dios. Blood congealed on his left arm, but at least the flow there had ceased. McPhail's final bullet had taken him in the meat of his right thigh, which more than made up for the arm.

None of it mattered.

A few more twists and bends, and he would be with Janie again.

He found her glade just as he remembered it. Her stone-covered grave lay unmolested in the dappled shadows of the trees. The bloom of little purple flowers had passed, but the view of the Jefferson plains below in the afternoon sun remained as breathtaking as ever.

To mount the horse, Will had used his arms to drag his body up onto her back. Climbing down now, his right leg remained a dead weight he had to muscle up over the saddle with his arms and would not support him when he slid to the ground. He collapsed and had to drag himself the last stretch to the little cross that served as Janie's headstone.

The rocks dug into his skin, cold and hard and sharp. "I'm sorry, Janie," he whispered. "I tried my best. I'm going to stay here with you now."

He rolled over to push himself into a sit and stared out across the plains. One more sunset would be nice. He had the bullets if it came to that, but the leg wound would serve. Despite the afternoon sun, he already felt a chill, and his energy seemed to be seeping into the earth with his blood, the last of his life force burrowing down in an attempt to find what remained of hers.

As he sat there, Will imagined Janie sitting next to him, maybe a little further out on the rock ledge, dangling their feet over the edge together. The warmth of her body would brush against him. The wind would blow strands of her hair across her face, and they would laugh together.

The hole where his heart beat ached worse than the one in his arm or the more serious one in his leg. How far away Tranquility now seemed, like some strange dream of a life without sorrow or pain. He could still picture George and Molly and Kalirose, but they were images with less and less color, becoming paler with each passing day. Janie hung there in front of him vivid as ever, calling to him across the veil separating one life from the next.

Just like the image of his adopted family, the color drained from the landscape of Jefferson laid out before him. His eyelids grew heavy, and Will laid back despite the growing cold.

Somewhere, a dog barked.

Cold tickled his forehead, and Janie's voice murmured in his ears. "I'm coming, Janie," he told her.

The dog barked, closer this time. A cold nose nuzzled his cheek followed by the lap of a warm tongue. Will winced at the subsequent bark so close to his ear.

Two voices, one male and one female spoke in a babble he could not comprehend. Janie's whispers became insistent underneath the other voices. "I'm trying," he said. "I'll be there soon."

Warm hands grabbed him and shook his face along with more incomprehensible gabbling from the male voice.

"He can't understand you," the female voice said. "Wake up, Will. We're here to help."

The light hurt his eyes when Will squinted out at the blurry faces, dark tanned skin under black hair, but neither was Janie, and he allowed his lids to slide closed. "Le'me 'lone. Goin' ta Janie." His mouth felt full of cotton, and Janie's voice echoed far away in his ear.

"Argh," the young man grunted. "Shut up, Ghost Girl. We're trying."

A gentle hand lifted his head while another placed a canteen to his lips to pour in a splash of water. "You need to drink, Will," the young woman said. "Bidziil, bind his leg."

That name connected with the blurry face in Will's fading consciousness. He fluttered his eyes open to look at the young woman. Someone from the pueblo? "Nascha?"

"Drink." Nascha poured another sip of water into his mouth. "Klah told us to follow you, and Janie's been guiding us."

The water splashed in the back of his throat, preventing Will from asking what she meant. After he swallowed but before he could form words, pain stabbed up his leg and out through the top of his head as Bidziil muscled his leg off the ground to pull the bandage tight. He cried out and his vision swam again.

"Oh, sorry," Nascha said, but she did not seem to be apologizing for her brother, rather she spoke to someone else. "I forgot the other bracelet."

The dry of her hands took his wrist. "Here, Will, let me put this on." A warmth like sitting close to a campfire encircled his wrist, and then Janie's voice, a faint whisper tickling at the back of his mind before this, roared into life in his ears as if she, not Nascha, knelt over him.

"Will, it's me. It's Janie. I've been searching for you, and I'm here now. You can't die on me."

Will tried to lift his head to look around the clearing. "Janie?" And then all the sorrow of the past month, the fatigue from the chase across the desert, the gunfight, blood loss, and shock at hearing Janie's voice became too much, and Will's world went black.

Once he and Nascha lugged the white boy to a straw pallet in the nearby cave, Bidziil headed back down the mountain with Maikoh, the dog, and left his sister to gather firewood and prepare the camp by herself. It would have pleased him to pass off his smoke bracelet to the pale boy and avoid the Ghost Girl's yammering entirely, but once Nascha placed Tsela's onyx bracelet on the boy's wrist, Ghost Girl seemed content to flutter about his prone body like a worried mother bird. The boy would not die, at least not tonight from his wound, maybe later from infection or a hemp rope if more cowboys caught up with them, or maybe from his own hand if Ghost Girl irritated him as much as she did Bidziil, but the boy would not die this night. With their initial mission from Tsela and Klah fulfilled, Bidziil had other duties to attend to.

He spent the last of the sun tracking down as many of the horses as he could. The poor creatures remained tame enough that they meandered around their former masters, frightened perhaps by the smell of blood, but lost as to where to go. He unsaddled each one. The saddles he left where they fell, but the saddlebags he collected first on the backs of his own pony, but then on the backs of two other fine-looking stallions among the herd.

The horses themselves would be valuable either back at the village for their work or for the money they would bring. Bidziil knew though that if anyone came across two tribespeople and a wanted paleface boy leading a tethered string of two dozen horses, they would be lucky to only lose the horses and receive a beating. More than likely, they would all hang from the nearest tree as horse thieves, which might not be too far off the mark, all circumstances considered. Keeping only one horse each seemed safest.

Maikoh helped drive the remaining horses before him and shooed them back down the path toward the plains below. Once one horse, a big bay, took the lead, the rest followed, leaving Bidziil and his three horses to make their way back to camp past all the paleface bodies and their unsettled spirits. He hoped Nascha had enough sense to hang wards near their camp. Tonight he would burn offerings to the spirits. Yes, the white boy had done the killing, but sometimes even the spirits of white men would vent their frustrations on the People as they had in life.

Around the campfire that night, inside the wards Nascha indeed had placed, and after performing the rituals to honor fallen adversaries, the siblings sorted out the food, guns, ammunition, knives, flint and steel, money, and other useful items from each saddle bag. When he looked over their new cache, Bidziil regretted not keeping one more horse to serve as a pack animal.

The pale boy slept, and, praise the ancestors, the Ghost Girl seemed to sleep as well.

The first light of dawn brought the less pleasant of Bidziil's duties. He spent the day searching each of the bodies along the trail for items of import. With too many bodies and too few hands to help, he could not bury or burn them properly, but he took each cowboy to a gully beyond the pass and once more said the prayers to a fallen adversary as his father had taught him and rolled the bodies down the hill.

At noon, Nascha carried some food down from the hideout, and they sat together in the shade, sipping cool mountain water from canteens and eating trail food from the procured saddle bags while Maikoh dozed at their feet.

"How is the boy?" he asked.

"The boy is as man as you, I think, and his name is Will."

Bidziil snorted, but considering all the bodies the boy had left behind, perhaps his sister had a point.

"He took some water and the herbs Klah sent with us in a broth and is sleeping again," Nascha said.

"And Ghost Girl?"

"Janie is worried, but is calmer than last night." Nascha looked at his wrist with reproach. "Klah and Tsela told us to keep the bracelets."

Bidziil waved a hand. "It's at the camp. It would only have caught on things here. We found him anyway." Also, even with the bracelet, despite all his attempts, Bidziil could only ever hear Ghost Girl talk, never see her. Stronger in the Sight, Nascha could reach out to Ghost Girl and see her and shadows of her world while Klah and Tsela could search the kin world of Ghost Girl with ease. An idle part of his mind wondered if the pale-skinned boy would have any better luck seeing Ghost Girl or if her voice would only echo in his head as she did in Bidziil's. Although that would give a base part of his soul some small amount of pleasure, he hoped, after all the trouble of this journey, the boy — all right, man — would be able to do more than just hear Ghost Girl.

The only body Bidziil exempted from the mass grave was the Ranger McPhail. The Ranger had been a friend of Bidziil and Nascha's uncle, Atza. Whatever reason the Ranger and the white boy and the Ghost Girl had come to odds, the Ranger deserved the rites appropriate to a blood brother of the tribe. Nascha helped Bidziil prepare a pyre and before the sun set that night, they set it ablaze and released the Ranger's spirit to the ancestors and the plains beyond the veil between one life and the next.

The white boy, even closer to the color of snow than he had been months ago in the pueblo, propped himself on a stick for a crutch and joined them to watch the Ranger's spirit turn to smoke and fly off to the ancestors in the river of stars across the sky. He remained silent while the branches crackled and snapped in the flames and the corpse of his dead mentor settled into the ashes. The entire time, he fiddled with the black bracket on his wrist.

Although his bracelet still lay in his bedroll at the camp, from the way Nascha and Will's bracelets had become smoke rings, Bidziil knew that Ghost Girl too bore witness to the passing of the Ranger.

The breeze rattled the branches of the trees around the clearing and ruffled cool air through his hair. Dried pine needles and shriveled brown flower petals lay scattered across the broken ground and between the stones over Janie's grave. They crunched under Will's boots when he shifted his weight from good leg to crutch and back. His eyes directed themselves to the patch of earth near her grave, darkened by his blood, but inside his head, dual realities fought for supremacy.

In one reality, the comforting figure of Nascha stood to his right, her warm fingers curled about his elbow to offer support while a grey and white dog snuffled about the edge of the clearing until it found an interesting scent to paw at.

In the other reality, Janie stood on his left, near his bad leg. One of her arms wrapped about his waist. Despite the gentle wind tugging at his shirt, a band across his low back remained warmer than the rest of him. Somewhere around Janie stalked a smoky feminine outline, like the shadow of a fish below the surface of a murky pond or the outline of a bird lost in foggy air, passing in and out of his line of sight, but never drawing into focus. Sometimes Janie spoke to this effervescent ghost, whom she called Madison, and from those snippets, Will gathered Madison saw even less of him than he did of her.

"You know what I think?" The distortion of the two worlds left Will unsure which woman he spoke to, and he did not wait for an answer. "I think I'm dying. McPhail shot me, I rode up here, and I'm probably laying right there next to your grave." He looked left into the pained expression on Janie's face. "I'm not dead yet though, that's why I can't see and feel you all the way."

Janie shook her head, but Nascha spoke on his right. "No, Will. You live." She held up his wrist. "The bracelet gives you the gift of Sight into Janie's world."

"That's right, Will. You're alive, and so am I." Janie stepped in front of him. The wind prickled his low back, but now a faint warmth cupped his cheek. "We can be together again."

He pulled his arm from Nascha to point at the cairn before him. "But you died. I held you in my arms, and you died."

Both of Janie's hands attempted to grab his cheeks, to focus his eyes on hers, not the cold sharp stones on the earth. "And I held you in my arms when you died, and I buried you in the same spot with the flowers and the view, just like you did for me, but we're also both still alive, and where there's life, there's hope."

Will tore his face from her hands, they were no stronger than air, perhaps less so, and looked to Nascha. "As I'm dying, I go mad."

The young woman's shoulders slumped in weariness.

"What I don't understand is why you and Bidziil are here. Why not Finn and Kali, or my parents to guide me on? We only met once. Why are you here to take me to the next world?"

"My brother asks me the same," Nascha confided, though she doubted Bidziil's reticence came as a surprise to either Janie or Will. She looked to Janie. "Let me talk to him, Janie, explain to him. He's been alone and lost too long and does not know the lore of the People. Go now, and we will call you when he's ready."

Will could tell she did not want to go, but Janie's ghost nodded. "I'll be here, Will." Her arms wrapped about him in a hug, and on reflex, his good arm came up to hug her back, but after a moment, like a puff of air, she vanished, and Will's arm cradled emptiness.

"Let's go sit at the stream." Nascha led Will in a hobble away from Janie's grave.

His leg screamed at him when Will lowered himself to sit on the rock. He would have hoped that dying would have spared him more pain. Given the plethora of physical aches and fatigue combined with the existential pain in his soul, he supposed death was less likely than madness. Maybe infection had set in his leg, and Janie, the smoke bracelet, and Nascha and Bidziil represented fever dreams.

Maikoh trotted over to sniff Will before sticking his muzzle in the stream to lap up a few mouthfuls of water.

Speaking to herself in her own tongue, Nascha sat down next to Will. He knew none of their language but recognized the name Klah. Both the tribespeople and Janie had spoken the shaman's name. "What did you say?" Will asked.

"That I wished Klah were here. He could explain better than I can, but he had to stay in the pueblo and speaks even less of your tongue than Bidziil." She gave him an anemic smile. "You're not dead, Will, and, in a sense, neither is Janie." She pointed to the ebony bracelet on his wrist. "You can hear her and see her with that."

Will rubbed the cool stone between his thumb and fingers. "Yes."

"These bracelets connect our world to hers."

"Her world? Heaven?"

"No." Nascha ran a hand through her hair. "Think about all the decisions in your life. You could go fish or go hunt. You went fishing, but perhaps a reflection of your spirit, what we call a kin spirit, went hunting."

"I don't understand."

"Shh. The universe does not ask that you understand all of its mysteries, but this is what I have been told and what we both have seen." She waited for him to nod in acquiescence.

"Our kin spirits live in kin worlds much like ours, different only in some of those small little choices in life. In this one, Janie died, and you lived. In another of those kin worlds, Janie did not, and she has found a way to reach out to us, to you, from that world."

Will held up his wrist. "Through this bracelet."

"First she used the Smoke Room, a place where all the kin worlds meet. Later, Tsela and Klah made the bracelets from that initial connection. With it, you can reach out to her whenever you want."

"How?"

"How does it speak across worlds? For that, you must return to our village and speak with Klah and study the rituals and lore until you grow old and grey and blind like Tsela and then perhaps you will understand." The corner of her mouth twitched in a smile stronger than the previous. "How can you call to Janie? That I can answer."

When she lifted her own bracelet, Will pushed her hand back down. "But if I do, is she *really* Janie? *My* Janie?" He felt the warmth of Nascha's hand cover his own and stared deep into her warm brown eyes. Flecks of chestnut swam in their irises, and more memories of Janie stabbed at his heart.

"She *is* Janie. The same spirit that gave her life in this world spreads its wings in hers. All our kin spirits are one."

Will felt the pull of the pile of rocks across the clearing, and his head began to swing toward them of its own accord. "But she died."

Nascha grabbed his chin to pivot him back. "Don't look there. Don't think about what lies beneath those stones." She tapped first his ear and then his chest over his heart. "Think about what you can hear and see with the bracelet. Forget about your fears, and feel what is in your heart. Did Janie ever die inside of you?"

Will shook his head.

"She lives, and she is calling to you. All you need to do is answer."

"And then what?"

Nascha shrugged. "In times of need, we believe the ancestors will guide us. What do your people believe?"

Bidziil's voice spoke from over Nascha's shoulder. So entranced by Nascha, Will had failed to hear the young man's approach. Nascha's eyes flared, and she snapped something back.

"What did he say?"

"It's time to change your dressing," she said.

Although a reasonable answer, Will doubted she had translated her brother's words. The frown on Bidziil's face bolstered that belief. Despite his injuries and feelings of disassociation since hearing Janie's voice and seeing her visage, Will had noted the tension between the siblings and Bidziil's displeasure. He suspected the shaman Klah had enlisted Bidziil to undertake this journey with his sister. In addition, given that the young man had spent the last two days moving and disposing of bodies, Will could not blame him for a perpetual frown. Will nodded to Nascha and allowed Bidziil to pull him to his feet and lead him back toward the cave.

"This was supposed to be the easy part." Janie buried the heels of her palms into her eyes. She ought to have expected this. Will believed her dead. From that final gun battle to the ride up to her grave, Janie surmised that Will planned on dying himself next to the poor cross that served as her headstone. Nascha and Bidziil had saved him, but how could her sudden appearance at death's door make her seem other than a phantasm to him?

With her insubstantial arms, distant voice, and Will's ability to banish her in an instant, Janie existed as little more than a ghost in Will's reality. Expecting Will to accept the existence of a hidden parallel world and embrace Janie as he had only a month ago asked too much from his exhausted body, mind, and soul. She had built her plan around four main obstacles: finding him across the worlds, preventing him from dying, establishing a connection with him again, and finding a way to pass from one world to another. She had missed one crucial step, convincing Will she was real.

Boots crunched on nearby gravel, and Janie felt the swish of air when Madison sat down beside her on the log. She imagined Madison's arm hovering around her back, but after thinking better of it, folding that arm at her side instead. "What's happening?"

Janie tipped her head all the way back so her face pointed to the sky and sucked in a deep breath of warm mountain air. "Will thinks I'm a ghost, and Nascha is trying to convince him otherwise." She looked at Madison with a rueful shake of her head. "Apparently, I'm not very convincing myself."

Madison raised an eyebrow. "Well." She gave Janie's upper arm a gentle poke. "You don't feel like a ghost, but ... truth? If you're not a ghost, then is he?"

With a snort, Janie stood up and ran her hands through her hair while kicking at the loose stones around the log. Madison kept coming back to versions of that question, reminding Janie how much she kept concealed and how close her companion gleaned of the truth. Whatever kind of caretaker Madison's mother had been, she did not raise fools. "No, his heart is pumping just as strong as mine." When she turned back to Madison, Janie saw the same incredulous look on her face.

"Look, what if I show you? Will you believe me then?"

"You mean with that bracelet?"

Janie nodded. "You don't know how to find him, but I think I can show you." Janie sat back down on the log facing Madison, her right knee touching Madison's left. She slipped the turquoise bracelet from her wrist but wrapped the first three fingers of her hand through the loop. "Hold the other side."

Madison stared at the blue stone before reaching out a tentative hand as if the bracelet might sting her the moment her fingers got close enough. When she did not lose her first finger, she slipped three more inside so that her knuckles touched Janie's in the center.

"Good." Less oblivious to Madison's distrust of the bracelet than she had been in the past, Janie flashed her friend a smile. "Now, close your eyes."

Madison's lids slid down over her sapphire eyes.

"Keep them closed," Janie said and closed hers. She pictured Will as he had been at the pueblo all those months ago, hair trimmed but still with gentle brown waves to run her fingers through, two days' worth of stubble on his cheeks and chin, and a smoldering look in his eyes. The cool tickle of the bracelet wound from her fingers to Madison's and back as stone turned to that eerie blue liquid of the pools in the woods. No sooner had Will's name passed her lips than Madison's intake of breath came sharp in her ears.

As if perched in the branches of a pine tree, they seemed to hang above the little stream and pool on Mount De Dios that Janie knew so well, looking down upon a young man seated near a young tribeswoman. Behind them, a tribesman, a bit older than the woman, approached. Janie thought Nascha noticed the change of black stone to silky smoke around her wrist but chose to ignore Janie's intrusion. The two tribespeople helped Will to his feet, and he limped off toward the cave that served as their home on the mountain.

Janie opened her eyes and found Madison staring back at her with mouth agape. In their fingers, the bracelet reverted to stone, which Janie slipped back over her wrist.

"That really was him. I recognize him from the wanted posters." For the first time since Janie revealed the bracelet's secret, belief flooded Madison's eyes.

"The woman was Nascha, and the man was her brother, Bidziil."

"Where are they?"

"Across the state on Mount De Dios, at our old hideout."

"So he didn't die in Victory like the papers said."

Painful memories made Janie flinch in the corners of her eyes. "No, he didn't."

Madison caught the prevarication and narrowed her eyes. "So what happened, and why does he think you're a ghost?"

Steeling herself, Janie closed her eyes. "I told you, we got separated after Victory. It was a crazy fight, and we all should have died." *Did die in lots of worlds*, she thought to herself. "Anyway, did you believe this bracelet could talk to people across the state?"

Madison shook her head.

"Neither did he. He will, though. He's just been through too much. He'll come around." Janie's voice trailed off and her gaze drifted to the side, eyes defocused, while inside all her fears swirled about like a dervish. She spoke the words aloud to bolster her flagging confidence within.

This time Madison's arm did snake out around her waist, and she drew near to Janie, the length of their bodies pressed together. "He'll come 'round for you. You'll be okay, Janie, and I'll be with you all the way."

Janie smiled but turned her head so Madison's kiss hit her cheek instead of her lips.

Madison sagged against her and her forehead bowed to Janie's shoulder.

"I'm sorry, Madison. I told you all along I'm looking for him. This just isn't right anymore." Her words pushed away, but she wrapped Madison into an embrace with her arms.

"I know," Madison whispered. "You love him, don't you?"

"I've never even told him. He knows, but I've never even said it to him. I never got the chance."

"If he doesn't, he's a fool. It's written all over your face." Madison disentangled herself and trudged away.

Janie let her go.

Together they sat around the campfire arranged at the four points of the compass, three flesh and blood figures, and one spectral image seen best with eyes closed. Maikoh lay with his head in Bidziil's lap, oblivious to the ghost in their midst, and off and on, Will caught a glimpse of a shadow stalking about them, the girl who had become Janie's new companion, not really part of their parlay, too distant and disconnected from Will's world, but present at the edges of Will's vision when she passed close to Janie. Somehow even more disconcerting than the phantasms, when Bidziil spoke, which was not often, his words entered Will's ears in the language of the tribespeople, but echoed in Will's mind in English, like having twin brothers speak over each other.

Will's leg kept interrupting his train of thought with its own throbbing monologue. Yesterday, chills had skittered up and down his bones but receded overnight under Nascha's regular administration of the sour broth Klah had sent on the journey. Today, his stomach had accepted some bread and strips of meat, and the appetite of his eyes had returned, though less so the appetite of his stomach. The smell and taste of food enticed him, but after a few bites, his stomach would clamp shut for an hour or two.

"We cannot be here when someone comes and finds the bodies of the dead cowboys," Bidziil said. A day of inactivity had rankled the young man, and although he was still healing, Will knew he would feel the same in a few short days.

"He is not yet ready to travel," Nascha hissed at him in their tongue, but thanks to the bracelets, each word echoed in Will and Janie's heads.

Out of the corner of his eye, Will saw Janie open her mouth, but he held up his hand to forestall her. "He's right. Someone's bound to come looking for the posse eventually, and someone down in the plains must have heard all the shooting. They'll get curious or just be traveling through."

"But I can keep an eye out for you and warn you long before anyone makes it up the mountain," Janie countered.

"You can see that much here?" When Will used the bracelet to call to Janie, she appeared clear in his mind's eye but lost in a sea of dense fog. That Janie could see clearer surprised him.

"She is stronger in the Sight than you or me." Nascha switched back to English. Will wondered if her words now echoed in Bidziil's head. She looked to Janie. "Perhaps as strong as Klah."

"Until Nascha told me, I thought all of you could see everything in my world too, but yes, I can watch over you. You'll be safe here."

Will shook his head. "We need to go. Once Hogg realizes his Agents are dead and I'm still alive, he may send the whole army after me." Janie shivered at that, Nascha blanched, and Bidziil scowled. "I want to be far away when that happens."

"Where?" Bidziil asked.

"To our village," Nascha answered. "Klah and Tsela will know what to do, how to connect Janie to our world."

"Or Will to mine," Janie said.

"We can do that?" Will asked Janie.

"Klah said we can."

Even though she seemed more ghost than real, Will read the hope battling doubt in Janie's eyes and wondered what the Spirit Guide had told her. "You know we're at our old hideout. Where are you?"

"In the mountains, near the south end of the Elephants."

"Then you should meet us at the pueblo." Out of the corner of his eye, Will saw Nascha and Bidziil share a look while Janie's eyes dropped down in sadness.

"I can't go there, Will." She looked back up at him with a face filled with as much guilt as sorrow. "In my world, Governor Hogg sent the army after me and took the mesa." She looked to Nascha. "Klah hasn't told me what happened, only that it's too dangerous for me now."

Emphasizing their family resemblance, Nascha wore a face as grim as her brother's. "Klah has not shared the tragedy with us either, only that we need to take care with all that we do. That is why we should return to the village as quickly as we can, once you are well enough to travel."

"The pueblo is still safe in your world," Janie assured them. "You need to go there even if I can't and find out how we can cross over."

Will contemplated his boots. If David McPhail had been the most wanted man in the state, once word got back to San Alonso of Will's ambush of two dozen of Hogg's men, he would catapult to the head of the line. Anywhere he traveled, hard men would follow with guns and little conscience for the innocents around him. "No, we can't put your tribe in any more danger." He looked up into Janie's eyes. Traveling any trail that led farther from her felt wrong in his heart. "I want to go to you." She was in the Elephants. They could meet at Gorseman's Pass and their buried treasure, but that lay at a crossroads too close to San Alonso in either world. The town of Sanctuary and the tail end of the Elephants might be safer, but Will had earned the nickname Deadeye Kid in that hamlet, and Finn had made his final stand in Sanctuary. Will could not fathom the thought of returning to the site of his cousin's sacrifice. "What about Fortitude?" For some reason, the word "Endurance" echoed in the recesses of his brain.

Janie's eyes widened at the suggestion. "We're actually headed that way, to meet someone."

"Who?"

Janie shook her head. "It doesn't matter. Being there won't help. We won't be able to reach each other any better than we can now."

"Maybe yes, maybe no," Will said. "I need to be where you are. If this is real, I need to be near you again. We'll figure out the rest later. When are you going to be there?"

"The new moon."

Will wrinkled his head in concentration, trying to remember when he last minded the phases of the moon and the distance from Mount De Dios to the abandoned town with its lone ferryman, all while contemplating how his wounded leg would feel after a single day in the saddle let alone a week. "I can do it. I can rest for another day or two here and make it there by the new moon."

Janie's face shown with worry. "Are you sure? That's a long ride."

"Not terribly longer than to the pueblo from here." Given the diagonal cut across the state the journey entailed, all four recognized the stretching of truth in that statement, but the more the idea sat in his head, the more correct it felt in his heart. "It just feels right. We'll meet in Fortitude." *Endurance,* said the echo. When Will looked back into Janie's eyes, he saw relief painted in them. *She wants us in the same space too,* Will thought, *even if it makes no sense.*

Lifting his body with his arms, Will shifted half a foot closer to Janie even as his leg whined in protest. If he were to ride the length and width of the state, he would have to learn to tolerate a good deal of pain. Hell, just riding all day left him saddle sore by the night, though less so than it had all those months ago on the cattle drive. An aching thigh should be no problem.

Janie met him three-quarters of the way, the slight warmth of her ghostly hands caressed his face.

"We should give them time alone," Nascha said to her brother in their tongue, but Bidziil had already slipped the bracelet off his wrist, no longer smoke, but now just onyx-colored stone.

Will stretched up his hand. With his eyes closed, Janie appeared more substantial before him, more than just the mirage of a heat shimmer on the plains. His palm cupped a feather's touch of air representing her cheek.

"What do you see, Will?"

"You, Janie. You're sitting on a rock, in the woods I think, but it's all fuzzy like there's clouds all around you." He looked left and right, but the shadows faded into nothingness. "I can't see your friend, but she was around earlier."

A tinge of color touched Janie's cheeks. "That's Madison. She went to gather more firewood. Do you believe this is real?"

Before answering, he paused to consider. "I want to, but it all seems like some strange dream."

He expected a wince of pain across her face, but instead, she flashed him a crooked smile. "I feel that same way too sometimes." She reached up to caress his hand on her cheek, and now a subtle warmth encircled his fingers. "Whatever happens, Will, I'm glad we have this time together."

A heat that was not subtle at all rose in his chest. "Me too."

"I want you to know that I love you. I love you more than anything or anyone."

"I love you too, Janie, probably from the time I first set eyes on you."

Proving beyond a doubt she was Janie, she arched her eyebrows at him over smiling eyes. "Even when I pulled a gun on you?"

A grin stretched across his face at the thought of their first meeting. How long ago it all seemed, even though only three short seasons had passed since that day. How young and green he had been, scared shitless there in the town of Mercy (*Compassion*, a part of his mind insisted), crouching beneath the gallows trying to release the noose from around the neck of a choking young woman. Despite the shapeless raggedy canvas dress, the dirty tangled hair, the raised purple bruise swelling her left eye to a squint, and the wild, angry look in her good eye, Janie had entranced Will. Back then, he never would have been able to walk to his own gallows the way Janie had: strong, proud, and defiant. Love had come later, but in those first few moments, the pull of her gravity had trapped him in an orbit that would only spiral tighter over time. That he had marched here to her grave attested that her power over him had not died with her. Maybe that draw really could transcend worlds. "Okay, maybe not exactly when you pulled a gun on me, but I've always been grateful you didn't pull the trigger."

"I would have regretted that."

"So, I'll see you at the new moon?"

Janie held up the wrist with the blue bracelet. "For now, we can see each other anytime with these."

"Yes, but I'll see you for real at the new moon." The confidence in his heart was condensing into a conviction that the doubts in Janie's eye could not dissuade.

"Will, I don't think that's how it will work."

"I do, Janie. I'm not sure why, but you can feel it too. We need to be together, in the same place. We'll know what to do then." Just as she had under the gallows when he'd pulled the executioner's black bag from her head, the look in her eye said she wanted to believe him, and then as now, she had no other choice but to trust and see what happened.

For the first time in more than a month, since the morning they saddled up and road to the town of Victory, Janie kissed Will. While the press of lips spoke of longing and desire, in the end, across worlds, it held no more warmth than being woken before the culmination of a dream, the memory foggy and fading and lacking substance in the cool light of dawn. "I love you, Will," she whispered to the breeze and clamped her eyes tight shut against the tears that tried to force their way between her lids.

Will was alive and recovering. She could talk to him, and he to her. If he did not believe in his core, who could blame him? Despite any doubts, he was coming to her. Klah had implied crossing over was possible. They would find a way.

And if not?

Janie opened her eyes. Madison hunkered down near their fire, stirring another pot of stew. She had stumbled across some fragrant herbs the previous day, and their pungent smell mixed with rabbit wafted on the wind. Maybe her culinary skills had grown over the previous days, or maybe they both were growing hungrier, but the aroma made Janie's stomach growl and mouth water.

If not Will, at least she had found a devoted friend in Madison.

Strange how when Janie had first met Will, his touch had repulsed her, and now she longed to feel his arm wrapped about her waist and the heat of his lips press to hers. His kindness and patience had allowed her to lower her walls and open the gates to her heart.

Now, she had spent the last weeks spying on him, dreaming of him day and night, and with each passing day, the yearning burgeoned and left her with a fizzy feeling in her chest that tingled outward up and down her body, a restlessness that refused to let her settle.

"Madison?"

Madison turned and flashed a smile.

"I need to move," Janie said. "I'll be back. I just need to hike around some and get out some energy."

"Okay. Dinner'll be ready when you get back. Don't get lost."

"I won't." Janie adjusted her gun belt and pointed herself upslope. A ridge of bare rock jutted out of the mountainside above them and beckoned to her with the view from its peaked edge. It seemed a worthy and achievable goal in the remaining daylight of these lengthening days.

Most of the trip traversed a low grade, but the last few hundred feet to the rock shelf involved an upward scramble that left her winded and sweaty. The exertion served its purpose to burn off a measure of the tension but still not enough.

From the tip of the rock, Janie looked down over the plains. To the north she could make out a dusty ribbon of road and a cluster of buildings, forming a little hamlet. Deeper in the west, she could make out the outlines of a ranch and herd of cattle. Farther than that, the shadows of the Serenity mountains rode the horizon, and amongst their folds lay the valley that had been Will's home while somewhere at their base lay the town of Purity, home to Madison's beginnings and Will's young cousin, Kalirose's, ending.

When Janie looked back down the mountain slope, she followed the dissipating curl of smoke out of the sky and down to their campfire and the tiny figure of Madison wearing the browns and greys of life on the trail that camouflaged her against the mountain chaparral. She must have been watching Janie's outline against the sky because she raised an arm in a wave. Janie waved back. She took a few more deep breaths of the crisp evening air and began her descent.

Even with the assistance of gravity, the journey back took longer than Janie expected with the lengthening of the shadows obscuring her landmarks. As the shadows grew, the dancing light of the fire served as her beacon home.

They ate dinner together in companionable quiet.

For the past several nights, Janie and Madison had relegated themselves to sleeping in lonesome bedrolls on opposite sides of the fire. Janie had gone on her hike to clear her head and exhaust the anxious, needy buzz inside her, but the heat still pumped through her veins. Will's effervescent kiss had inflamed her, and now he slept a world away, beyond her reach. Was it so wrong to yearn for the feel of someone's touch in the night?

"Madison?"

"Yeah."

"So, it's still pretty cold at night." The little devil of Need on Janie's right shoulder shouted louder than the little angel of Guilt on her left, and she slipped the azure bracelet from her wrist. *Only for a short time*, she told herself. "Maybe we can keep each other warm tonight."

Madison's throat bobbed with a swallow. "I'd like that."

The dining room of the Desert Rose teemed with patrons during the lunch hour, but the jostling crowd left a halo around the corner table by the window where Alistair Hogg sat reading the afternoon broadsheet with his long legs crossed and extending into the aisle. Across from him, Horace Weatherwax scribbled in a ledger between bites of bread and chicken. Outside, noontime crowds bustled up and down the street and carriages kicked up dust that settled on the window glass.

Had he deigned to look through the thin haze of dust, the Governor would have seen a black-clad figure ride up to the hitching post not far from the Desert Rose's entrance and lash the reins on the end. The bay dipped his nose in the watering trough while his master shouldered his way across the wooden sidewalk and into the hotel.

A handful of seconds later, the man in black stepped into the dining room and made his way to the Governor's table.

When the man cleared his throat, Horace glanced up with a sniff and returned to his books while the Governor took a placid look down the rest of the page before acknowledging his visitor. "Agent Nazario, please have a seat." Hogg waved a hand at the third and final chair at the table.

The chair legs scraped across the floor and the seat creaked when Ovidio Nazario sat. "Thank you, sir."

Hogg folded the broadsheet. "You have news, I take it?"

"Yes, sir. Head Agent Warren headed out this morning with the big one and the blackie. Said he was headed toward Truth to check on things."

"Yes, he told me he was making his patrol rounds and might go as far as Victory." Hogg folded one hand over the other on the table and tapped his fingers.

"Well, they started off that way but took a turn south."

Hogg raised his eyebrows. "Indeed?"

"Like you suggested, I had McMaster and Heath tail behind to make sure what they were up to. Heath came back about twenty minutes ago. McMaster is still following 'em, but as of about two hours ago, they was definitely headed south." Nazario beamed in triumph. "Ain't no way he's headed to Truth. He's up to something."

Hogg leaned back in his chair. Dick had always been secretive about that Jamieson woman and her ranch of fallen women, which Hogg presumed was why the Agent avoided the area whenever possible. Given Dick's history with Henrika Jamieson and the current Mrs. Warren's feelings about Dick's old flames, Hogg could not blame the man. Odd that Warren would choose to check on her again so soon, but maybe Hogg had gone a bit too far in implying Agent Nazario and his new posse might pay the ranch a visit. As long as the woman kept her reform views sequestered on her ranch and far from the capital, Hogg was happy to let her be. Of course, Warren checking south on a hunch implied that De Casas had visited the ranch at some point and therefore might return once she ascertained that her friends in the pueblo could be no help to her.

"Wait," Hogg said. "Did he turn around and cross the bridge?" San Alonso sat at the elbow of the Great River where its westward course ran against the Elephant Mountains and forced it to make a southward swing. Only one bridge crossed the Great River, and it lay at the southern outskirts of the city.

A note of confusion crossed Nazario's face. Like many of the men in the state, he led a blissful life, unaware of the Jamieson woman. "Nope, he just headed south."

Which meant Dick and his two Agents were headed south between the eastern banks of the Great River and the foot of the Santo Domingo Mountains. The Jamieson woman's ranch lay on the western bank. What lay down to the east?

Hogg rapped the top of his secretary's ledger. "Horace, get back to the mansion and have them prepare my coach. We're going to follow Agent Warren." He turned back to Nazario. "Have your man Heath catch back up with McMaster. I want them to keep Warren and his men in sight, and give us updates. You'll come with me, and we'll put Agent Warren's shenanigans to rest." *Once he leads me to De Casas*, Hogg added to himself.

From the smoothing pass of pestle over mortar and the diminishing of the crunching of the seeds, Tsela could tell that he had almost reached the proper grain. A hint of their sharp aroma wafted toward his nose. In another few minutes, to be positive, he would run the smooth powder through his fingertips, but he knew his mixture would be even and ready for use.

Since losing his sight when Klah was just a babe in swaddling, all of Tsela's other senses had honed themselves to a sharp edge: the feel the of ingredients grinding finer and finer, the smell of the stew pot next door with a bit too much spice for his taste, the brush of air along his neck as Klah stepped back inside, the slapping of bare feet on stone as the four children ran back to their homes. And even more so than the senses of his body, the ability of his mind to peer into the kin-worlds beyond had grown as he aged and his vision for the world before him dimmed. The bracelets aided in the focus, but his mind had grown strong enough that he no longer required their power to peer into the kin-worlds of the spirits.

While his fingers and hands worked their skills, Tsela's mind drifted. That was both the boon and the curse of age. He could think on many tasks at once, the milling of the seeds for the rituals for instance, but also listen to the murmurs of the women on the roof of their home next door as they discussed the news of the village, and the cries and shouts of the men down the mesa, and at the same time let his inner eye wander the worlds of the kin-spirits. Sometimes, though, his mind would flit like a child's from thought to thought and then become lost in memory.

Today, he thought on his departed wife, Ajei, who had moved on to the world of the ancestors when Tsela was still a young Spirit Guide and before the spirits had seen fit to take his vision. At first, when a spirit departed the Land of the People for the stars and lands of the ancestors, they would return to visit and check on those left behind, and Ajei had visited him in his dreams along with the son who had passed on with her at birth, the son who had died unnamed but never forgotten in Tsela's heart. Yes, then he still had his older twin sons, Hastiin and Shilah, and a daughter, Lina, but with time, they had grown and made families of their own. Lina still lived in the pueblo with her husband and children and a new granddaughter, but Hastiin had moved to the village of his wife, and his twin, Shilah, had died while hunting a boar years ago. Shilah's children still came to pay respects to their grandfather. As was only right and proper, as time flowed on, Ajei and his youngest son, too, had drifted away on the currents.

What would happen when Tsela took his turn to cross over? Would he remain stooped with age and blindness? Would Ajei still be the same young mother holding a newborn babe in her arms, or would she have turned grey and frail as her husband? And what of his son? In his dreams, the babe had become a boy, though. his look had changed to resemble first Shilah, then Hastiin, and even Lina, or some blend of all three. Would the son be a grown man, or trapped forever as a newborn, always a spirit yearning to grow but never able to leave his mother's breast? Perhaps all the spirits stood with bodies in their prime but minds sharp with the wisdom of age. Tsela would find pleasure in revisiting the body of his youth, full of vigor and shorn of the aches and pains and swellings life had chosen him to bear, and taking Ajei in his arms as he had on the eve of their wedding, but would he then even recognize the children who had passed before him or his own parents and grandparents, aged as they had been when he had known them in his youth? Many questions remained that even Tsela could not answer.

Klah would continue to be a strong Spirit Guide for the pueblo when Tsela passed on. After him might come the girl Nascha. She had the Sight, and with nurturing, she could grow in strength, just as Klah had grown. Perhaps she had been born a bit too early. Klah could serve as Spirit Guide for two or three tens of turns of seasons before choosing a successor, but in the history of the People, some periods had been blessed with two Spirit Guides. The next few years might again provide the same blessing to the People.

Early on, when Tsela had first noted Nascha's nascent gift, he thought perhaps the spirits hoped for her to be a companion and wife to Klah. Though younger than he by several turns of seasons, Nascha was not too young that a match between them would be considered improper, and he was not so much older that she might find the match objectionable, but Tsela had divined that Klah was one of those men who would never choose a wife.

Like Tsela, many Spirit Guides, be they man or woman, married and raised families, but a handful would never find a bond in marriage, and so they chose to bond with the spirits of this world and all the worlds. Klah was one of those. Tsela had confirmed this in his mind when he gazed out over the expanse of kin-worlds to the fluttering kin-spirits of his young protégé and seen those in which a kin-Klah did find a worldly bond to share his heart. Tsela understood the varieties of the human heart, but many did not appreciate the breadth of those varieties, and so Tsela set aside his search for a companion for Klah in this world, content that Klah would choose the most proper path for himself in this one.

The air tickled the back of Tsela's neck when Klah climbed back out onto the roof of their home, and his sandals scuffed across the dried bricks as he approached.

"Have you any word of our lost lamb?" Tsela handed the bowl to Klah so he could empty the powdered seeds into the gourd for storage. Although he could do much despite his clouded eyes, Klah would more easily pour the fruits of Tsela's labor through the small hole.

"Janie? She speaks with Will Covington now, but she remains lost, I fear."

Tsela's ears detected the grains filling the shallow container and the scrape of Klah's fingers as he emptied the mortar. "Her heart wavers, but she is less lost than either you or she think."

"How so?"

"She heads south," Tsela said as if that alone sufficed to explain all.

Klah exhaled for several heartbeats in thought. "I am sorry, master. I do not see."

Tsela broke into another grin. He might be old and frail and of little use out hunting or making bricks and building homes and might even spill most of his powders if he had no help, but he still had much to teach the younger Spirit Guide. "Remember, the People are not the only ones who can see across the worlds. She may yet find the connection she seeks."

Again, Klah fell silent and looked out to the world of Janie De Casas with his inner eye. The quick intake of breath demonstrated he had seen the possibilities. "Many still pursue her."

"They do."

"And a crossing always requires sacrifice."

"It does."

"Should we warn her?"

That gave Tsela the briefest of pauses. "She knows the danger, and she is strong. She has asked for our help once and will do so again if she needs to, but first, she must solve the riddles of her heart. I fear meddling too much in the affairs of the kin-worlds lest they choose to meddle in ours. For now, we will wait, and Janie De Casas will attend to herself."

PART FIVE

ENDURANCE

Janie and Madison avoided the thin ribbon of road when they approached the banks of the Great River the evening before the new moon. The ground here rose and fell in small undulations and, from the crests of those hills, the roofs of the dilapidated buildings that comprised the ghost town of Endurance peeked into view.

Janie called a halt in the hollow behind one of the taller ripples in the land. After tethering their mounts to a gnarled tree, she and Madison crawled to the top of the rise on their bellies and surveyed the tableau before them.

A faded, dusty line of trail meandered its way toward the river and a small dock. Here the river spread its placid surface perhaps thirty yards to the opposite bank and a larger dock where a ferry bobbed in the gentle current. Beyond the dock, fifteen buildings stood in varying stages of disrepair while grass and bushes pushed themselves from the hard-packed earth that had once been streets. Past the buildings, flat plains stretched out to the east, while north, more hill country followed the banks of the river toward distant San Alonso.

Only one building showed any signs of life. Grey smoke

curled from the chimney of the cabin adjacent to the docks and, snuggled against its side, sat a well-tended garden of neat rows of vegetables. The curtains over the windows lay open, but from their vantage, neither Janie nor Madison could make out more than a shadow moving inside.

"What are we looking for?" Madison spoke in a whisper, though they hid too far for anyone in the town to hear.

"Smoke. Signs of life." Janie's eyes locked onto one building for several seconds and then jumped to another in concentrated focus.

"Umm, right there." Madison's extended hand pointed to the cabin on the docks.

Janie gave a quick shake of her head. "That's Marvin. He's harmless, more or less. I want to know if anyone else is there."

"Like Warren?"

"Or some of his cronies. This is probably a trap."

"So why are we here?"

Janie sighed. "Because for some damn reason, I trust Warren. I said I'd hear him out." She shrugged. "Plus, short of swimming, this is the only place to cross, and Will is on the other side." She felt Madison's accusing eyes jabbing into her, but continued her survey of the town. "Check out the hills." Janie gestured north of the town. "They might be camping up there."

"They're not supposed to be here 'til the new moon."

"Neither are we. Just look."

They lay there for another fifteen minutes, but even with the shadows spreading out and the cold creeping in, no new fires appeared in any of the abandoned buildings or the nearby hills. Once, a figure did pass by the window of the cabin on the docks and then later drew the curtains. The outline might have worn a mop of shaggy hair, but from so far away, Janie could not be sure.

As satisfied as Janie could be, the pair returned to a cold and dark camp and worked their molars over tough, dried meat and bread. Probably Madison could have ridden into the last town they passed to buy supplies, but Janie was too worried that Agents Macon and Neems might have added Madison's picture to the wanted posters. Perhaps they could persuade Marvin to break into his larder for them.

After the unsatisfying dinner, Janie used the bracelet to speak with Will. He, Nascha, and Bidziil sat around a merry fire maybe thirty miles east of Endurance (*Fortitude*, her brain whispered underneath). Will's leg pained him more than he would admit, but he refused to let the wound retard their progress. For the past week, Nascha urged Will to rest more, but in his taciturn way, Bidziil approved of Will's doggedness, which egged Will on more than Nascha's worries could hold him back.

Over the past fortnight, a sense of normalcy had crept back into Janie and Will's relationship, if Janie could call holding a seance with a ghost a relationship. Much as they had done riding the trails together, Janie would feel him reach out to her during the day. Sometimes his touch felt like the faintest brush of a breeze, as though she had crossed his mind and activated the bracelet without intent. Other times, his voice and visage swam into her mind, as he did now each night before falling asleep. These goodnight messages in turn encouraged Janie to enforce awkward walls between her and Madison. In her dreams, Janie lost track of which dreams belonged to her and which belonged to Will. With the normalcy, the intervening weeks had brought a degree of acceptance and hope that Janie could tell Will strained to keep in check. It was the same hope that struggled in her own heart.

Since Janie refused to let Madison light a fire, they curled up together under blankets. Janie stared at the dark clouds and between them the wisps of the Milky Way. She permitted Madison's arms to hold her near. When she closed her eyes, Janie pretended the heartbeat against her arm belonged to Will, and that the kiss on her cheek came from his lips.

The clouds above blotted out most of the stars and whatever sliver of moon hung in the sky this night. Chill winds blew down the length of the river and in their wake more dark clouds roiled.

Big Ben tossed another branch onto the fire and rubbed his hands to warm them. "Bad season to be out. Storm'll be blowing in next."

"We'll be in Endurance tomorrow. I'll make sure to get you a nice cozy bed," Moses said.

Big snorted at that. "Place is a ghost town, except fer that crazy ferryman. Anyway, you promised her we'd stay away."

Moses shook his head. "If it's stormin' she won't mind us holing up in one of them old houses."

"I wouldn't count on that. She's liable to start shooting 'fore we can get close enough to ask her permission."

Dick Warren had remained silent while his men jawed, but now he stood and dusted off his pants. "Looks like we may not need to worry about what our young friend thinks." He nodded across the fire toward the road. "His Governorship has arrived."

Big and Moses looked in the direction Warren indicated. Indeed, out of the shadows rocked a large coach pulled by four horses. A nicker behind Warren caused all three men to turn in the opposite direction in time to see two more horsemen materialize out of the night. One rested a rifle across his horse's neck, not quite pointing in the Head Agent's direction but not stowed in a friendly fashion either. The lead horseman reined in his mount with one hand while the other rested on the grip of the six-shooter on his hip.

"Evening, Ovidio," Warren said and touched the brim of his hat.

"Evening, Dick. The Governor would like a word with you."

Janie and Madison woke stiff from the cold of the night and the unyielding ground. Overhead, grey clouds turned the sun into a hazy blob while dark black clouds to the north and south portended a brewing thunderstorm. By the time they broke camp and made their way down to the ferry docks, fresh smoke puffed from the chimney of the cabin across the way. If Janie closed her eyes, she could just make out the off-tune notes to some little shanty that drifted toward them over the sloshing of the current against the pier.

A green, weathered brass bell with a frayed rope stood sentinel at the foot of the docks. Janie climbed from her mule. Before ringing the bell, she let her eyes drift over the other chimneys in Endurance and then over to the northern hills, but the ferryman's house manifested the sole signs of human habitation in their vicinity.

Despite its age and look of fragility, the peel of the bell sounded clear and crisp over the water and echoed back toward Janie and Madison from both the town and the hills behind them.

Before the final echoes could die away, the upper torso of a shaggy-haired man leaned from a window of the cabin. His chest was bare save for the suspenders over his shoulders, and the white on his face suggested shaving cream. "Hi-de-ho," he boomed across to them and waved his arm in a vigorous greeting. "Ole Marvin'll get movin' in a jiffy." With that, he ducked back inside.

A few minutes of banging and a minced oath or two ensued before the figure flung open the door and clomped out onto the far docks. Over the suspenders, he now wore a buttoned denim shirt faded almost to the muddy beige of the river and a floppy tan hat crammed down over the untamed brown curls on his head. He futzed about for a time going over his ferry, but presently cast off and began cranking the handle that pulled the ferry along the cable tether and across the river to his passengers.

As the ferry approached, Marvin resumed his off-tune and

off-lyric singing. The sight brought a smile to Janie's lips and an eye roll from Madison. "He's a little strange," Janie said. "But he was one of the nicest people we met on the trail." The kindest had been the nun who reminded Janie of her mother.

"Given the sort of people you attract, 'nicest' doesn't count for much," Madison said, but a soft smile crossed her eyes and lips when she said it.

Another ten minutes elapsed before Marvin arrived at the near dock. Up close they could see little beads of sweat across his forehead that he had worked up despite the chill of the weather. With a few deft twists, he moored the ferry to the dock and then stood to send the two women a grin bright enough to chase away the clouds, if, that was, one could ignore the crooked and stained teeth.

"Howdy, there," Marvin said, looking first to Madison on her tall steed. "Name's Marvin, and I'm the ferryman of these here parts." His eyes swung down to Janie astride her mule. "You two need to cross over?" Deep furrows spread across his brow when his eyes settled on Janie, as though he was trying to place her in his memory. "Are you sure you're goin' the right way, miss?"

Taken aback, Janie exchanged a look with Madison before turning back to the ferryman. "Yes, Marvin, I am. I'm meeting someone on the other side."

Marvin stared back at her with that strange half-recognizing expression on his face. "Yes, you are." He nodded his whole upper body. "Yes, you are." Then the beaming grin re-emerged. "Well, 'all aboard' as they say on the railroad, or at least that's what I been told." He swung open the gate. "Easiest to walk 'em on. They like it better that way."

The women dismounted and led their respective animals onto the ferry as it rocked and bobbed in the current. Marvin whispered something into the horse and mule's ear as they passed from dock to ferry, and the beasts took to the movement of the water with docile equanimity. Once he had secured the gate and released the ties, Marvin began turning the winch to pull the ferry back to Endurance.

"You gotta new friend," Marvin puffed.

While he pumped the winch, Marvin appeared to be trying to keep an eye on the river and the winch and his passengers all at once which left him cross-eyed, and Janie wondered whether he was speaking to her or Madison. "Yes, I'm surprised you remember."

"A ferryman always remembers his passengers; that's what me pappy told me." They were approaching the middle of the river, and the current increased its tug. A few mists of moisture fell from the sky, not quite a drizzle or perhaps just the spray from the river. Marvin faced forward and put his back into cranking harder. "Your other friends be here soon."

With the heaving of Marvin's breath, Janie could not tell if that last sentence had been a question or statement, nor to which friends he referred. She gazed toward the northern hills and fingered the blue bracelet around her wrist. When she turned to look back at the town, she longed to see Will standing on the docks to greet her. Instead, as expected, cold air and what was becoming a low drizzle awaited her.

The ferry bumped against the town docks, causing everyone but Marvin to take a lurching step to keep their balance. The ferryman had resumed humming a ditty to himself as he lashed the ferry into place and tightened the knots. "Storm's a-comin'. Hope you don't need crossin' over today. It'll get rough."

Janie tightened her coat against the wet. "We're actually looking to stay until tomorrow. Are there any rooms available?"

"Knew you was waitin' on friends." Marvin beamed and swung his arm wide at the opening of the ferry gate. "Welcome to Endurance. Most any of the buildings is fine, though Marvin don't check their roofs no more. I is a ferryman, like my pappy and his pappy and some more pappies afore them, I reckon, not a roof man."

"At least you know who you are." Janie felt her lips curl in a smile suffused with a wistfulness. "How much do we owe you?"

"Dere's always payment for a crossin'. This crossin' were the easy one. Coin each, or whatever you can spare for Marvin, the poor, lonely ferryman."

After leading her mule off the ferry, Janie dug about in her saddle bag for the small purse of coins. "And we'd be mighty obliged if you could spare some food and a fire too."

Even more of Marvin's failing teeth flashed in his smile. "Aww, Marvin's always got food and fire for old friends. You two come on in afore it gets too wet out here."

Before they joined Marvin in the warmth of his cabin, Janie chose a small paddock, overgrown with weeds and prairie grass, to house their horse and mule. Madison fetched water from the river to fill an old trough under an overhang of the adjacent home. As a bonus, the paddock lay on the south side of the cabin, giving their animals some concealment from the northern hills where Warren and his men would arrive. The home looked to be dry enough inside for her and Madison and would shelter them from the worst of the wind. Janie wanted the only fire in town to come from Marvin's chimney in case the Head Agent decided to pay them an early visit.

As the afternoon wore on, the drizzle turned to bouts of sprinkles interspersed with showers. The banks of the Great River crept up so that the waves splashed the bottom of the docks and would have rendered them slick had not the rain already accomplished that task. Marvin ventured out several times to check on his ferry and the cables, but all his tethers remained tight.

For most of the day, Janie and Madison remained inside near the potbellied stove, though Janie stalked the room from time to time in impatience. She gazed out the windows, but as the day wore on and showers turned to a downpour, the distant hills became dark, muddy blobs. If anyone did approach Endurance, Janie realized she would not be able to spot them until they were knocking on Marvin's front door. Of course, given the weather, she would hardly be able to begrudge Warren and his men if they sought shelter of their own from the storm.

While Marvin roamed outside, Janie would use the bracelet to speak with Will. In his reality, the storm assaulting Endurance transformed into a light shower. Despite the mud and cold, the trio had made good time and hoped to reach the vicinity of Fortitude by nightfall and if not, by early the next morning. The raincoats, pilfered from the gear of the men who had trailed him to Mount De Dios, kept Will, Bidziil, and Nascha reasonably dry and warm, and Will in good spirits.

Janie tried to let Will's enthusiasm buoy hers, but the storm, rumblings of thunder, and Warren's impending arrival tethered her back to earth.

An hour or so before sunset, Madison excused herself to the outhouse, leaving Janie and Marvin alone. He had returned from the docks and stood dripping a puddle and warming himself by the stove. "So you gonna cross when he gets here tomorrow?"

The abruptness of the question caught Janie off guard. "I guess it depends on what he has to say. We may keep heading east. How do you know Warren is coming?"

Marvin's eyes grew wide. "He wants to cross too? Been a long time since so many crossed. Is he comin' your way, or are you goin' his?"

"What are you talking about, Marvin?"

"Good ole Will, of course." Marvin goggled at her as if she was an idiot. "He's comin' with two, and youse only got one. Ain't Marvin's, no, never mind, I is just the ferryman, but that cross is expensive. I'd say two is cheaper 'n three, but if old man Warren is wantin' ta cross, who knows who he'll bring, and then that's a mighty big pickle, that is."

Janie froze, and her throat went dry. She pushed back the chair and stood. "You know about Will?" Her voice came out as a croak. Her stomach rolled, and her blood pooled in her boots, making her feel as if she would swoon.

Marvin looked at her cross-eyed. "Youse and he and Finn and the scary one all came and visited Marvin. Then Will and Finn came back." Here Marvin's face scrunched up. "Later they came back with the preacher man, though mostly they wasn't here at all, and that all makes Marvin's head hurt and sad." His whole body slumped into a frown, and he stared at the wall. Just as abruptly, though, he brightened back up. "Any ho, that's the hard crossin'. Needs the blood sacrifice of someone dear. Preacher man wouldn't like that, but a fare's fair if that's what the fair fare is, and Marvin don't set no rules. He is only the ferryman, and the ferryman ferries. That is his job."

The front door caught in the wind and banged out of Madison's hands when she scampered back inside. The curtains flapped. Janie collapsed back into the chair while Madison tugged the door shut and latched it.

"You can cross me over to Will." She still felt a daze. Will had been right about coming here. Somehow he had known.

Marvin seemed not to hear and went back to humming tunes and bustling about his kitchen.

"What's going on?" Madison sat down next to Janie and touched her hand.

Janie said nothing but stared at Madison's hand over her own. Back in the room of woods and pools, Klah had said to her, "You ask much and know not the price." Marvin had just named the price, and the thought left her cold.

Marvin lent them some straw to cushion against the drooping floorboards of the little cabin. A leak in the roof of the bedroom had led them to set up their makeshift bed in a small space that might have once been a larder. Sagging shelves lined two of the walls, and the smell of bygone potatoes still permeated the air. The closeness of the room helped trap the warmth of their bodies, and since three walls of the room faced inside, only a small draft snuck through the cracks between the outside boards.

After Janie had regained contact with her lost love, Madison could feel the yo-yo bouncing of Janie's attraction to her. Janie loved Will and longed to be with him, but she burned with a desire for love and attention here and now. Will could not yet fill that need, but Madison could, each and every night.

Only Janie would no longer let Madison play that role to its fullest.

Of course, given the sword of Damocles that hung above their relationship, Janie's withdrawal benefited them both, but Madison was all too happy to welcome Janie back into her embrace. That night in the mountains, when Janie had suggested they "keep each other warm," as they lay in each other's arms and covered each other in kisses, sweat and twined limbs, Janie had let out a low moan and said, "Just like that, Will." Madison doubted Janie had even realized she'd said his name out loud, but those words demonstrated whom she pictured when she kissed Madison.

Despite playing second fiddle to a ghost (she still did not believe Janie's fanciful story and her eerie, mind-stealing, glowing bracelet), Madison still reveled in the fantasy of love when she lay next to Janie in the night, even if Janie now relegated their love at a clothed embrace and chaste kiss on lips or cheek.

And then this evening, she had walked in on something between Janie and the ferryman. Madison overheard them talking about crossing over while she stood near the window under the eaves. The conversation confirmed Madison's suspicion that Janie did not plan on crossing another river. She wanted to invite a ghost back to the land of the living with a blood sacrifice. Despite how preposterous the idea sounded, the thought chilled Madison. Janie was communing with the ghost of her lost love and believed she could raise him from the dead like Lazarus.

Why did she keep looking for comfort in the past? Why was Madison's love not enough? She could make Janie happy if only Janie would let her. She could help Janie forget Will.

The wind howled over the loose shingles and banged doors and shutters around the town. The rain pounded down like a thousand hoof beats punctuated by the rumbles and roars of near and distant thunder. Bright flashes of lightning lanced in from outside, setting monochrome shadows to dance at intervals in their room.

Through it all, Janie slept, perhaps dreaming that Will held her close even when Madison's arms entwined her waist. At one point, well past midnight, after a flash of lightning and roar of thunder had descended as one beast and shaken the walls of their abode, Janie stirred enough to roll to her side away from Madison.

Since then, Madison had drifted in and out of drowsiness, staring at the dark ceiling and listening to the storm attempt to drown the world. She had lost all proper sense of time, while the steady persistence of rain, wind, and thunder extinguished the last of her ability to sleep.

She sat up in bed and stared out the doorway. Next to her, at the movement of the blanket, Janie shifted but did not rouse.

Madison heaved a sigh and stood up. She pulled the blanket over Janie's shoulder, stepped into her boots, and walked out into the old kitchen at the front of the house.

The chimney pipe created a patter of indoor rain where an old stove must have stood before the former owners of this cabin hefted it into the back of a wagon with all their other worldly possessions and headed out for parts unknown. In the blackness of the night, Madison could no longer see the puddle running along the floorboards before disappearing into the cracks in the floor, but the splashes made her suspect that the ingress from the chimney pipe was winning the equilibrium battle with the egress into the mud beneath the cabin. Given the ferocity of the storm, Madison wondered if those same drops might start scrambling back up those cracks as the entire world began to flood.

Now that she was upright, a pressure rose from her bladder, but not an urgency. She contemplated making a run for the outhouse, but given the storm decided she could hold it a mite longer.

Her boots clicked on wood as she walked to the window to peer out the shutters. Outside, clouds blotted out any trace of the moon and stars. Even when her eyes adjusted to the darkness between the lightning flashes, she could no longer make out the black bulk of the other buildings against the equally dark landscape. When her eyes traveled up, the heavy ebony of the earth gave way to the charcoal black of the sky.

The next flash of lightning made her swear aloud. Across the way, her horse, Black Bessie, hugged the side of the opposite cabin. The lightning and thunder must have frightened her or Janie's mule into breaking out of the paddock. Perhaps the good luck of the Fates had woken Madison before Bessie bolted and drowned in the river or become lost in the hills. Madison did not waste time going back for her coat. She threw open the door and ran out to grab Bessie's bridle lest the beast disappear into the night. She was one step out the door onto the moldering patio with rain already soaking into her shirt from the broken eaves above when her brain asked how Bessie could possibly have saddled and bridled herself. Before she could halt her second step into the rain and retreat, a cold callused hand clamped on her wrist and yanked her the rest of the way into the rain and mud.

A flash of lightning illuminated three dark figures in Agent's black. If she screamed in surprise or fear, the following thunder drowned her out even in her own ears.

The oil lamp hanging from the ceiling cast images of dancing flames on the walls of the coach. Outside, the wind and rain battered against the walls and shutters sealed over the windows. Drops of water crept through the edges of the door when the rain pelted sideways across the landscape and the edges of the windows when it ran down the sides of the coach, but the roof remained waterproof. Above, the branches of the tree scratched at the roof, and the stronger gusts of the storm rocked the body of the coach on its springs as if it jostled on a pleasant afternoon ride behind a team of trotting horses.

Governor Hogg reclined across the rear bench of seats, the glasses on his nose reflecting the lamp light while behind them his eyes flickered across the page of his book.

Dick Warren lay on the forward bench with a blanket pulled up against the chill and his coat bundled beneath his head for a pillow. He watched the lantern swaying in the air and strained his ears to hear beyond the sounds of the storm: the rain pelting against the wood of the coach and the sodden mud covering the ground, the wind tearing across the hills, and the rumble and roar of thunder punctuated by bright flashes of lightning. Of course, he might not even hear the return of Agent Nazario and his men until the Agent swung open the coach door to announce their arrival back at camp.

But Warren doubted Agent Nazario would be returning this night.

Dick Warren had risen to the position of Head Agent because he was smart enough, dogged, and told his men exactly what he thought, blunt, but not harsh, unless the moment called for a little harshness. If Horace Weatherwax could be believed, Dick had also risen because Governor Hogg respected those thoughts and opinions. Well, if that were true, it was time he spoke his mind, and if Horace was mistaken, well, Warren was on his way out anyway, and speaking his mind stayed true to his nature. He pushed his big body upright on the bench. "You know, you signed their death warrants."

Hogg continued reading and turned a page in his book before replying. "You know, you could join your men or the coachman in a tent out in the rain. I'm perfectly content in here reading by myself." His eyes continued their run over the new page.

Dick swung his legs off the bench to face the Governor. "You've said I should speak my mind with you. I'm speaking it."

Hogg sighed. He slipped the ribbon that dangled from the book's spine down over his page and snapped the volume shut. "They are three trained Agents, Dick. They can handle one young lady in the night, I'm sure."

"But they aren't real Agents."

Hogg raised his eyebrows. "They're wearing the same black as you, Dick."

"Stick a collar on a pig, and it still ain't no parson."

Hogg shook his head and gave a wry smile. "You're just upset I interrupted your plans for a tête-à-tête with Miss De Casas."

"If you say so, but you're upset because I wasn't doin' my job the way you wanted me to," Warren said. "I should be riding in to meet her, calm and alone just like I promised her. Nazario and his thugs are Revenue Men, not Agents. They're used to intimidating shopkeepers, farmers, and ranchers. When things get hot, they always call in the Agents."

"Fair enough." Hogg nodded his head. "But Agent Nazario was head of the Revenue Men. He knows his men and how to handle a gun."

"In my book, that just makes him head accountant and a bully to boot, not an Agent."

"You've never cared for Ovidio much, have you?"

"Like him or not, I hate to see goo..." Dick paused to search for a more appropriate word. "...valuable men wasted, especially when all they're gonna do is scare her off, and I'll never get a chance to talk to her and bring her in peacefully." In the back of his mind, Dick doubted he had hoped to bring Janie in, but he would still pretend to himself that had been his plan in asking her to meet in Endurance.

"Come now, Dick." Hogg wagged a finger in admonition.

"Three trained men — despite what you may think, they are trained and worthy of being Agents, are going to ride into a ghost town, under the cover of night and a raging storm. They'll nab our quarry while she's still asleep. They'll have her before she knows what happened."

"You can't honestly believe it'll be that easy.

"More so than I can believe I've signed their death warrants."

"She's Janie De Casas."

Hogg laughed. "She's one woman, not some demigod."

Following Warren's lead, Midnight and Big had kept their mouths shut regarding the young woman who rode with Janie, and Warren continued to avoid disabusing the Governor of the belief that she traveled alone. "She's Arthur's daughter."

Hogg snorted. "Even if he was an ace shooter, he was a drunk, and it doesn't mean his daughter can shoot half a damn."

"She ran roughshod over this whole state all last year. How many men did she kill?"

Hogg shrugged. "No way to know. She had three other guns with her, including David McPhail."

"Whom she killed," Warren said.

"We don't know she killed him, or if she did, how she did it."

"She drew iron on him and beat him. I'd bet my life on it." Warren stared the Governor in the eye. "And if you were so sure she didn't, you'd roll this coach right into that town to watch Nazario in person."

"Pish, Dick. I'm the Governor of the State. A little prudence on my part is necessary." Hogg reopened his book. "Even a blind squirrel will find a nut every now and again. We can't have her getting a lucky shot at me." He gave another shrug. "And if Nazario isn't up to the task, I still have my faithful Head Agent to keep me safe and finish the job." Hogg's voice dropped from casual banter to menacing. "Now shut up and get some shut-eye, Dick. Open your mouth again, and you'll be out in the rain and perhaps out of a job."

Warren crossed his arms, but Hogg ignored him. After

a full minute passed, Dick flopped back down on his bench. "Yes, Sir," he grumbled. Hogg might retire Dick as Head Agent when this was all over, but God willing, Dick would stick it out to the end. He owed it to himself, to the Governor, to Jefferson State, and to that one lonely young woman, Janie De Casas.

Ovidio Nazario had always considered Dick Warren soft for a Head Agent, too mired in his past as a Territory Ranger, too placating and gentle. Yes, he was smart enough to bamboozle Governor Hogg into allowing him to rise through the ranks, but in the end, the man was more a nattering old biddy than a strong enforcer. Governor Hogg led the State with a firm hand, and his most trusted lieutenants ought to do the same.

Nazario ran the Revenue Office in the same manner his daddy had run their household, with fear and respect. He might offer a sweet hand now and again, but only if the other one stayed rolled up in a fist, and he never let them forget the fist. Let Mommy sew that seam on his shirt crooked or short him a chunk of beef in the stew, POW, just like that, he'd set Mommy on her rump with a red mark across her cheek if she were lucky and a blackened eye if she weren't. Same thing with the kids. Once, Nazario didn't tip his hat quite proper when Daddy's boss passed them on the street, and as soon as that boss man was out of sight, Daddy whipped him proper across his rear with a switch.

Nazario grew up fearing God and fearing his Daddy, and that meant he respected them. The men in the Revenue Office and the little folk in the towns Nazario oversaw learned right early to start jumping before Nazario had to tell them it was time to jump.

His first assignment had been in the town of Forgiveness. He and his cadre of Revenue Men arrived early in the morning in their wagon and set up outside the general store, a place called Mitchinson's. Three Revenue Men stopped by each establishment to remind the townsfolk taxes were due while Ovidio and Pearson stayed by the strongbox and ledger. Over the course of the day, the townsfolk and neighboring farmers stopped in to pay their tithe to Governor Hogg and the State. The last shopkeeper, the owner of the local barbershop, arrived late in the day just before sunset and an hour or so after the blacksmith to pay his due.

"The Governor don't tolerate tardiness," Ovidio told the man while Pearson logged the payment in the big blue ledger.

The barber, a fair-haired man with a beet red face, bristled. "Ain't tardy. I'm here to pay."

"Yeah, but you're the last one in town who come by," Ovidio said. He whistled to the other three men under his command. "Next time, be early."

They burned the barbershop to the ground before retiring to the local saloon and brothel for the night and rode out toward the next town in the morning with the ashes cooling behind them.

When Ovidio and his Revenue Men returned to Forgiveness the following year, they found the entire town standing in line before the sun reached its zenith with the barber first in line.

Governor Hogg wanted Janie De Casas brought in. Dick Warren, in his weakness, had failed in that duty. Agent Ovidio Nazario would finish the job tonight.

The three Agents, Nazario, Heath, and McMaster, rode tall and proud into Endurance like specters come to claim the living, oil black coats flapping about them in the storm. Above the constant noise of the rain, Ovidio could just make out the jangle of stirrups and bridle and the huffing of their horses' breath. The flashes of lightning lit their way.

The only smoke and light came from the ferryman's cabin by the docks, but Ovidio had encountered the raggedy man often enough to know the man would squawk like the dickens if they roused him. If De Casas was here, he wanted to check the rest of the town first, lest the yelps of that addled-brained denizen of this ghost town forewarn her of the danger.

They started on the eastern edge of the town square. The first building's roof had collapsed, and they passed it by. The second stood empty, and Nazario was headed to the third when Heath slapped his arm and pointed. A horse poked its head out from a paddock three buildings over.

Nazario smirked. "Easy. Spread out, boys. Let's bring her in. Heath, you go first."

The three men crept up to the cabin. Their boots squelched in the mud, but the sound could not carry far against the rain.

Heath reached for the front door while Nazario and Mc-Master fanned out behind him. A curse from inside pulled all three up short, and Heath flattened his back to the wall. A second later, glory of glories, Janie De Casas came running into the night. Heath seized her wrist and yanked her off balance to go tumbling into the mud at Nazario's feet.

Nazario let go with a belly laugh. All this fuss over the past year over a mite of a girl. This just proved how incompetent Warren and his vaunted Agents truly were. All Nazario had to do was show up, and she went scampering out the front door like some scared jackrabbit and right into their arms. "Well, lookee here, boys. We done caught ourselves the most wanted woman in the state."

Covered in mud, the woman at his feet shivered, a dark blob in the night. He bent down to grab her collar and yank her to her knees. "I'd say I'm disappointed, but I'm not surprised. Don't know what the Governor wants with the likes of you, but I knew them stories were just tall tales.

Lightning flashed again to reveal pale doe eyes dripping with fear, but her hair was short and brown, not long and black, her nose was too big and upturned, and the face too round compared to the poster hanging back in the Revenue office in San Alonso. "Who the hell are you?"

Instead of answering, the girl spat in his face.

Nazario cranked her neck back, and the girl cried in pain. "Oh, you'll pay for that, honey."

"Her name's Madison. I'd thank you to let her go." The voice was quiet but stung with a cold, sharp edge.

Nazario straightened to look toward the cabin. The figure was a shadow against a shadow, indistinct, edges softened by the rain, perhaps not even there at all. He pointed his gun at the girl by his side. "I'd thank you to raise those hands miss, less'n your friend here gets hurt."

"That would be a very bad idea," the cold voice said.

The calm assuredness of the voice sent an involuntary shiver down Nazario's spine, but maybe that was just the rain getting inside the collar of his shirt. Heath and McMaster stepped away in flanking positions, hands on their guns. Nazario yanked Madison to her feet to stand beside him.

"The Governor wants you alive, Miss De Casas. He didn't say nothin' 'bout any friends of yours." Nazario pressed his pistol into the girl's ribs. "I'll start with hurting, but'll go farther if need be."

Madison shifted and trembled in his grip, trying to wriggle free of the barrel.

"Madison, stop moving." The shadow's voice softened, but the words ordered in a way the gun in the girl's side did not. "Remember my second day on the ranch?"

Madison's body went from hanging atremble from the end of Nazario's arm to as rigid as the gun barrel pressed against her ribs.

Lightning arced sky to ground just outside of town, turning night to day and hammering down on them with thunder louder than all the blacksmith hammers in the world. Janie De Casas stood illuminated before him for one long second. Even sodden with rain, she was no more than a slip of a girl, scrawny and trail worn, but she stood there with boots planted, hands at her hips, folded on the grips of her pistols, bigger than the ones Nazario and his men carried. Her eyes seemed like black sockets, and their pupils glinted red like Satan's in the dazzle of light.

For that one second, the world stood awash in color, and then the darkness returned, but Nazario had seen enough. A natural killer stood before him. To hell with what Hogg wanted. Nazario would rather take his chances with a length of hemp rope around his neck than the creature before him. He swung his gun from the girl at his side and fired.

Janie woke to a draft as the blankets shifted and Madison sat up, but Janie lay still. Warren and Will would both arrive in the morning, and all her secrets would be revealed. Facing Madison became more painful each day, and now seemed almost unbearable. Unbearable now because of Marvin's words: a blood sacrifice of someone dear. Only Will and Madison remained dear to her, and she would have to sacrifice one to be with the other.

When Madison slipped from the room, Janie rolled to her back and stared toward a ceiling she could not make out in the dark. She really ought to have sent Madison back to Henrika weeks ago, but her need for companionship on the trail overruled the compass of conscience in her head. Maybe, deep inside, Janie had known Madison had another role to play.

Janie tossed back the blankets and sat up to follow, but even as she did, Madison's swear echoed back to her from the front room. A cold blast of air curled into the pantry with the opening of the front door. Instinct made Janie reach for her gun belt even before Madison's choked-off cry of surprise demanded Janie to.

Within seconds, Janie hid behind the edge of the open doorway and peered out into the night. Lightning flashes gave her glimpses of three black-clad figures hovering over a fourth figure sprawled in the mud.

Once again, Janie had placed her faith in a man and been betrayed. Warren's promise to come alone, to only talk, had been a ruse. None of the three seemed as large or dark as the two men the Head Agent had originally sent to arrange this parlay, but only Warren or his men would have known to meet her here on this day.

The Agent in the middle bent down to pull Madison to her knees, and Janie stepped out into the night.

She might as well have stepped into a cave at midnight as this storm. Her eyes could make out only the vaguest of shapes of buildings among the backdrop of hills and the closer figures who struggled in the lightless night which greyed by only a shade or two up into the clouds.

Marvin spoke of payment and sacrifice if Janie hoped to reach Will. Maybe the claim was just more crazy blather, but somehow he knew about Will, about her, and the thousands of shining worlds out there. A ferryman to ferry her across the thin blue squiggles connecting the worlds and into Will's arms, but the toll required the blood of someone dear.

Three Agents held Madison and stood between her and Will. Or perhaps they offered her a gateway. The strange pull of Warren's invitation on her and the rightness she felt when Will insisted on meeting her in Endurance had become clear. Destiny led her to this moment in this place offering her the chance to fulfill her heart's desire. All it would take is a single bullet amid the firefight to come. Janie was an expert shot. She could make Madison's sacrifice fast and painless.

Yet Madison had followed Janie and held her close in the night. How could Janie even think of sacrificing her friend and lover so callously?

But Will had pulled her from the darkness. How could she not finish this quest to reunite with him?

The patter of rain onto the mud and puddles muffled the Agent's words and rang a meditative rhythm in her ears. The tension slipped off her body like the rain running through her hair. She knew what to do.

Janie De Casas had been born for moments like this. Arthur De Casas had groomed his daughter all of her young life. David McPhail had added the finishing polish. Live or die in this sorry excuse for a town, a literal world away from the man she loved, if tonight she would step over to join him or meet him on the plains of the Lord, Janie would find joy in that. If not, in the morning, she would search again.

The raindrops fell on her scalp, each one somewhere between a cool tickle and a needle prick. Her rough cotton shirt soaked up the drops and clung to her shoulders and breast. The water in her hair tried to tug her down with it.

She brushed strands from her eyes before she spoke to the Agent accosting Madison. "Her name's Madison. I'd thank you to let her go."

The words caught the man unaware, and he jumped but recovered quick enough. "I'd thank you to raise those hands miss, less'n your friend here gets hurt."

"That would be a very bad idea."

"The Governor wants you alive, Miss De Casas. He didn't say nothin' 'bout any friends of yours. I'll start with hurting, but'll go farther if need be."

Talking to the man had been necessary, but the outcome of this conversation came as unstoppable as the storm washing over them. "Madison, stop moving. Remember my second day on the ranch?"

Madison did.

Janie waited. Her boots stood planted firm in the mud, but the four figures before her remained indistinct blobs. Two of the Agents had shifted toward the edges of her peripheral vision, flanking out of each other's line of fire, but she could not take a chance just yet.

And then the lightning came down like a wrathful ray of sun.

The images burned themselves into her mind. Three Agents,

center, left and right, none of whom she recognized, Madison held to the middle Agent's left side with her head and wide eyes at his shoulder. Where was Warren? She filed the question away for later if she had a later in which to contemplate it.

As abruptly as light bathed the world, darkness returned, even deeper than before. The brief flash wiped out her night vision. Neither side could see the other, but Arthur De Casas had taught Janie one all-important lesson for a gunslinger: how to shoot with her eyes closed.

As soon as the light evaporated, Janie drew.

Her first two shots roared straight ahead toward Madison and the Agent accosting her while the thunder still rolled over them. The flanking Agents would be drawing even as her arms swept toward them. Though it would affect her accuracy, and although she longed to join Will more than anything, years of self-preservation made Janie drop to one knee just before her arms found their marks, and she fired again, two bullets toward each Agent. Something buzzed over her head, but maybe that was just a storm-thrown leaf or twig. Another something dug into the mud near her right leg, but maybe that was just more rain.

Her night vision began to coalesce once more. Two figures lay sprawled before her on the ground. Two more thudded to the mud on either side.

Janie jumped to her feet and ran forward. She dropped to slam her knee into the first Agent's gut. He spasmed and tried to bring his gun hand back up, but Janie placed the muzzle of hers against his chest and fired again, twice into his heart. Warm drops splattered against her face and lips leaving the taste of salt and copper to mix with the rivulets of rain.

Splashing and a groan came from the right. Janie spun, gun extending out over Madison's prone form, and fired into a dark blob in the mud that was struggling back to its feet. The force of her shots spread the man out in the mud for good.

She continued a full rotation to the third figure, but it remained motionless under the outpouring of the clouds.

The rain washed down. From the direction of the docks, a voice yipped in the night and a doorway banged open.

Janie turned back to the small prone figure before her. "Madison?" She reached out to her friend's shoulder, and a small, cold hand gripped her wrist.

"I thought you were gonna shoot me." Madison pushed herself to sit. "I'm your sacrifice."

Tears streamed from Janie's eyes even as the rain splashed them away. "I could never hurt you, not even for Will." She pulled Madison into an embrace, and they sat there together, crying as the rain doused them as if in baptism.

Overnight, the storm spent itself and moved east. By morning, thin rays of the sun shone down on Endurance, but the parched greedy ground had already slurped up most of the puddles, leaving firm moist earth. In a matter of days, all the thirsty plants would push forth flowers of gratitude, and brilliant oranges and yellows and pale blues and purples would wash across the desert just as the storm had done.

Janie huddled under a rough woolen blanket on the porch steps to Marvin's cabin. In her hands, she clutched a tin cup of coffee from which she took sips and warmed her hands. At the end of the porch, on a post that served both cabin and dock, hung her gun belt and rosewood revolvers that had once belonged to Will.

In the night, Marvin had found Janie and Madison sobbing and shivering in the rain. He brought them to his cabin, stoked the fire, and laid out their clothes to dry while the women trembled under blankets from the cold and ebbing adrenaline.

At dawn, Marvin and Janie dragged the three dead Agents to lie in a row outside the cabin they had perished raiding. Madison could not go near them, but she helped unsaddle the horses and fed and watered them in the paddock behind the cabin.

Now the three had retired to the far end of town, and though in shadow, the bodies pulled at Janie's attention. She did not recognize any of the dead men, which meant that Warren might still be on his way.

Janie tore her gaze away and looked north. She set down her mug and toyed with the bracelet on her wrist. "I'm sorry, Will." She kissed the bracelet. "I wasn't strong enough."

After a time, out of the hazy morning sun reflecting off the river, a heavyset rider crested the ribbon of road over the hill and began to descend.

"Madison?" Janie called.

A few seconds later, Madison emerged from the cabin carrying a plate of eggs and boiled oats. "What is it?" Her voice caught on the last word when she too spied the black-clad rider. "Oh."

"Go hang up your guns down there." Janie gestured to where hers hung.

"But we'll need 'em." The rider had a good lead, but following him, at a leisurely roll, a coach flanked by two more riders crested the hill.

Even at a distance, Janie recognized the dark of Agent Macon and the bulk of Agent Neems. "I need you to be unarmed," Janie said without taking her eyes off the lead rider, now clearly Dick Warren riding slump-shouldered and head down. "It's too late for you to run, but if you aren't a threat, Warren'll let you be."

From her stance and grimace, Janie could read Madison's doubt, but the young woman assented and hung her gun belt next to Janie's. Then she returned to Janie's side and set the plate of eggs between them on the porch, her appetite extinguished.

Warren paused to hitch his horse across the way. When his eye alighted on the bodies farther into town, he shook his head. He ambled toward Janie, hiking his slumping pants as he came. He halted ten feet or so from them and tipped his hat back. His crooked half smile touched his lips with an escaping snort. "Feels like I've been in a similar position to this not too long ago."

Janie said nothing, but beside her, Madison shifted as if in understanding.

"The Governor caught up with me on the way down." He gestured a thumb over his shoulder at the coach still bumping down the road. "I didn't send those men last night."

"Just like you didn't send the one into the Governor's little playground either," Janie retorted.

Warren grimaced. "Yeah, pretty much just like that." He did have the good grace to bow his head and look chagrined. "Look, Miss De Casas, I'm sorry. I really was hoping you and I could just talk, find out a little of what you know maybe, and figure a way to end this mess. Now, well, it don't look like we have much time."

Janie shook her head. "I'm sorry I listened. You're right though, we don't have much time."

"Can you really speak to them other worlds?" Warren asked. The coach rolled to a stop in the town square behind him.

Janie's eyes left Warren's to follow the coach and horsemen. The coachman climbed down and made to open the door, while Agents Macon and Neems dismounted. "Madison has nothing to do with this. She doesn't even know me." Janie spoke low but urgent so her voice would not carry further than Warren's ears.

Warren's eyes jotted to Madison and back. "Me and my men have never seen her before. She's just a friend of the ferryman."

Janie gave a fraction of a nod. "Yes, I can speak to one of them, anyway, but I won't let Hogg have it." The coach door swung open and disgorged the spindly white figure with the greying handlebar mustache.

Warren's chest heaved with the force of his sigh. "I didn't think you would."

Janie shrugged off the blanket and stood.

Spinning his walking stick as he came. Governor Hogg squelched through the remaining mud. He tapped Warren's belly with the cane. "Looks like I owe you an apology, Dick. She did kill them. I guess Nazario wasn't cracked up to be an Agent after all." A wolf smile graced his lips when he turned to Janie. "Ahh, good Miss De Casas. Finally, we meet again."

"Too soon, if you ask me."

"Tut, tut, now." Hogg waved his hand. "Has this been any way to repay my generosity? I welcomed you into my home, to my most personal sanctum, and you killed one of my trusted men and ran away with my property."

"You sent your 'trusted man' to spy on me, he tried to beat me and rape me, and I have nothing of yours." Despite that, she covered the bracelet on her wrist with her other hand on reflex.

"Well, I can't be held responsible for the actions of some lone wolf who decided of his own accord not to follow my orders." Hogg had not missed Janie's movement, though, and pointed to her wrist with the muddied end of his cane. "But I do believe you have something that belongs to me."

Janie cupped a protective hand tighter around the bracelet, but the iridescent blue glow spilled out from her fingers. Will bore witness to the confrontation, and perhaps so too did Nascha and Bidziil and even Klah and Tsela. "This isn't yours. It was given to me by a friend."

"A friend I dare say who took it from the Map Room." Hogg extended his hand. "You can talk to the other worlds with it. Give it to me."

Janie shook her head. "No, you can't have it."

Neems and Macon had approached the tableau but still hung back. A nod of Hogg's head drew them closer. "My dear, you are in no position to argue. You will give me that bracelet. Then we will all climb back into my coach and have a nice peaceful ride back to San Alonso while you tell me all about how it works and how you plan on reaching your young man. If you do all of that willingly, I may be so inclined to allow you to join him. Contradict me again, and you will still tell me everything I want to know, but it will be much less pleasant for you, and I doubt I will ever let you see that young whelp ever again."

"That's okay. I know I'll never be able to hold him again anyway." Janie closed her eyes for a brief second and called Will to mind. There he stood on the docks just feet away with deep lines of sorrow on his face. "I'm sorry, Will," she whispered.

Before she could hear his reply, Janie yanked the bracelet from her wrist. She spun in one movement and flung the bracelet far out into the river. Sunlight played along the wobbling edges of the bracelet and sent bright sparks of blue dancing in the air before the grey-brown waters swallowed its beauty in a dull gulp.

Janie turned back to face the Governor.

His eyes widened in livid circles and his nostrils flared for six or seven breaths before he mastered himself enough to speak. "Then I guess I have no use for you. Kill her, Dick."

Janie remained standing impassive on the steps. To one side, Marvin had taken hold of Madison and pulled her away despite her cries. In her mind, Will's voice echoed, but without the bracelet, he was only a whisper, a breeze, the beating of a moth's wings on the other side of a wall. She ignored Warren and his men and kept her eyes riveted on the Governor. Where weakness had overcome her last night, now she had the strength to know she would be rejoining Will in the plains of Heaven. She only regretted not telling Madison about his grave on Mount De Dios. She would have liked to die knowing that her bones might lie next to his for eternity.

Out of the corner of her eye, Dick Warren shook his head and drew his gun. He left it hanging at his side and bowed his head.

"Dick," Hogg bellowed. "Kill her now, or my next stop will be at a certain ranch upriver."

Years ago, Territory Ranger Dick Warren had deserted his friends and brothers when Governor Hogg arrived to take the reins of State. He had served the man for close to twenty years now, and although he did not always agree with the Governor, he respected the man's leadership and at times even considered him a friend. That leader and friend had just given him a direct order, and as Head Agent, Warren had a duty to the State to fulfill, the same duty he had sworn to back in the Territory Rangers: to defend the citizens of Jefferson and keep order.

Dick Warren raised his gun and shot Alistair Hogg in the side of the head.

Janie flinched at the sound of the bullet, expecting to feel the sharp pain of lead in her chest. Instead, Governor Hogg toppled to the ground like a pine tree severed by the woodman's axe, and Janie could still not make sense of what had transpired.

Dick Warren did not even look at her. He just holstered his gun with a hangdog look on his jowls.

Behind him, Agent Neems screwed up his face in consternation.

Agent Macon broke the ensuing seconds of silence. "God dammit, Dick. You just killed the Governor." Macon threw his hat to the ground and stomped the earth.

Warren turned to him. "Looks like I did, Moses. Looks like I did."

Macon swore again. "Don't have no choice now, Dick. God damn you." He drew his gun and shot Warren twice in the chest.

The sight of his friend and mentor collapsing to join the lanky body of Governor Hogg shook Agent Neems from his stupefaction. "Jesus Christ, Moses, why and the hell did you do that?"

Agent Macon had turned away to swipe tears from his eyes. "He killed the Governor, God dammit. He shot the mother-loving Governor. That's a capital crime, that is."

"But you killed him. You killed Dick."

"I know I killed him, you big oaf. What the hell else was I supposed to do? I loved him like a brother, but he killed the Governor."

Janie might have stood there another eternity listening to the two men shout themselves hoarse, but a firm hand grabbed her elbow. "Get while the gettin's good, missy. Marvin don't like guns, no siree. Too much blood and sacrifice for poor ol' Marvin." The ferryman drew Janie and Madison with him up the docks. That faraway look Janie had seen yesterday swept over his eyes. "Time's a-wastin' and rivers want crossin'."

Janie scooped up the gun belts as she passed the post and stumbled with Madison onto the ferry. Marvin unlashed the moorings and swung the gate shut behind them. "This crossin's gunna be a little rougher'n you're used to. Better hang on tight." With that, Marvin threw himself at the winch and churned away with a happy tune on his lips despite the bloodbath taking place on his doorstep.

Behind them, Agents Macon and Neems seemed to have realized that the object of this debacle was slipping away over the river. Janie watched them mount the docks, but their voices were unable to bridge the divide between dock and ferry. A heavy fog turned their dark uniforms into blobs and muffled their voices.

As the voices of the Agents faded, dull chimes echoed from far away, but each turn of the wheel drew them closer, their volume climbing with each toll until Janie had to cover her ears, but even that gesture failed to dim the sound. Beneath the chimes came a buzz whose pitch increased into a crescendoing whine.

Madison had already collapsed to her side, trying to cover her ears and hold her belly all in one motion.

"Starts ta get rough here," Marvin called over the chimes and the whine. "We done lost your pretty guide," he yelled. "Need you to concentrate on him. Think hard, lessin' I get us lost." Then his lips puckered back into a tune Janie could no longer discern amid the cacophony about her.

Janie thought of Will as she had glimpsed him on the docks before she tossed the bracelet, forlorn but with understanding in his eyes as well.

Waves rocked the ferry and water ran over the deck and soaked Janie's jeans. Without realizing, she had dropped to her knees beneath the beating of the chimes, and she stared dumbly at the water soaking her clothes. The whine continued to climb to such intensity that it drowned out the noise of the chimes.

Janie called to mind Will's thin frame and broad shoulders. She pictured him when he pulled the canvas executioner's bag from her head, when he bandaged her ankle the first night, when he sat next to her by the pond and offered her friendship, when he twined her arm in his while she walked the streets in the maroon dress, when he held her by the fire after nearly drowning in the river, when she drew him after her into her bed in the pueblo.

The pressure of the world crushed in on Janie, bending her double while her insides inflated until she knew she must burst, but then the whine reached its apogee and began a long slow slide down into the waves on the river. The pressure, both inside and out, eased. The chimes clanged against her ears, but either they had deafened her, or they were chasing the whine back from whence it came.

Janie looked up. The world had shifted like a reflection in a looking glass. When Janie had last looked, Madison lay to her left, but now she curled on her side to Janie's right. Marvin manned the opposite side of the winch, and the ferry crawled toward the docks in Endurance (*Fortitude*, the wind whispered).

Ahead, grey fog shrouded the docks in shifting tendrils, but each creak of the winch peeled them away one by one. Three hazy shadows awaited them.

"Why are we going back?" Janie's voice cracked on the words as though it had lain in long disuse, not a scant handful of seconds. She struggled back up on wobbling legs. "They're waiting for us."

"Waitin' at the crossin'," Marvin sang. "Marvin told you he could cross you over. That's what a ferryman does."

When Janie looked back to the docks, the last of the fog evaporated. White and grey feathers of clouds broke up the heavens into streams of blue, and rays of sunshine bathed the dock enough to make her squint, but there he stood.

The breeze ruffled the waves of his brown hair. A dirty scruff of week-old beard covered his pale face. He held his right leg at an awkward angle, and his clothes hung on his frame, gaunter than she remembered, but if she had a mirror, Janie supposed she would look leaner and more trail-worn than she had before Victory changed everything.

Will Covington stood on the docks waiting for her. Beyond him, Nascha and Bidziil stood with Maikoh wagging his tail at their feet.

Behind her, Janie could hear Madison sitting up, and Marvin grunted one last time as the ferry bumped against the docks.

None of that mattered to Janie. She leapt over the ferry railing and onto the docks even as Will hobbled toward her.

They came together under the warm rays of the sun. She stopped him with her hands on his chest. His hands cupped her shoulders, and they gazed into each other's eyes.

"You're here, you're really here." She reached to cup the coarse scruff of his cheek.

Will's eye stretched wide as if trying to drink all of Janie in at once. "It's like a dream. Are you really my Janie?"

If that thought gave her pause, Janie did not let it show. After everything she had braved to find him, all the time she played his guardian angel looking over him, hearing his voice again these past few weeks, she knew the answer. "Yes, and you're my Will."

And then she pulled him into a kiss that would erase all doubts.

ACKNOWLEDGMENTS

Janie was a story that demanded to be written. Almost as soon as I pushed away from the keyboard after finishing *Gunslingers*, Janie started whispering in my ear incessantly. I missed her too much, and she had more stories to tell. Perhaps it was reading too many *What If* comics growing up, but once the premise appeared, the rest just kept rolling out.

As always, thank you to my family, friends, and early readers who supported me through early drafts and tolerated the need to hide away and write the story.

Once again, the Atmosphere Press team shepherded me through the process with their usual tack, dedication, and encouragement. My editor BE made me examine and re-examine what I wanted to say. They helped me clarify passages and bring out a sharper picture of Janie and her world. Sarah and Chris did the heavy lifting of copyediting and fixing all my punctuation and those pesky spelling errors that split through spellcheck. Ronaldo and his design team put together another awesome cover. Alex once again helped organize the entire gang, and by the time you read this, another whole team will have put together the interior layout and pushed me through the final publishing hoops.

Thank you to everyone who read *Gunslingers* and let me know how much fun they had reading it. I hope *Janie* gave you even more enjoyment.

To my family, I love you. I never would have been able to write these stories without your love and support. Thank you.

ABOUT ATMOSPHERE PRESS

Founded in 2015, Atmosphere Press was built on the principles of Honesty, Transparency, Professionalism, Kindness, and Making Your Book Awesome. As an ethical and authorfriendly hybrid press, we stay true to that founding mission today.

If you're a reader, enter our giveaway for a free book here:

SCAN TO ENTER
BOOK GIVEAWAY

If you're a writer, submit your manuscript for consideration here:

SCAN TO SUBMIT
MANUSCRIPT

And always feel free to visit Atmosphere Press and our authors online at atmospherepress.com. See you there soon!

ABOUT THE AUTHOR

Kendall Roberts lives in California. In his spare time, he enjoys writing, biking, and board games. *Janie* is his second novel.